The Proposal
LINDA TURNER

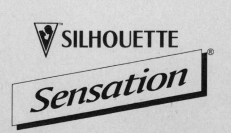

Silhouette, Silhouette Sensation and Colophon are registered trademarks of Harlequin Books S.A., used under licence.

*First published in Great Britain 1998
Large Print edition 2000
Silhouette Books Limited,
Eton House, 18-24 Paradise Road,
Richmond, Surrey, TW9 1SR*

© Linda Turner 1998

ISBN 0 373 04662 6

*Set in Times Roman 16¼ on 17¼ pt.
34-1200-76119*

*Printed and bound in Great Britain
by Antony Rowe Ltd, Chippenham, Wiltshire*

LINDA TURNER

began reading romances at school and began writing them one night when she had nothing else to read. She's been writing ever since. Single and living in Texas, she travels every chance she gets, scouting locales for her books.

Prologue

She had a reputation for being hard as nails and cold as ice. Hanging Judge Thompson. That's what the hotshots in San Antonio's legal community called her, sometimes to her face, and it wasn't because she was known for handing down the death sentence. *That* her critics could have accepted. No, she was hard on lawyers and even harder on men. She prided herself on always being fair, but any man who dared to think he could take advantage of her softer side got hung out to dry, and not by his thumbs.

Worse things had been said about her, especially over the course of the last eight months, but none closer to the truth. Yeah, she was tough, and had been from day one, when the governor had chosen her to finish the term of a judge who had died in office. She'd been new in town and young, barely two years out of law school but already on the fast track to the top. And that had caused nothing but trouble with older, more experienced lawyers who'd felt that they should have gotten the governor's appointment instead of some snippy upstart who didn't know the difference between a tort and a trust. They'd set out to teach the new kid on the block a lesson and challenged her at every turn. If she hadn't dug in her heels and stood her ground on the little issues, they would have eaten her for lunch on the bigger ones.

Three years and one election had passed since those awful first days, and while she might not have earned everyone's liking, she had earned their respect, and that was more important.

Lawyers knew they'd better be prepared when they came into her courtroom, and they'd damn well better be on time. When a case had been on the docket for weeks, she saw no reason short of a major emergency why they couldn't be in their places and ready to begin when they were supposed to.

Frowning over the top of her reading glasses at the defendant's table, where the accused in an assault case that had just been called sat conspicuously alone, she said, "Mr. Jackson, are you representing yourself?"

"Uh—no, ma'am. I mean, Your Honor." Color surging under the skin of his thin cheeks, he squirmed under her steady gaze. "Noah Baxter's my lawyer. He was supposed to meet me here, but I guess he got held up."

"So it appears," she said tartly. Noah Baxter had appeared before her only a couple of times, and then only for plea bargains, but it was a well-known fact that she didn't like to be kept waiting. Especially by cocky, brash lawyers who thought schedules applied to everyone else but themselves.

"Have you tried calling him?" she asked the defendant. "Or paging him? We don't have all day, Mr. Jackson, and I don't intend to let Mr. Baxter's tardiness throw this court off schedule for the rest of the day just because he has a problem with punctuality. If he doesn't present himself before this court in the next five minutes, I'll have no choice but to reschedule the entire proceedings."

"But that's hardly fair to the victim," the assistant D.A. argued. "She wants to put this behind her and get on with her life, Your

Honor. She can't do that as long as she has the trial hanging over her head. If we have to reschedule, it'll be fall before we can get back on the docket.''

She was right, which left Sadie between a rock and a hard place. Mr. Jackson was entitled to have his lawyer present, so they couldn't very well start without him, but the victim was entitled to see that justice was carried out in a fair and timely manner. A delay now, after waiting months for the trial, made that impossible.

''I realize that after all the victim has suffered, a postponement at this stage of the proceedings is outrageous,'' she told the prosecutor. ''I'm not happy about it, but I can't see that there is anything else I can do. I can't, in good conscience, force Mr. Jackson to appear before the court without benefit of council. And appointing another lawyer would still result in a delay. Therefore, I must—''

Before she could reschedule the proceedings, the heavy wooden doors at the entrance to the courtroom suddenly swung sharply open and Noah Baxter strode in, already apologizing with an engaging smile. ''I beg your pardon for my tardiness, Your Honor. I was unavoidably detained.''

Far from impressed with his boyish grin and wicked blue eyes, Sadie didn't even blink. She knew all about the infamous Mr. Baxter and his way with women. Rumor had it that he'd never been turned down for a date, and she could believe it. Good-looking didn't begin to describe the man. Square-jawed, his sensuous mouth bracketed by deep dimples, his dark, wavy hair cut conservatively short, he should have been in Hollywood making movies. Instead, he was in her courtroom and obviously expecting to charm not only the jury, but her, as well. It wasn't going to happen.

Studying him over the top of her glasses, she narrowed her eyes at him like a teacher calling a student on the carpet. ''Were you in some kind of accident, Mr. Baxter?''

''No, Your Honor.''

''Is one of your loved ones in the hospital dying?''

''No, ma'am. As far as I know, everyone's healthy.''

''So there was no family emergency, no accident or even a breakdown,'' she concluded coolly, scowling at him. ''You've just kept this court waiting for a good half hour and I've yet to hear why. I suggest you come up with an excuse, Counselor, and damn quick, or you're going to find yourself in contempt of court. Do I make myself clear?''

Nodding solemnly, Noah didn't doubt for a minute that she meant every word. It was a well-known fact that she didn't suffer fools lightly. In her courtroom, she expected legal eagles to be as prim and proper as Victorian maidens at tea. That didn't, however, stop him from daring to grin at her as he gave her the explanation she demanded.

''I would have been here on time, Your Honor, but I had to rescue my sister from a skunk.''

As far as stories went, it was an outrageous one. But what the hell was he supposed to do? Come up with a lie when the lady judge had eyes like a hawk? He didn't think so. So he stuck to the truth and waited for her to jump all over him. Instead, she leaned back in her chair and lifted a delicately arched brow at him. ''A skunk, Mr. Baxter? Are we talking the two-legged kind or one that walks on all fours?''

Encouraged, he flashed his dimples at her.

''Which one will get me out of a contempt-of-court fine?''

Too late, he saw he'd made a mistake. The smile that made most women melt like hot wax only made her stiffen in disapproval.

''Neither,'' she said coldly. ''Nothing short of an emergency is a valid excuse for keeping this court waiting. The fine is two hundred fifty dollars, payable to my favorite charity. You can pay my clerk when we adjourn.'' She reached for her gavel and struck it firmly. ''Now that that's settled, let's begin.''

Swearing under his breath, Noah had no choice but to accept the ruling and join his client at the defendant's table.

Chapter 1

Sadie trudged tiredly up the stairs to her apartment, her arms laden with work she'd brought home with her and the groceries she'd had to stop and buy for supper. The day had been too long, her feet hurt from the new shoes she'd made the mistake of wearing without breaking in first and she felt as if she was coming down with a summer cold. All she wanted was a long soak in a hot tub, but she knew she wasn't going to get it. Not tonight. Not when her briefcase was bulging with paperwork and she had a pile of motions that had to be studied and decided on by the time court started tomorrow.

Groaning at the thought, she stopped before her front door and was fumbling for her keys when she heard her phone ringing. Once, she would have let her machine get it, but that was one of the little luxuries, along with half the house and car and 401K plan she'd had before she'd ever married, that David, her ex-husband, had been awarded in their divorce eight months ago.

Annoyed that just the thought of him could still knot her stomach after so much time, she shied away from the still-painful memories and finally unlocked the door. Rushing inside, she dumped her things on the couch and reached the phone on its fifth ring. "Hello?" she said breathlessly.

"Sadie? This is Alice Truelove, the landlady at the Lone Star Social Club," her caller said cheerfully. "I know it's been ages since we talked, but I felt sure you'd remember me. You stopped by about seven months ago to see about renting an apartment."

"Alice! Of course!" Pleased, she sank onto the couch and slipped off her tight shoes. "It's been so long, I'd almost forgotten."

She and the landlady had talked the same day she was forced to put her house on the market in order to raise the money the judge had awarded David in their divorce settlement. She'd needed a place to stay and had hoped to rent one of the highly prized apartments at the Lone Star Social Club. But the beautifully restored Victorian mansion that had once been a gathering spot for cowboys in search of good women in the decade after the Civil War seldom had a vacancy. Alice had promised to give her first shot at the next apartment that became available, but she hadn't been able to hold out any hope on when that would be. There were only eight apartments and the tenants lucky enough to have a lease didn't often give them up.

"I hope you're calling to tell me you have a vacancy," Sadie said eagerly. "I know you said people don't move out very often, but the social club is so incredible, I'd just love to live there."

"Then start packing your things," Alice replied, chuckling. "The couple in 1A moved to Dallas yesterday, and their apartment will be available this weekend. It's yours if you want it."

Sadie didn't even hesitate. "I want it."

The older lady laughed. "I knew you would say that, but you don't have to decide right this second, dear. Don't you want to look at the place first?"

Settling more comfortably against the couch, Sadie only had to glance at the somber, bare walls of her current apartment to know that she wanted out—out of an apartment that had never been a home to her, out of the stagnant existence she'd fallen into since the divorce. She'd been treading water, getting nowhere, barely living. She hadn't seen her friends in months, couldn't remember the last time she'd gone to a movie. It was time for a change, and she couldn't think of a better one than the Lone Star Social Club.

"I don't need to see it—I know I'm going to love it," she assured her. "Would you like me to bring you a security deposit tonight? Or I can stop by tomorrow after work if that would be more convenient for you. After waiting so long, I don't want to take a chance on losing it."

"Oh, you're not going to lose it, dear," Alice replied quickly. "We have a deal, and as far as I'm concerned, the apartment is yours. If you're going to move in on Saturday, we can do the paperwork then."

Sitting on the bench day after day as a district judge, Sadie seldom encountered trust, especially from someone she hardly knew.

Touched, she said, "You don't know how much I appreciate this, Alice. I'll start packing tonight."

"Wonderful! You're going to be on the ground floor at the back on the right, right across the hall from me, and I can guarantee that you're going to love it. There is, however, one thing you should know. Since you're single, it's only fair that I warn you…"

When she hesitated, Sadie prompted, "Warn me about what? What does my being single have to do with anything?"

"Oh, everything, dear! You see, the house seems to have a special power over the unmarried tenants. I don't know how it works—I guess it's some kind of magic held over from the days when this really was a social club—but every single person who's moved in here has ended up falling in love and getting married within a year."

"Oh, c'mon, Alice," she scoffed, amused. "You don't really believe that, do you? You're pulling my leg."

"No, I'm not," she replied somberly. "There's something about this place that just seems to bring soul mates together. I don't know if you're interested in getting married again, but I thought you should know that if you move in here, you won't stay single for long.''

If she hadn't been so serious, Sadie might have laughed at the irony of the situation. Despite her ill-fated marriage to David, falling in love had never been one of her goals in life. She'd seen firsthand what damage love could do to a woman's life, how it could make her bitter and disillusioned and so miserable that all she wanted to do was crawl in a hole and drag the dirt in after her. Her mother had made the mistake of falling head over heels in love with a soldier being shipped off to Vietnam. He'd promised to love her forever, to come back to her, but when she'd written him two months later to tell him she was pregnant, she learned to her dismay that not only was he married, he had no intention of getting a divorce to marry someone he barely remembered.

Relatives had told her that her mother had once been young and carefree and impulsive, but Sadie had never seen any sign of that woman. Determined that her daughter would not make the mistakes she had, her mother had warned her time and time again as she was growing up that men only used women and couldn't be trusted. It wasn't until her mother died and she'd met and married David when she was so lonely she didn't know what she was doing that she realized just how right her mother was.

"I appreciate the warning, Alice," she said dryly, "but I've already been there and done that and don't intend to make that kind of mistake again. In fact, I can pretty much guarantee that there isn't a man alive who could tempt me to say *I do* again. Not after tangling with David. He made out like a bandit when we divorced and nearly robbed me blind."

"I know, dear, and I'm so sorry that you had to go through that, but you don't understand. This isn't something *you* have any control over. If you move in here, like it or not, you *will* fall in love again within a year."

She sounded so sure that Sadie hesitated, half-tempted to take her seriously. But then she remembered David's greed and betrayal, his vindictiveness, and almost laughed at her own foolishness. After everything she'd been through, it would take a heck of a lot more than some kind of spell to make her ever trust a man again.

"I'm sure the house has a special magic,"

she told the older lady, "but at this point in my life, I don't think even magic could help me fall in love again. I hope you won't be disappointed when I break the spell."

Unperturbed, Alice only chuckled. "Oh, no, dear. You won't be the first person to move in with that attitude, and I'm sure you won't be the last. And it really has nothing to do with me, after all. I just want everyone to be happy. I guess we'll just have to wait and see what happens, won't we?"

"Or what doesn't," Sadie replied, grinning. "It should be interesting."

"It always is," the landlady assured her. "But that's something you'll have to find out for yourself. I'll see you on Saturday."

The next two days whizzed by in a whirlwind of activity. Given a choice, she would have made arrangements to take the time off from work, but with so little notice, that was impossible. So she lined up friends to help her make the move, then rushed home from the courthouse both Thursday and Friday after work and started packing. It should have been a snap. She'd gotten rid of everything that reminded her of David and sold all but her most prized possessions to satisfy the divorce settlement. Still, there were clothes to pack, not to mention towels and linens and everything in the kitchen. And when had she gotten so many shoes?

By the time Saturday morning arrived, boxes were piled to the ceiling. It would probably take her a month to find everything again and settle in, but she didn't regret the move. She'd never been happy in the small, plain apartment, and the social club just took her another step further away from David and the disillusionment of the past. If for no other reason than that, she was going to love living there.

She was doing one last check of all the closets and cabinets to make sure nothing had been forgotten when her friends arrived. One second she was surrounded by the silence of her own thoughts, and the next she was being hugged and congratulated and teased about the move.

"Are you sure you want to move into that spooky old mansion?" Bob Whacker teased as he swept her up in a bear hug. "You know it's haunted, don't you? They say you can hear people talking and laughing when there's nobody there and the ghosts hold parties in the attic."

Jane Garrison, Sadie's best friend and roommate during college, rolled her eyes. "Leave it to you, Whacker, to believe in ghosts and goblins and things that go bump in the night.''

"Hey, now, don't go picking on the big guy," Tommy Harper scolded playfully, slinging an arm around Bob's linebacker-sized shoulders. "He can't help it if he's more brawn than brain."

"Speaking of brawn," Tommy's wife, Nancy, drawled. "Isn't that why we brought you two lugs along?"

The two men immediately straightened and saluted sharply. "Yes, ma'am!" Tommy teased. "Crack that whip, ma'am. What d'you want us to load first?"

Sadie had to laugh. Nancy, at five-two, was a good foot and a half shorter than her giant of a husband and could wrap him around her finger with just a lift of her brow. "The bedroom furniture," she said. "Then the couch. Are you sure you guys don't need any help?"

When Bob just looked at her, insulted, she grinned. "Did I spit on Superman's cape? What was I thinking of? All this testosterone in here must have scrambled my brains."

"I do seem to have that effect on women," he retorted, leering at her. "It's a gift."

"Please...spare us," she groaned, laughing.

"We've all seen just what kind of effect you have on women, Romeo, and it's not pretty."

Amid much good-natured ribbing and teasing, they carried Sadie's things out to the small moving truck she'd rented, and it was just like old times, when they'd all been in law school together. They'd helped one another out through thick and thin and somehow still always managed to laugh.

Right from the beginning, they'd been a tightly knit group, more like family than friends, and that hadn't changed much over the years. Except when she'd married David, Sadie was forced to admit. No one had ever said anything, and they'd tried to welcome him into their midst, but she'd always sensed something was wrong. When she'd seen less and less of the gang, she'd attributed it to the fact that they were all busy with their own lives. It wasn't until later, when her marriage had fallen apart, that Jane had told her about the times David had gone behind her back to con her friends into investing in his get-rich-quick business ventures. By then, she'd already figured out that he'd married her only because of the connections she'd made as a judge with the city's upper crust, but she hadn't had a clue that he'd gone to her closest friends for money. She'd been mortified.

Using her was one thing, but not suspecting he was using her friends was something she would always regret. They, however, had been much quicker to forgive her than she'd been able to forgive herself. When she filed for divorce, they were right there beside her, offering support and sympathy and legal advice. And when David spread hateful gossip about her and their private life, it was all she could do to keep Tommy and Bob from going after him and taking him apart, piece by piece. They'd wanted her to sue him, to contest the divorce settlement, to hotly defend her honor and expose her ex for the miserable worm that he was.

She wasn't a wimp and would have given anything to do just that, but she knew how the rumor mill worked. The more she protested the lies David spread about her, the more they would be believed. She was damned if she did and damned if she didn't, so she did the only thing her pride would allow her to do. She said nothing.

It was the hardest thing she'd ever done in her life. For nearly eight months, she'd lived a nightmare, and things hadn't gotten much better with the passage of time. She still couldn't walk through the courthouse corridors without being aware of the whispers behind her back, the stares, the jokes that circulated in her wake. And every day she came home from work and walked into her miserable excuse for an apartment, she was reminded of David and all he had taken from her.

But that was about to change, she thought with a quiet sigh of relief as she followed Bob and Tommy outside and supervised the loading of the last of her things into the moving van. The Lone Star Social Club might only be across town from her old apartment, but it was a world away from the mistakes she'd made in the past. Maybe now she could get on with the rest of her life.

After slamming the back door on the moving van, Bob joined her and the others on the sidewalk. "All right, that's it. Lock, stock and barrel." Holding out the keys to the truck to Sadie, he arched a brow at her. "It's your move, Judge. You wanna drive?"

He didn't have to ask her twice. Snatching the keys from him, she grinned. "Today, you couldn't stop me, Whacker. C'mon. Let's go."

* * *

Alice Truelove had warned Sadie that the first-floor apartment at the rear of the Lone Star Social Club was small and it was, but it had all the character of the old lady herself. There were two fireplaces with Italian tile, fourteen-foot ceilings that gave the impression of spaciousness and stained-glass windows that overlooked the rear gardens and the River Walk. She took one look and she was in love.

In spite of the size of the place, however, it took the rest of the day to arrange and rearrange the furniture and get everything where she thought she wanted it. Bob and Tommy playfully teased her about not knowing her own mind, especially when she asked them to move her bed for the third time, but they did as she requested and would have even helped her unpack all the moving boxes if she'd let them. But they'd already done more than enough, and she couldn't take advantage of them any more than she already had. She called out for pizza, brought out the beer she'd had the foresight to buy earlier and gathered everybody at the kitchen table for an impromptu pizza party. They laughed and joked with one another and devoured enough pizza to feed a small army. It was just like old times, and the perfect way to break in her new apartment.

By the time everyone finally left, it was going on ten, and Sadie felt like a day laborer who'd been hard at work since dawn. Muscles she hadn't known she had ached, and all she wanted to do was take a hot shower and crawl into bed. But she couldn't do that until she found some sheets and towels.

She was bent over headfirst in a large cardboard box, searching for her linens, when a loud thump from upstairs had her straightening in surprise. Glancing up, she frowned as something hit the floor so hard in the apartment directly above hers that it shook the old-fashioned light fixture suspended from *her* ceiling. Before she could blink, it happened again, then again.

What the devil was going on up there? she wondered, frowning. It sounded as though whoever lived upstairs was dropping blocks of concrete on the floor. And if they kept it up, the light fixture was going to shake loose and come crashing down on her head.

Swearing under her breath, she hesitated at the thought of going upstairs to complain. It was her first night in the social club, and confronting the neighbors about the noise they were making wasn't the way she wanted to meet them. She'd give them a few minutes, she decided, warily eyeing the light fixture that was quivering over her head like an accident waiting to happen. Then, if things didn't quiet down, she'd go upstairs and quietly remind whoever lived above her that they weren't the only souls in the universe.

She wasn't a woman who lost her temper easily—she couldn't and maintain control of a courtroom with any degree of decorum. So when she started up the stairs to the second floor nearly twenty minutes later, she was calm and cool and more than willing to be friendly. After all, it wasn't as if the Lone Star Social Club was some kind of rowdy low-rent dive whose occupants made a habit of disturbing the peace. According to Alice, all the tenants were professional people who were quiet and peaceful and minded their own business. For all she knew, whoever lived in the apartment above her didn't even know that someone had moved in downstairs. She would introduce herself, explain that she had rented the place below them, and they would no doubt apologize for disturbing her on her first night in her new home. They would stop whatever they were doing, and she could finally go to bed—it was that simple.

But when she knocked on the door to apartment 2A and her new neighbor came to see who was calling at nearly ten-thirty at night, the friendly smile that hovered at the corners of her mouth abruptly disappeared. Stunned, she stared in disbelief at Noah Baxter.

He'd been lifting weights. Behind him in the living room, a set of barbells sat on the floor where he'd dropped them, and somewhere in the back of her head, Sadie realized that the repeated thud she'd heard in her apartment was the sound of the weights hitting his floor. That thought, however, barely registered as her widened eyes took him in from head to toe.

She'd only dealt with the man a few times in her life, and then he'd been shaved and combed and properly dressed for court in a suitably conservative suit. And while she was prepared to admit that he cut an impressive figure in a courtroom, nothing could have prepared her for the sight of him dressed in gray sweat-dampened shorts and nothing else. Good Lord, the man was big! And hard as a rock. Who could have guessed that beneath his tailored suits was a lean, rangy body that looked as though it belonged in a Calvin Klein underwear ad?

Her mouth dry and her heart thundering, she couldn't stop her gaze from wandering from his bare feet all the way up the long, magnificent length of him. She'd heard the gossip about him, seen the way women, including her own clerk, sighed over him whenever he strode down the courthouse corridors, and had never understood what all the fuss was about. Granted, with his chiseled jaw, sensuous mouth and dimples, he was attractive, but no more so than several other good-looking attorneys in town.

But now, as her brown eyes lifted to his blue ones and she saw the self-directed humor there, she understood why females of every age tended to make fools of themselves over Noah Baxter. He knew his effect on women and found the fairer sex's fascination with him more than a little amusing. And here she was, ogling him like a schoolgirl who'd just stumbled across Tom Cruise, making his day, and there wasn't so much as a spark of recognition in his eyes.

Furious with herself, she stiffened like a poker, the neighborly little speech she'd planned flying right out of her head. "Do you have any idea what time it is, Counselor?"

Hot and sweaty from his workout, Noah stared down in amusement at the small, petite woman who stood before him like a cute little bantam hen with ruffled tail feathers. He'd have sworn he'd never laid eyes on her before, but she seemed to know him, and if she wanted to stand in the hallway and discuss the time, who was he to argue?

Propping a shoulder against the doorjamb, he grinned. "I've had women knock on my door to borrow a cup of sugar, but this is the first time one has asked me for the time. I believe it's going on ten-thirty. Do I know you, sweetheart?"

It was an innocent enough question…and obviously the wrong thing to say. The lady drew herself up to every one of her sixty-four inches and gave him a look that should have stripped the skin from his bones.

"Yes, you do, and don't call me 'sweetheart'! I'm perfectly aware of the time, Mr. Baxter. *You're* the one who doesn't seem to have a clue. For your information, some people like to go to bed at this time of night, but they can't because you're making enough racket to wake the dead!''

Hardly hearing her diatribe, he frowned in confusion. That voice. Dammit, he knew that voice from somewhere! That tone that put a man in his place faster than his own mother could. But from where, dammit? Who the hell—

Recognition came from out of the blue. Blinking like a man who'd been knocked on his backside by a blow in the dark, he stared down at her searchingly and told himself it couldn't be. There was no way the small, slender woman who stood before him could be Hanging Judge Thompson. Not in faded jeans and a stained UT sweatshirt that showed off some damn enticing curves. It just wasn't possible.

From what he'd heard, the woman slept in her judicial robes, and rumor had it that not even that sleaze of an ex-husband of hers had ever seen her hair down. She kept it screwed up in an ugly knot on the back of her head, not flowing down past her shoulders in a mass of wild, reddish brown curls that begged a man to touch it, to bury his hands in it up to his wrists.

Shaking his head, he frowned at his own

musings and tried to convince himself that his imagination was just playing tricks on him. But that voice. And those eyes. He'd never seen the straight and rigid judge without the old-fashioned, wire-rimmed reading glasses she always wore in court, but he'd been caught in the trap of her narrowed gaze enough in their short confrontations in her courtroom to know what her eyes looked like. Dark brown and straight-forward, the kind of eyes that could see right through a lawyer's—and a man's—line of bull. And this woman had those same eyes.

Damn, damn, damn! What the hell was she doing here?

For your information, some people like to go to bed at this time of night....

Not liking his sudden suspicions, he hid them behind a crooked grin. ''I beg your pardon, Your Judgeship. I didn't recognize you without your gavel.'' If it had been any other woman, he would have told her she looked damn fine, but that wasn't something a man told Hanging Judge Thompson, not if he wanted to keep his head on his shoulders. So instead, he settled for, ''You look...different.''

He might as well have told her she looked

like a hooker. She sent him a glare that should have slain him on the spot.

"You will address me in an appropriate manner, Counselor—"

"I wouldn't dream of doing anything else," he said agreeably. "When we're in court."

Narrowing her eyes at him, she glared at him in growing frustration. "And what I look like is not the problem here!"

"No, that's right. You mentioned something about not being able to sleep, didn't you?" Devilment sparkled in his blue eyes. "Am I keeping you up nights, Ms. Chief Justice?"

"No, of course not!"

"Then what are you doing at my door at this time of night? I didn't even know you knew where I lived. Another man might think you were looking for an excuse to come calling," he teased. "Is that what you're doing, Your Honorableness? 'Cause if it is, I gotta tell you, I'm flattered. I didn't think you were that kind of woman."

If he'd wanted to push the lady's buttons, he couldn't have found a better way. She gasped, outraged, and for a second there, he thought she was going to split a gasket. Watching her struggle to control the emotions that swept across

her finely drawn face like the turbulent winds
before a thunderstorm, he found himself fascinated. From what he knew of the lady, she had
a reputation for being as constrained as a
maiden aunt bound up in an old-fashioned cor-
set. Who would have thought it took nothing
more than a little teasing to shake that famous
self-control of hers?

Making no effort to hold back the grin that
pulled at the corners of his mouth, he stepped
toward her in playful concern. ''You okay,
Judge? You're turning a little purple. You want
to come in for a drink or something?''

''No!''

Retreating like a scared rabbit before she
stopped to think, Sadie took a quick step back,
then could have cursed herself when she saw
the laughter twinkling in his eyes. What in the
world was the matter with her? Noah Baxter
was an outrageous flirt who, as a matter of
sheer principle, made a habit of charming anything in skirts. Only a fool would take him seriously, and she was nobody's fool.

She just had to look at the wicked amusement in his eyes to know that life was a game
to him, enjoyed to the fullest and not to be
taken seriously. If she needed further proof of

that, she got it when a movement behind him in his apartment caught her attention and she looked past him through his open front door just as a willowy blonde stepped from his kitchen into the living room. Dressed in a T-shirt and cutoffs that were designed to show off the long, beautiful length of her legs, she was model-gorgeous…and barely eighteen if she was a day.

Sadie told herself she shouldn't have been surprised that he wasn't alone. But she hadn't thought he was the type of man to flirt with one woman, even if it wasn't seriously, when he had another one just in the other room. That was something an opportunist—and David— did, and just the thought of her ex was enough to bring her temper back under rigid control.

Reminding herself that she didn't give a fly- ing leap what Noah Baxter did in his apartment at that time of the night as long as he did it quietly, she told him coolly, "Save your flirting for someone who appreciates it, Mr. Baxter. For your information, this isn't a social call. I just came up to tell you that I moved into apartment 1A this afternoon, and your weight lifting is shaking the hell out of my bedroom light fix- ture. If you must exercise, I would appreciate it if, in the future, you would do it earlier in the evening. Just because you want to stay up half the night doing God knows what doesn't mean that I do.''

Her shoulders back and her spine ramrod straight, she pivoted on her heel and took the stairs down to her apartment with the regal grace of a queen who had handed down an edict and was confident she would have no further problems with a troublesome subject. Staring after her, Noah felt as though he'd just tangled with the wrong end of a buzz saw.

In the silence that followed, his sister Alex said dryly, ''Well, that's a first—a woman who doesn't drop at your feet when you turn on the pearly brights. What'd you do? Kill her cat?''

''No!'' Shaking off the daze she'd left him in, he shut the door with a decided snap. ''Dammit, doesn't the woman know it's the weekend?'' he grumbled. ''Who goes to bed at ten-thirty on a Saturday night?''

''Apparently she does,'' Alex retorted in amusement. ''Who is she? And why doesn't she like you?''

''Because I'm a man,'' he growled, ''and I actually had the audacity to smile at her in her courtroom. She's a judge, in case you hadn't figured that out. Judge Sadie Thompson. 'Hanging Judge Thompson,' they call her around the courthouse.''

''Why?''

''Because…'' Suddenly remembering he was talking to his seventeen-year-old baby sister, he scowled. ''It doesn't matter. Let's just say she hates men. Ever since she divorced her jerk of a husband, she's had a real ax to grind with the male of the species.''

''And now she lives downstairs.'' Delighted at the thought, Alex warned, ''You're not going to be able to make a move without her calling you on it.''

He snorted, not impressed. ''It'll take more than a lady judge to cramp my style,'' he assured her brashly.

But later, after he took Alex home and quietly let himself back into his apartment, he couldn't help but be aware of the woman who slept in the apartment below him. What had he ever done to deserve Hanging Judge Thompson?

Chapter 2

"What do you mean, the Greenwood case is going to be heard by Judge Thompson at eleven?" Noah demanded when his secretary informed him of the change in scheduling the minute he walked through the door of his office Monday morning. "McGowen is hearing that at two this afternoon."

"Not anymore he's not," Susan replied as she handed him his phone messages. "He had a heart attack this morning, so his caseload's been divided between Thompson, Sanchez and Whitaker. I've already called Ms. Greenwood and informed her of the change of plans. She'll meet you outside Judge Thompson's courtroom at ten forty-five. Oh, and your sister Rachel called to remind you not to forget softball practice tonight. It starts at six.''

His thoughts already jumping ahead to eleven, Noah nodded curtly, irritation fisting in his gut. Dammit all, the last person he wanted to see this morning was Sadie Thompson. Since Saturday night, he'd managed to avoid the woman like the plague, but that hadn't stopped her from making her presence felt. He couldn't walk across the floor of his apartment now without wondering if she was down there, listening to his every move, and it annoyed the hell out of him. He paid his rent. He shouldn't have to walk around on pins and needles in his own home just because the prissy judge downstairs didn't want her ceilings to squeak. That's what happened when you lived in an old house. If she wanted quiet, she should have moved into one of those newfangled soundproof places that had about as much character as a stainless-steel box.

But nooo! he thought resentfully. She had to make her nest right under his, so even when he couldn't see her, he was aware of her disapproval. And now he had to face her again in court, and he wasn't looking forward to it. She had a reputation for being as hard on crime as she was on men, and his pro bono client, while she might appear like a beautiful angel, was the best little scam artist he'd ever had the misfortune to represent. McGowen might have gone easy on her, but Noah had a feeling Thompson wouldn't take kindly to anyone, man or woman, who scammed decent people out of their hard-earned money.

Wondering if it was too late to work out something with the D.A., he arrived at the courthouse two hours later in a grim mood that only got worse when his client informed him that she intended to plead guilty and throw herself on the mercy of the court.

"Trust me, Belinda, you don't want to do that," he said flatly. "You've got priors, remember? Judge Thompson—"

"Is easier on women than she is on men," she cut in smugly. "I know. I heard about her ex and what he did to her. Men are jerks, and when I tell her how my old man dumped me, too, and left me with a sick baby and no money, she's going to feel real sorry for me. She might even let me walk."

Noah doubted that, but the story might have earned her a more sympathetic sentence...if it was true. It wasn't. Belinda Greenwood didn't have a baby, sick or otherwise, and the state knew it. ''If you stand in front of Thompson and try to scam her in her own courtroom, you're going to get the book thrown at you,'' he warned coldly. ''So I suggest you let me do the talking for you and see what kind of deal I can work out with the D.A. Otherwise, we're talking jail time, and I'm sure you don't want that.''

She didn't, and she sullenly agreed to let him handle things. He had a hurried conference with the assistant prosecutor and was able to cut a decent, though not great, deal for his client. She would have to serve some jail time, but considering her past record and her confession the night she was arrested, things could have been a lot worse.

Satisfied that he'd done the best for her he could, he escorted Belinda to the defendant's table and stood as the case was called and the charges against her were read by Thompson. As expected, the lady judge was stiff and formal in her judicial robes, and all business. With her hair scraped back and twisted up and her Ben Franklin reading glasses perched on her nose, there was no sign of the petite, surprisingly attractive blue-jean-clad woman who had fumed at him on Saturday night. Her expression impassive, she met his gaze without so much as a flicker of emotion before turning her attention to his client.

"Do you understand the charges against you, Ms. Greenwood?"

At his side, Belinda nodded respectfully. "Yes, ma'am."

"And how do you plead?"

"Guilty, Your Honor," Noah answered for her.

The prosecutor then explained that the defendant was pleading guilty in exchange for a one-year sentence, and all that was left to do was the formalities. Perusing the paperwork the D.A. handed her, the judge glanced over the top of her glasses at Belinda. "Do you understand the plea bargain, Ms. Greenwood? And the rights you are giving up by pleading guilty? For the record, I need to know that you understand what you are agreeing to and that no one forced you into agreeing or signing anything against your will."

A simple yes, she knew what she was doing, and no, she wasn't forced into anything, would have ended the proceedings and tied everything up with a nice, neat bow. Noah had already gone over everything with her—all she had to do was respond correctly. But before he could begin to guess her intentions, Belinda stepped forward. "I don't know if I can do that, Your Honor," she replied. "I know I done wrong, but a year in jail is an awful long time. Just the thought of being caged up that long gives me the willies."

Surprised, Sadie glanced up sharply as Noah swore under his breath and tried to shush his client. "I understood that you were willing to accept a plea bargain, Ms. Greenwood. Are you now saying that you want to change your plea from guilty to not guilty?"

"Oh, no, ma'am. I did it," she admitted without a smidgen of remorse. "And I'd do it again in a heartbeat. But I had my reasons, and you being as understanding as you are about men who dump their women, I thought you should know why I did what I did. You see, my baby was sick—"

Swallowing a curse, Noah immediately stepped forward to shut her up. "Your Honor, I need some time to confer with my client. She's obviously not feeling well."

"I'm feeling just fine, Mr. Baxter," Belinda said tartly. "Don't you go putting words in my mouth. I need to talk to the judge, and I'm going to.''

''This isn't smart, Belinda,'' he warned her in a hiss that wouldn't carry to the bench. ''Step back and let me handle this before you shoot yourself in the foot.''

Observing them through narrowed eyes, Sadie said quietly, ''Ms. Greenwood, I'm willing to hear what you have to say, but you should know that anything you say to the court can be used against you. If your lawyer advises against you saying anything, you should listen to him. He's here to protect your rights.''

''I don't need him to protect me,'' she said stubbornly. ''I know what I'm doing.''

''Your Honor, I must object—''

''Your client has spoken, Mr. Baxter,'' Sadie replied coolly, cutting him off. ''She's been apprised of her rights and knows the risk she's taking. If she wants to speak, I won't stop her. Continue, Ms. Greenwood.''

''But, Your Honor—''

''You heard me, Mr. Baxter,'' she said curtly. ''Don't push me.''

Muttering curses, he shut his mouth with a snap, and Belinda immediately began entertaining the court with the pathetic tale that had led her to this mess in the first place. And even to his own ears, Noah had to admit it sounded good. Damn good. But Sadie Thompson was as sharp as a tack, and he could see by the set of her jaw that she knew a con when she heard one. Belinda, however, was too bent on having her say to notice that the judge was less than sympathetic to her tale of woe. She rambled blithely on, damning herself with every outrageous word.

"So you see, Your Honor," she concluded earnestly, "I had a good reason for what I did. I know it was wrong and I shouldn't have lied, but what else could I do? My husband left me without a penny to my name, and my baby was sick. I needed money."

Outraged by her blatant lying, the prosecutor started to sputter a protest, but Sadie stopped him with a wave of her hand. Never taking her eyes from Belinda, she asked silkily, "Are you willing to swear that what you've just told this court is nothing less than the truth?"

"Oh, yes, ma'am." Quickly crossing her heart, she said, "I would never lie to you."

"I'm glad to hear it," Sadie replied promptly. "Then perhaps you can explain to me where this sick baby of yours is. From what I understand, you don't have any children.''

Caught red-handed in the lie, Belinda didn't even have the grace to blush. Without missing a beat, she came up with another lie. ''Well, I never actually said the baby was mine, Your Honor. It was my sister's. She just ran off and left it with me without so much as a diaper to change its poor little wet bottom. I was desperate—''

The prosecutor, no longer able to hold his tongue, exploded. ''Your Honor, I can't stand by while that woman lies through her teeth. She hasn't got a sister or any other kind of family. If you'll check her file, you'll see that it's a matter of public record that she was raised in an orphanage until she was sixteen. Since then, she's supported herself by conning anyone who's stupid enough to be taken in by her lies. The same night she got out on bail for this charge, she hit up tourists on the River Walk by claiming she was a tourist herself and got mugged the first night she was in town.''

Wincing, Noah ground his teeth on an oath. This was just what he'd been afraid of. By admitting she was guilty and insisting on having her say, Belinda had opened up the proceedings to a whole kettle of worms and there wasn't a damn thing he could do but object. "Whatever happened on the River Walk is irrelevant to these proceedings, Your Honor," he stated smoothly. "My client hasn't been charged with anything—"

"Only because she gave all her victims on the river the same sob story she told us about the nonexistent baby," the assistant D.A. said hotly. "They fell for it and wouldn't press charges."

"Or they decided they hadn't been conned after all and let it go," Noah argued. "Either way, the result is the same. My client has only been charged with one crime, which, I might add, she has already pleaded guilty to. We're not here to bring up every transgression she's ever made, but to decide her sentence."

"You're entirely right, Mr. Baxter," Sadie said before the prosecutor could come up with another argument. Glancing at Belinda, she said, "Do you have anything else to say in your own defense, Ms. Greenwood?"

Standing at Noah's side, confident that one woman wouldn't send another one to jail, she smiled easily. "No, ma'am. I'm sure you'll do the right thing."

"Yes, I will," Sadie said confidently. Her expression grim, she looked the other woman straight in the eye and said, "You've admitted your guilt, and I have to commend you for that. But," she added sternly when Belinda started to smile, "I'm outraged that you stood before me and lied to this court. You show no remorse for what you've done or the people you've cheated. You have a history of preying on others' naiveté and generosity and have shown by your behavior here today that you will continue to pull your scams as long as you're allowed to get away with it. Because of that, I have no choice but to make your punishment so severe that you're forced to realize the seriousness of your crime and change your ways. I therefore sentence you to seven years in prison without parole—"

"Seven years!"

"Your Honor, you can't be serious!"

"*And,*" she added over Belinda and Noah's shocked protests, "fine you two thousand dollars, to be paid to your victims." Banging her gavel, she said, "Bailiff, take the defendant into custody—"

Scowling, Noah stepped forward. "The punishment is excessive for this type of crime, Your Honor—''

It was the wrong thing to say in Hanging Judge Thompson's courtroom. She hit him with a sharp glare that would have had a lesser man fumbling for an apology immediately. When Noah just glared back at her, she snapped, ''I'm not interested in your opinion, Mr. Baxter. This case is closed.''

''But it's outrageous!''

''And so is your behavior in my courtroom, Counselor. You're in contempt and fined five hundred dollars. You know who to make the check out to.'' Striking her gavel, she looked him square in the eye and just dared him to say another word.

He wanted to. God, how he wanted to! It wasn't in his nature to back down from a confrontation, and he'd known he and the lady judge were going to butt heads again ever since Saturday night. But she had an unfair advantage in her courtroom; all the power was hers. If she found him in contempt a second time, the punishment would be a hell of a lot more than a mere five hundred dollars. Even then, he was tempted to push his luck, but he liked to think he wasn't an idiot. This was a battle he couldn't win. Without a word, he strode over to the clerk and wrote out a check to the Battered Women's Shelter.

Another man might have been fuming when he walked out with pockets considerably lighter than when he walked in, and he was more than a little ticked. But he'd always liked a woman who wasn't afraid to put a man in his place when he needed it, and his dear, sweet neighbor had certainly done that. As much as it galled him to admit it, she'd had every right to call him on the carpet. The sentence hadn't been that far over the line and, considering Belinda's priors, no more than she deserved. He'd had no right to question Thompson's judgment, but there was just something about the lady that made him want to challenge her and see those brown eyes of hers spark with fire. He'd get another chance, he promised himself with a small smile of anticipation, and next time, they'd be on more equal footing. He was, he found to his surprise, looking forward to it.

The opportunity presented itself sooner than he anticipated nearly a week later in the old red-stone courthouse across the street from the county's new justice center. On his way up to the fourth floor, he pushed the button for the elevator, but when the doors parted, the car was already crowded. There was only room for one more person, and he almost passed it up. Then he saw Judge Sadie Thompson crammed into a corner at the back. Her eyes locked with his, her mouth curled in a slight smile that was more than a little superior, and just that easily, the lady issued a challenge he couldn't resist. Grinning mockingly, he eased into the car, turned his back on her and pressed the button on the control panel for the fourth floor.

As the doors swished shut in front of his face, the crowd behind him was as quiet as the proverbial mouse. He could almost feel Sadie's eyes on him, boring a hole in the back of his head; then the car reached the second floor and he was jostled from all sides as people tried to stream out around him. In self-defense, he moved aside and held the doors open until the crowd had exited, then he repeated the process on the third floor. When the elevator finally started climbing to the fourth floor, he and Sadie were the only two people left on it. Things couldn't have worked out better if he'd planned them.

Given the chance, he figured she would have

looked straight ahead and ignored him like he was some kind of lower life-form that didn't warrant her attention, but he had no intention of letting her get away with that. Devilment dancing in his eyes, he leaned a shoulder against the far wall of the elevator car and grinned at her. ''Looks like it's just you and me, Your Honorness.''

That brought the fire to her eyes, but her voice was as cool as spring water as she said to the wall directly in front of her, ''If you must address me by a title, Mr. Baxter, 'Judge' or 'Your Honor' will do just fine. Anything else is unacceptable.''

''You got it, Lady Justice,'' he said easily, flashing his dimples at her. ''How's tricks?''

That earned him a glare that would have melted lead.

''I wouldn't know. I don't *do* tricks.''

''I don't know about that,'' he drawled playfully. ''The word on the street is you got the Dominguez trial, and every other judge in town is grumbling about it. I can name at least four who thought they had that one in the bag and could ride the publicity it's going to generate all the way to the state supreme court. Did you bribe somebody or are you just living right?''

He was joking—he didn't doubt for a minute that the biggest trial to come down the pike in years was given to her for any other reason than she was the best. And it would take the best to keep the trial from turning into a media circus. Dominic Dominguez, the defendant, was not only accused of killing a popular San Antonio businessman, but was also suspected of have connections to the Mexican mafia. The latter had never been proven, but there wasn't a doubt in anyone's mind that it would come out at the trial, and reporters from all over the state would jump all over it.

If the good judge had any ambition at all, she could write her own ticket to the top with this one. But before Noah could tease her about that, the elevator came to a sudden, jarring halt and almost threw both of them off their feet. A split second later, the lights flickered, then went out altogether. When they came back on a few seconds later, they were half as strong as they had been before.

"What the hell!" Swearing, Noah frowned at Sadie in concern. "Are you all right?"

Nodding shakily, she pushed back tendrils of hair that had pulled loose from the twist at the back of her head. "What happened?"

"I don't know." Glancing up, he studied the weak lights and the old-fashioned, half-moon brass dial over the door, which showed the floor they were on. The indicator sat unmoving between the third and fourth floors. "That storm that's been threatening all morning probably hit and knocked the power out. Looks like we're stuck."

"Stuck? No! We can't be!"

She was so adamant, he couldn't help but laugh. "Sorry to disillusion you, Your Judgeship, but you don't seem to have any say-so about it. This baby's stuck and God only knows when it's going to move again."

"Then call someone!" she cried. "Don't you have a cell phone with you? There must be someone in maintenance who can get us out of here."

She was close to panicking and definitely not amused. Making no effort to pull his phone from his pocket, Noah studied her suspiciously. "You're not claustrophobic, are you? Tell me you're not going to wig out on me and start climbing the walls or something. I can handle anything but that."

"*I am not claustrophobic!*" she said through her teeth, struggling for patience. "I just don't want to spend the rest of the day cooped up in this box.''

Not with him. Not with a flirt and a playboy who, lately, had been turning up in her life with the regularity of the proverbial bad penny. As much as she loved her new apartment, she couldn't step into it without being aware of his presence overhead. And the irritating thing about it was that ever since that first night when she'd stormed up to his place to complain about the noise he was making, he'd been extremely quiet. She should have been relieved, but she found herself listening for him, instead, wondering what he was doing whenever she heard him walk across the floor above her, who he was with. It was enough to drive a normally sane woman right out of her mind.

And then there were those encounters with him in the social club's entrance hall, not to mention the corridors of the courthouse. Every time, he was with a different woman. An alley dog would have been more discriminating. Not that it was any of her concern how many women he saw, she assured herself. She couldn't have cared less, and for some reason that seemed to amuse him no end. Every time he saw her, he got this infuriating smirk on his face that made her just want to smack him one.

And now she was stuck with him for heaven knew how long in a space that was hardly bigger than a piano crate, and there was no emergency phone in the old elevator to call for assistance. God, how could this be happening? Thanks to David, she'd been the punch line of more jokes than she cared to think about over the last eight months. Lately, though, the talk had died down and she'd hoped that it wouldn't be too much longer before it disappeared completely. So much for wishful thinking, she thought dejectedly. When the gossips got hold of this latest tidbit, she wouldn't be able to walk down the corridor without hearing the snickers.

Did you hear about Noah Baxter? The paramedics had to treat him for frostbite after he got out of that elevator with Hanging Judge Thompson. And it's the middle of summer!

Wincing inwardly, she cursed her too-vivid imagination and dragged in a calming breath. "Do you have a cellular?" At his nod, she sighed in relief. "Thank God! Johnny Valenzuela is in charge of maintenance. He should know what to do."

She couldn't give him the number off the top

of her head, but he phoned the operator, instead, then quickly punched in the call. When he hung up a few minutes later, his eyes were rueful. ''You'd better sit down, Your Judgeship. You're not going to like this.''

''What else is new?'' she retorted. ''I can't think of a single thing about this situation that I do like. Give it to me straight, Counselor. I can take it.''

''Lightning hit the building and knocked out all power in a twelve-block area.''

''What!''

''That's not the worst of it,'' he warned her. ''The backup system was pretty much fried by the lightning and is struggling just to keep the lights on. Emergency crews are doing everything they can, but no one's sure when there'll be enough power to run the elevators again. We could be here awhile.''

She paled. ''What do you mean by *awhile*? Ten or twenty minutes? An hour? What?''

''Let's put it this way,'' he said dryly. ''I hope you had a big lunch, because supper could be a long ways off.''

It was worse, much worse, than she'd expected. He was talking *hours!* ''I can't believe this,'' she murmured. ''What do they expect us to do all afternoon? Just sit on the floor and wait?''

His eyes got that devilish glint, the one that for reasons she couldn't explain invariably made her heart lurch in her breast and her temper simmer. ''Oh, I'm sure we can think of something a little more interesting to do to pass the time than that,'' he drawled, daring to wink at her. ''The last time I got stuck in an elevator with a woman—''

''Was no doubt highly entertaining for you but of no interest to me whatsoever, Mr. Baxter,'' she said primly. ''So if you don't mind, I'd just as soon not hear about it.''

''I was only going to say that we played—''

''If I wanted to know about your adventures with your harem, I would read the gossip columns,'' she cut in stiffly. ''Now, if you don't mind, I'd like a little peace and quiet. I have work to do, and this is the perfect time to do it.''

As regal as a queen, she moved to the corner farthest from him and sank as gracefully to the floor as the straight skirt of her black crepe suit would allow. She felt his eyes on her—his amusement, damn him!—but never spared him a glance as she positioned her briefcase on her lap and snapped 'it open. Seconds later, her reading glasses perched on her nose, she had a brief spread out before her and appeared totally engrossed in it. She'd have died before admitting that not a single word registered.

Still, she was prepared to ignore him, and for well over an hour, she put on a good show of doing just that. Neither of them spoke, and the only sound was that of the small emergency fan whirling overhead. She half expected him to try to distract her, but he surprised her by sinking into his own corner, leaning his head back and closing his eyes for a nap. When she dared to peek under her lashes at him, she found him watching her as if she were some strange new being from outer space he couldn't quite figure out. And that in itself was a distraction. Her head bent, she could feel his eyes touching on her bare neck and tried not to twitch.

"It's hot in here," he finally said gruffly, breaking the long silence.

She never looked up. "It'd be hotter without the fan."

"Maybe for you. You're sitting right under it."

He sounded like a grumpy little boy who always got beat out by the bigger kids. Her eyes trained on her work, Sadie struggled not to smile. Next, he would be complaining that she was taking up more than her fair share of the floor space.

"I'll be happy to move if you like," she volunteered. "God forbid that you should be hot."

"Don't get snippity, Ms. Chief Justice," he growled. "I was just making an observation. Keep your narrow little fanny right where it is. There are other ways to get cool."

Her head snapped up at the mention of her bottom, her gasp of outrage turning to one of shock as he slipped out of his suit coat and the meaning of his announcement suddenly hit her. Alarmed, she jumped to her feet, legal papers flying everywhere. "What are you doing? Stop that!"

For an answer, he loosened his tie and pulled it off. Grinning, his blue eyes challenging, he held it right in front of her nose and dropped it.

She should have laughed and called his bluff. After all, it wasn't as if she hadn't seen a man strip before. It would serve him right if she told him to go ahead and peel down to his Hanes; he didn't have anything that she hadn't seen before. But even if she had managed to get the words out without choking on them, he never would have believed she was that brazen. Not when her ex had spread it all over town that she was an uptight, frigid little witch who couldn't please a man if her life depended on it.

Then his fingers moved to the buttons of his shirt, and heat climbed painfully into her cheeks. Damning her fair skin, she jerked her gaze up to his, only to find his eyes laughing down into hers. Oh, he was enjoying himself! Fuming, she snapped, "You stop right there, Noah Baxter! Or I'll...I'll—"

"You'll what?" he taunted in amusement. "Find me in contempt of court again? I don't think so, Your Honor. In case you hadn't noticed, we're not in your courtroom now, and I don't have to do what you say."

Her eyes narrowed dangerously. "So is that what this is? Payback time?"

The rat had the nerve to look wounded. "Would I do something like that?"

"You're a lawyer, Counselor. That makes you capable of just about anything."

"Said the pot to the kettle, Ms. Legal Eagle," he retorted. "You weren't appointed to the bench by the governor because you were at the bottom of your class in law school.'' When she just scowled at him, he said in exasperation, ''Look, sweetheart, it's hotter than hell in here, and I'd just as soon avoid a heatstroke. It wouldn't hurt you to loosen a few buttons yourself.''

''As if I would!''

His grin broad, he arched a brow at her. ''What's the matter? You afraid if you show a little skin I might jump your bones? Relax, Your Honorableness. You're safe with me. I only accost judges in courthouse elevators on Tuesdays and Thursdays, and today's just Monday.''

He was teasing, but she'd heard enough about Noah Baxter to know that while he might be the world's most outrageous flirt, he was a gentleman who generally liked and respected women. And they loved him for it. He'd never stoop to forcing his attentions on anyone. Especially Hanging Judge Thompson.

Oh, yes, she knew what she was called behind her back, as well as every hateful word David had said about her and their sex life after their divorce. He'd told anyone who would listen that all their problems stemmed from her coldness and lack of responsiveness, so she wasn't surprised that Noah felt the need to assure her that she was safe with him. He was a man who obviously had strong sexual appetites—the last thing he would want was a woman like her.

And it hurt. For the life of her, she couldn't explain why. If she'd learned anything from her marriage and divorce, it was that she just didn't have what it took to make a relationship work. And she was okay with that. Some people were better off going through life alone, and she was obviously one of them. She should have been overjoyed that Noah Baxter wasn't interested in her as a woman. Instead, he'd kicked her in the heart with his teasing words of reassurance, and all she wanted to do was cry.

She didn't, of course. She would have died first before letting him see that he'd hurt her. Stooping to pick up her paperwork, she said stiffly, "Then I'll be sure to stay out of the elevators on Tuesdays and Thursdays. In the meantime, I'd appreciate it if you'd keep your clothes on. You may be an exhibitionist, but I'm not."

He would have laughed at the idea of anyone under eighty labeling him an exhibitionist just because he had his shirt unbuttoned, but he didn't feel much like laughing when he caught a glimpse of the lady's face as she bent to stuff her papers into her satchel. There were tears in her eyes—tears he knew *he* had somehow put there—and the sight of them was like a punch in the gut. What the hell had he said?

"Judge? Are you okay?"

She didn't answer; she wouldn't even look at him. She couldn't have picked a better way to make him feel like dirt. And he didn't even know why. "Look," he began gruffly, "I don't know what's going on here—"

The weak overhead lights suddenly surged brighter as the power came back on, and in the time it took for them both to glance up, the elevator jolted into motion. Swearing, Noah quickly began to button his shirt. He was only half-done when they reached the fourth floor.

If he lived to be a hundred, he didn't think he would ever forget the sight that met his eyes when the damn doors parted. What looked like half the maintenance staff was there in the hallway in front of the elevators. No one said anything, but they didn't have to. He saw their eyes widen as they took in his disheveled appearance, the way Her Worshipfulness wouldn't look at him, the satchel she clutched protectively to her breast. The two of them couldn't have looked more guilty if they'd been caught in a hot clench, and it didn't take an Einstein to figure out that the story, embellished many times over, would be all over the courthouse by the first coffee break in the morning.

At his side, he could almost feel Sadie cringing in mortification, which only added to the appearance of guilt. She should have kept her chin high and acted as if nothing out of the ordinary had happened, and no one would have dared think anything else but the best of the straitlaced Judge Thompson. Instead, she blinked back tears, ducked her head and rushed through the crowd like the hounds of hell were after her, choking apologies all the way.

Chapter 3

The storm was directly over downtown and making its angry presence known. A premature darkness had settled over the city, and as streetlights sprang on long before they should have, lightning slashed across the gloomy sky, only to be followed by rolling claps of thunder that seemed to shake the very walls of the old courthouse.

Plunging down the central staircase of the building, Sadie winced as the lights once again flickered, but this time they held strong. There was no bell to signal the end of the day, but suddenly jurors and lawyers were pouring out into the hallway and down the stairs like a bunch of kids let out from school early, chattering and laughing and eager to be on their way. Caught up in the fast-moving tide, Sadie let them carry her along, away from Noah. Over the din, she thought she heard him impatiently call her name, but she couldn't be sure and she didn't look back. Like a wounded animal, she just wanted to go to ground and lick her wounds.

The social club was four blocks from the courthouse and well within walking distance, which was one of the things she loved about it. Before she'd left for work that morning, the weather forecast had called for a slim twenty percent chance of rain. That twenty percent was currently coming down in sheets. Hesitating with the rest of the crowd that had collected on the front portico of the old building, she swore softly. Her clerk always kept a spare umbrella—she only had to take the underground walkway that linked the courthouse to the justice center and her office across the street to retrieve it. But she'd had enough of the legal system for one day. All she wanted to do was go home and forget the last hour had ever happened. Pushing her way through the crowd that blocked the stairs down to the sidewalk, she stepped out into the rain and wind and rushed down the steps.

In the time it took to gasp, she was soaked all the way to the skin. Shivering, she hugged herself, the scent of ozone strong in the air as lightning flashed and sizzled all around her. Too late, she realized that walking home in the middle of an electric storm wasn't exactly the brightest thing to do, but she could see the social club down the street. In the time it took to turn back to the courthouse and fight her way back inside, she could be home. The decision made, she bent her head, leaned into the blowing rain and hurried on.

She was a block from home when she heard a shout behind her and looked over her shoulder to see Noah, as wet as she, his hair plastered to his head and dripping in his eyes, quickly eliminating the distance between them. Lord, didn't the man ever give up? He was furious—even in the unnatural darkness caused by the storm, she could see that steam was practically pouring from his ears. If she hadn't still been so upset herself, she would have found some humor in that. Instead, she turned her back on him and picked up her pace. Almost running, she darted into the street just as the traffic light at the corner turned green.

"Dammit, woman, what are you trying to

do? Get yourself killed?'' Noah roared angrily after her as she dodged traffic to a symphony of blasting horns. ''Wait up!''

She had no intention of doing any such thing. Finally reaching the opposite corner safely, she turned to find a sea of cars separating them like a raging river. Nothing could have pleased her more. Ignoring his repeated shouts to wait up, she waved jauntily, then turned and marched toward home. Stuck on the far corner, there wasn't a damn thing he could do to stop her.

More than one driver dared to toot his horn at him, and Noah didn't even count the ones who grinned at him like an idiot. Grinding his teeth on an oath, his shoes squishing with every step and his favorite suit clinging to his body, he tried to remember the last woman he'd made such a fool of himself over. The only one who came to mind was Mary Lou Gardner. Fourteen and suffering the pangs of his first crush, he had, much to the amusement of his entire high school, chased after Mary Lou like a puppy tripping over its own tongue. He'd sworn then he'd never be that stupid again, yet here he was, standing out in the weather like some kind of moron who didn't have enough sense to come in out of the rain.

He didn't even know what the hell he'd done to set her off, but he was going to find out, he vowed grimly. Through narrowed eyes, he watched her hurry down the street and reach the front porch of the social club. Wet and bedraggled, she still somehow managed to hold on to her dignity, and for reasons he couldn't begin to explain, that irritated the hell out of him. Oh, she was a cool one! But if she thought she could outmaneuver him so easily, she was in for a rude awakening. As soon as the light changed, he was after her like a shot.

He caught up with her just as she was unlocking the front door of her apartment. Dripping water across the old hardwood floors of the central hall, he growled, ''Hold it right there, Miss High-and-Mighty Chief Justice. I don't know what's got your tail feathers in a twist, but I think I'm entitled to an explanation.''

''Then you're doomed to disappointment,'' she said curtly, ''because this conversation is over. Now, if you'll excuse me, I'd like to change and get into some dry clothes.''

He should have let her go. It would have

been the smart thing to do. He wasn't in the best of moods and what he had to say to her could wait until another time. But the lady judge was used to giving orders and had a way of dismissing him that he'd be damned he'd accept anywhere but in the courtroom.

"No, I won't excuse you," he retorted, grabbing the doorknob before she could open the door and slip inside. "You've got a bee in your bonnet about something, and I seem to be the cause of it. You want to tell me what I did or do I have to guess?"

Half-turned away from him, her spine ramrod straight, she didn't say a word, didn't even look at him. Exasperated, he wanted to shake her, but he struggled for patience, instead. "Look," he said with a sigh, "I don't know what's going on in your head, but if I said something to hurt you, I'm sorry."

That got her attention. Whirling, she faced him, her brown eyes dark with hurt and temper. "Of course you don't know what you said. You're one of those charming men who speak without thinking, then figure a smile and an apology make up for anything. Well, just for the record, Mr. *Stud* Baxter, they don't. Next time, I'd appreciate it if you'd keep your opinion of me to yourself. I don't care that you don't find me attractive—''

Stunned, he said, ''Whoa! What are you talking about? I never said—''

''I don't *want* you to,'' she continued as if he hadn't spoken. ''In fact, I wouldn't have you gift wrapped on a platter. So save the assurances that I'm safe with you to yourself, Mr. Baxter. I never thought anything else. Am I making myself clear?''

Oh, she was clear, all right, he thought, glaring down at her. Clear as glass. If that wasn't just like a woman! He'd just been trying to make her feel more at ease in the damn elevator, and now she was all bent out of shape because he hadn't taken advantage of the situation. On top of that, she had to insult him. Wouldn't have him on a platter, would she? he silently fumed. Well, they'd see about that!

''If you're rejecting me, sweetheart—and that seems to be what you're doing—don't walk away without at least getting a taste of what you're passing up,'' he snapped.

That was all the warning he gave her. Giving in to impulse, he grabbed her and pulled her up on her toes to lay a kiss on her that was guaranteed to curl her hair. Later, he couldn't have said who was more surprised, him or the very prim and proper Sadie Thompson. She went stiff as a board under his hands, and too late, he remembered just who he was kissing. A judge. A criminal court judge who could make his life miserable in the courtroom. He didn't have any business touching her, let alone kissing her.

He should have released her immediately. After all, it wasn't as if she encouraged him. She didn't kiss him back, didn't unbend in the slightest. But Lord, she had a sweet mouth on her! Soft and enticing, with a seductive curve that no man with any blood in his veins could resist. If she would just loosen up a little…

The ice princess doesn't loosen up, a voice in his head jeeringly reminded him. Remember? Not even her husband could melt the ice in her. What makes you think you can?

Brought up short by the taunt, he jerked back abruptly to scowl down at her in confusion. Her cheeks were flushed, her mouth red and slightly swollen from his kiss, her brown eyes nearly black with temper and a shock that matched his own. She was pretty, he thought, disconcerted that he'd just then noticed. She didn't deck herself out in makeup and perfume—if anything, she did everything she could to conceal her femininity—but the classic lines of beauty were there in the curve of her cheek, the elegant sweep of her brow, the clear, translucent freshness of her skin. And it was all he could do not to kiss that sweet, sweet mouth again.

What the devil was going on here?

Swearing, he told himself to get the hell out of there while he still could. He didn't need to be told twice. His jaw rigid, he turned and stormed up the stairs. He took pride in the fact that he was a man who rarely lost control of his temper, but when he slammed the door of his apartment behind him a few seconds later, the force of the door shutting rattled the windows.

Damn! What the hell had he been thinking of? he wondered furiously. Sadie Thompson. God, he'd kissed Sadie Thompson! He must have been out of his mind. It was the only explanation. He'd walked home in that damn storm, and the electricity in the air had fried his brain. Why else would he have grabbed the woman and kissed her like there was no tomorrow? It wasn't as if he was attracted to her. She was so straitlaced that she probably creaked when she walked, and according to gossip, she was as frigid as ice water in bed. No man in his right mind would want to get mixed up with a woman like that.

I don't care that you don't find me attractive.... I don't want you to.... So save the assurances that I'm safe with you to yourself, Mr. Baxter. I never thought anything else.

The angry words she'd thrown at him echoed in his ears, suddenly, for the first time, making sense. He swore, cursing himself for his own blindness. Of course she'd heard the ugly whispers, the hurtful rumors about herself that had been circulating for months. How could she not? Gossips weren't often nice and seldom discreet. Not only was she aware of every malicious word that had been said about her, she knew that he had heard the comments, too, and thought he believed them. Taken in that context, his words of reassurance must have hit her like a slap in the face.

"Dammit to hell!" If he could have gotten his hands on her ex right then, he would have gladly punched him for her. God, he was a bastard! No matter what problems they'd had in the bedroom, Lincoln had had no right to trash her the way he had. He'd publicly hit her where a woman was the most vulnerable, then high-tailed it to Houston like the sniveling coward that he was, callously leaving her to the mercy of every scandalmonger in town. Talk about sleaze!

And he hadn't helped matters by first inadvertently offending her, then grabbing her like some kind of Neanderthal who couldn't control his own primitive urges. She'd had every right to slug him, but resorting to the physical wasn't the honorable Judge Sadie Thompson's way. Oh, no. She'd used her tongue to cut him to ribbons, instead, and he couldn't say he blamed her. He'd deserved nothing less.

He owed her an apology, face to face, the sooner, the better. Given his druthers, he would have bitten the bullet and marched back downstairs to deliver it right then and there, but he seriously doubted she would even open the door to him, let alone accept his apology. She was too upset. She needed time to cool off, and time was something he didn't have right now. Every Monday night, he had dinner with his mother and sisters, and he was already running late. Tomorrow, though, he promised himself, the lady would listen to him. Even if he had to camp out on her doorstep.

* * *

With one sister in high school, one in college and one each in law school and medical school, it wasn't surprising that getting everyone together, even just one night a week, was a major accomplishment. It was the only chance they all had to share a meal and catch up on one another's lives, and if you couldn't make it, his mother expected you to have a darn good reason.

He made it, but the rain and flooding streets held him up, and the second he walked into the old-fashioned bungalow-style home where he was raised, Alex let him know about it. Waiting at the front door, she pulled it open and flashed her braces at him. "You're late, and you know what that means. You get to do the dishes!"

"Hey, c'mon," he protested. "Have you looked outside recently? It's pouring out there! I'll probably have to rent a canoe just to get home tonight."

Rachel, in the process of setting the table in the dining room, wasn't the least impressed with his excuse. Twenty and sassy, she never let him get away with anything. "Wah! Wah!" she teased, imitating an infant's cry. "Poor baby thought he was going to melt if he got wet. The rest of us got here on time."

"I guess so," he snorted, tugging at one of her dark, short curls. "You just live around the corner, and Nat and Kelly aren't much farther away. I had to come all the way from downtown."

Picking up the gist of the conversation, Natalie sailed in from the kitchen with a full bowl of spaghetti and shot him a knowing look, her blue eyes, so like his, twinkling. "Late again, hmm? Who is she?"

"Who?"

Not fooled in the least by his innocent act, she laughed. "Nice try, Romeo. But the only time you're ever late is when you get held up by a woman. So who was it this time? Do we know her?"

A first-year law student, Nat might not know Sadie personally, but Noah didn't doubt for a second that she knew who she was. "A gentleman never mentions a lady's name," he drawled, winking.

Standing in the doorway to the kitchen, Kelly arched a brow at him, her grin wicked. "Well, that lets you out. So what's her name, hotshot?"

"It must be that Newman woman," Alex guessed. "The one with the big—"

"Alex!" Her tone scolding, her brown eyes laughing over the steaming bowl of meatballs she carried, Gillian Baxter tried to give her youngest a stern look, but the effect was ruined by the smile that kept tugging at her lips. "Innocent young girls don't go around talking about women's big... Ah, I mean... They don't talk about..."

Helplessly, she looked at Noah, who only grinned and took the bowl of food from her. Devilment glinting in his eyes, he prompted, "Don't stop now, Mom. A woman's big what?"

"Oh, you!" Laughing and blushing like a girl, she pulled off her apron and swatted him with it. "Her big feet, of course! You never took the time to introduce us properly, but I saw her once at the mall, and I swear, the woman had feet as big as Shaquille O'Neal's. Why, I bet I could put both my feet in one of her shoes and still have room left over!"

Chuckling, Noah didn't doubt it for a minute. Barely topping five foot, Gillian Baxter was a little thing, petite and delicate. Every one of her children towered over her, and it always amazed Noah that she was his mother. She was fifty-five, a widow for seven years, the mother of five children. As pretty and sassy as her daughters, with hardly a touch of gray in her dark, curly hair, she could have passed for a forty-year-old.

"You're probably right," he agreed. "Not that I paid that much attention. I wasn't looking at her feet."

That earned him another swat from his mother as they all took their seats around the table. "Stop that! You shouldn't talk like that about the woman you might marry."

Taken aback, he gaped at her. "*Marry?* I'm not marrying Gina Newman!"

"Or Tracy Richie, Susie Preston or Lynn Ford," Kelly said, her dimples flashing impishly. "And those are just some of the ones you dated last week. Who'd I miss?"

"Ellen Dunn and Jennifer Bernard," Alex said promptly over a mouthful of spaghetti. "Colleen Kerry always keeps tabs on who he's seeing in her gossip column in the paper."

"So when are you going to settle down with Miss Right?" Natalie asked him bluntly. "Mom wants grandchildren."

"I'll get around to it eventually. There are a lot of beautiful women out there—it takes time for a man to go through them all and find the

right one,'' he teased outrageously. ''Anyway,
I'm not the only one who can give her grandchildren, you know. What about you? Are you
still seeing that Madison character? What's it
been now? A year or two? Maybe I should have
a talk with him.''

''Oh, no, you don't! You stay away from
Tim. The last time you *talked* to one of my
dates, he never spoke to me again.'' When he
only gave her that big-brother look that told her
he'd do whatever he had to to watch out for
her, she turned in growing frustration to their
mother. ''Mom! Make him stop!''

''Now, children, don't fight,'' she scolded
playfully. ''Your food's getting cold.''

That successfully turned the topic of marriage away from him, but Noah knew it was
only a matter of time before the subject came
up again. His mother worried about him, worried that he had put his life on hold for his
sisters, and in a way, she was right. The last
thing his father said to Noah, right before he
died, was, ''Look after the girls.'' Noah, just
out of law school, promised him he would, and
he took that promise seriously. He was very
involved in their lives, emotionally as well as
financially, and had no intention of marrying

until the last one was out of college. And that was okay with him. He loved them, and looking out for them was no sacrifice. And it wasn't as if he'd had to pass up the woman of his dreams because of his commitment to his family. He liked women, enjoyed dating them, but he hadn't lost any sleep over one in years.

That did not, however, reassure Gillian Baxter or make her worry any less. As soon as the meal was over and his sisters had scattered, she joined him in the kitchen to help him with the dishes. ''Sweetheart, we need to talk.''

He knew that tone and quickly moved to cut her off. ''Sure, Mom. Did you catch the Rangers game the other night? It was a no-hitter—''

Smiling, she patted him on the cheek. ''Nice try, honey, but I'm not talking baseball and you know it. Don't you think it's time you found some happiness for yourself?''

''Mom, I'm not unhappy—''

''I didn't say you were. You seem content enough with the way things are, but that's only because the right woman hasn't come along yet.''

''And she won't,'' he assured her. ''Not until Alex is out of school.''

Humor glinting in her eyes, she chuckled at

his confidence. "Oh, how the mighty set themselves up for a fall. Sweetheart, I know you think you're in charge of your own destiny, but when Miss Right comes knocking on your door, trust me, you're not going to know what hit you. Whatever you do, please don't let the promise you made to Dad before he died keep you from grabbing her while you can. For some people, love only comes along once. It was that way for me and your father, and I think it'll be that way for you. Don't let it pass you by. You might not get a second chance."

Normally, he would have teased her that her real concern was for the future grandchildren she was impatient to love and spoil before she was too old to enjoy them, but her brown eyes were dark with concern and he knew she was truly worried about him. "All right, I'll keep my eyes open," he assured her. "I want what you and Dad had, too, Mom. But you've got to remember, they don't make girls like you anymore."

"Of course they do, sweetheart," she chided. "You're just not looking in the right place."

An image of Sadie Thompson flashed before his eyes. The button-down-collar, figure-concealing business suits, the dark hair scraped back into a no-nonsense knot. And that soft, soft, enticing mouth. A man could lose himself in that mouth.

"Noah? Son? What's the matter?"

Jerking back from his hot thoughts, he blinked and just barely swallowed a groan as he brought his mother's face back into focus. They were talking about Miss Right, dammit. So what the devil was he doing thinking of Sadie Thompson?

"Nothing," he said hastily, forcing a wolfish grin that didn't come as easily as he'd have liked. "I was just thinking of Honey Sue Greenwood. I met her at the car wash when she was washing her Jeep in a bikini. I guess a car wash isn't exactly the place to look for the mother of my children, huh?"

"Not hardly," his mother retorted dryly. "Especially if she was flaunting her big... feet."

They both laughed, but long after Noah had left and headed back to his apartment, it was images of Sadie Thompson, not Honey Sue Greenwood and her big *feet* that kept flitting before his mind's eye, teasing his senses.

When Sadie didn't sleep well, she refused to believe it had anything to do with Noah and a kiss that she wouldn't allow herself to dwell on. It was just the thunderstorms that rumbled overhead all night that kept her awake. When she overslept the next morning and was fifteen minutes late leaving for work, she knew it was going to be one of those days.

She couldn't have been more right. In a hurry, she'd hardly rushed into the courthouse when she became aware of more than a few speculative looks and snickers about her captivity with Noah in the stuck elevator the day before. Even her bailiff teasingly commented that she was probably late because she wisely took the stairs. If she could have gotten her hands on Noah, she would have gladly given him a good tongue-lashing.

Needless to say, she wasn't in the best of moods when she strode into her courtroom, and neither was anyone else. Everyone seemed to be short-tempered, including herself. When a defense attorney and prosecutor started going at each other like two heavyweights who wanted to pound each other into the ground, she would have liked nothing better than to let them have at it. That, unfortunately, wasn't an option.

Banging her gavel, she glared at both men

and warned, "This kind of behavior is not acceptable in my courtroom, gentlemen. You will act in a civilized manner or you're going to find yourselves in contempt." Striking her gavel again, she said, "We'll adjourn early for lunch to give you both time to think about your behavior. Court will reconvene at one o'clock."

With a swirl of her robes, she rose and proceeded to her chambers. She'd barely stepped inside, when her clerk appeared with the mail and a rose. Taking the letters, Sadie arched a brow at her. "You and John have another argument?"

Betty's husband was the gentlest of men, and whenever he lost his temper, he always felt horribly guilty about it later. He invariably apologized with flowers. "Nope, no arguments. Not even about this month's checkbook, and I really thought he was going to lose it over that." Smiling, she held out the flower to Sadie. "This time, it's for you."

"Me!"

Chuckling, she nodded to the stack of mail she handed her along with the rose. "There's a note and a card. Since you don't normally get personal stuff here at the office, I thought about steaming them open," she admitted with twinkling eyes, "but I figured you'd be able to tell. So who's the secret admirer? Anyone I know?"

Dazed, Sadie stared at the rose in wonder. "There's no one. It must be a mistake—"

But even as she sank into her big leather chair behind her desk, she knew. Hot color seeping into her cheeks, she reached for the note and tore it open:

You should have decked me. I'm sorry.

There was no signature beneath the bold scrawl, but she didn't need one. Noah. Only he would dare to apologize with a gesture that would just add fuel to the gossip stirred up by yesterday's elevator fiasco. All it took was one person seeing flowers being delivered to Judge Thompson's chambers, and someone would put two and two together and come up with five. By the time the tale completed its course through the courthouse, the single rose would have been exaggerated to a dozen and the rumor mill would have it that Noah Baxter had lost his mind and was trying to heat up icy Judge Thompson.

"Well? Who's it from?"

Looking up from her thoughts, she couldn't help but smile at the sight of Betty hovering in front of her, as curious as a cat, dying to get a look at the card. Normally, she wouldn't have hesitated to show it to her, but Betty would take one look and start asking questions she wasn't prepared to answer. Hastily she closed the card, then stuffed it back in its envelope.

"One of my new neighbors," she said off-handedly. "It's just one of those welcome-to-the-neighborhood gestures."

"Oh." Disappointed, Betty said, "Well, rats. So much for secret admirers. The other one's probably the same thing."

Curious—surely Noah wouldn't send her two cards!—Sadie pulled a cream-colored envelope from the stack of mail. Her name and address were neatly typed on it, but there was no return address. The back flap wasn't sealed, and with a flick of her finger, she opened it and pulled out the card inside. The second she saw the picture of a baby tiger on the front, she started to smile. Then she read the typed message inside:

Excuse yourself from the Dominic Dominguez trial or you'll regret it.

It wasn't the first threatening piece of mail she'd ever received, and it wouldn't be the last. She got letters full of hate and recrimination on a fairly regular basis from convicted criminals and their families, blaming her for everything from letting the prosecuting attorney get away with murder to accusing her of being vindictive and assigning too harsh a punishment. She'd learned not to take any of the correspondence personally, but it never failed to surprise her what people put in a letter.

"I don't think this is from one of the neighbors," she said dryly, handing it to her. "Take a look."

The other woman opened it, only to snort in disdain. "Somebody obviously doesn't know you at all or they'd know you wouldn't even blink at a little sissy threat like that. Who do you think sent it?"

"God only knows. There are a lot of nuts in the world."

"And all of them are cracked." Holding the card out in front of her as though it put off a stink all its own, she grimaced in distaste. "What do you want me to do with it?"

"File it with the rest of the unsolicited opinions," she replied, and laughed when Betty dropped it in the trash.

She had to thank him for the rose.

Staring at its delicate red petals after Betty

left for lunch, Sadie would have liked nothing better than to drop a quick, impersonal note of thanks in the mail to Noah, then forget that she'd ever had the misfortune to tangle with the man, let alone be on the receiving end of a kiss she'd wanted no part of. For hours after he'd left her last night, the only thing she'd been able to taste was his mouth on hers. It must have been three before she'd finally fallen asleep, and the last thing she wanted to do was see him again. But her pride insisted that she thank him in person.

Anxious to get the chore over with as soon as possible, she pulled out the phone book, looked up his office number and quickly punched it in before she could change her mind. She would keep things as impersonal as possible, she vowed, and meet with him at his office instead of the social club. Then she could leave when she was ready.

But when his receptionist came on the line, it was to inform her that he was in court with a murder trial and would be tied up for the next five or six days. If Sadie wanted to make an appointment, the earliest he could see her was a week from Friday. ''If you just need to talk to him for a few minutes, you'd do better to catch him at the courthouse, Judge Thompson. He's in Judge Quincy's courtroom.''

Tom Quincy's courtroom was just down the hall from hers—if they hadn't broken for lunch yet, she could pop in, wait for the recess to speak her piece, then be on her way. ''I'll do that,'' she told the receptionist. ''Thanks.''

Hurriedly shedding her judicial robes, she grabbed her purse, locked up her office, then strode quickly down the hall to the 284th district court. Through the glass sidelights flanking the entrance, she saw Quincy, complete with muttonchop whiskers and the pipe he boldly puffed on in spite of the No Smoking signs everywhere, sitting at the bench like an old-timey circuit judge. Relieved that he hadn't called the lunch break yet, she quietly slipped inside.

Noah was seated with his back to her at the defense table and never saw her find a seat in the crowded gallery. All his attention was focused on the testimony of the man in the witness box. A middle-aged minister with graying hair and a kind face, the witness answered the prosecutor's questions without hesitancy, placing the defendant at the scene of the murder, with the murder weapon in his hand, just seconds before the killing occurred.

Sadie knew better than to rush to judgment after hearing only one side of a case, but the minister's testimony was riveting—and damning. Everyone in the courtroom was hanging on his every word, and he was quietly confident of what he had seen. When Noah's turn came to question him, he tried to pick apart his story under cross-examination, but he knew better than to badger such a witness and chance losing any plausibility with the jury. Watching him in action, she had to admit that he was good, but not even he could do anything to discount that kind of testimony. She'd never seen him so grim.

Noah was, in fact, furious. When Jonathan Taylor had hired him to represent him, he'd sworn that he was innocent and this was all just a big mistake. He'd claimed he had an alibi, that there was no way he could be guilty of killing his own mother, and Noah had had no reason not to believe him.

He hadn't known then that the man was a pathological liar who couldn't be trusted to tell the time of day, let alone the truth. Over the course of the last two days, the state had produced one witness after another who'd looked squarely at the jury and sworn that Jonathan

Taylor was an ambitious, amoral man who would do or say anything to get ahead… including shoot his mother in the head while she was sleeping to get his hands on her money. When he wanted something, he didn't let anything get in his way.

Too late, Noah had realized that all of Taylor's sincerity when he'd come to him for help had been nothing but an act. And it was that, more than anything, that rankled. Taylor was scum, lower than dirt, but hardly the first piece of trash that Noah had represented. After all, he was a criminal lawyer, and few of his clients were lily-white. It was his job to defend them to the best of his ability and get them the fairest trial he could. But Taylor didn't want just a good defense—he made it clear that for the money he was paying, he damn well expected to walk out of the courtroom a free man. And everything in Noah rebelled at the idea of helping anyone get away with premeditated murder.

Jonathan Taylor knew it, and reveled in the fact that he had him between a rock and a hard place. He was too crafty to fire him, and Noah couldn't quit without raising questions about his client's innocence. If he did anything to cause a mistrial, he could be disbarred. He was stuck and he hated it. All he could do was his job and hope that the jury was smart enough to see the bastard for what he was—a cold-blooded killer.

With the ending of his cross-examination, Quincy excused the witness and called a break for lunch. Noah had no intention of spending the time with his client and quickly headed for the nearest exit. He'd only taken three steps, when he stopped dead in his tracks at the sight of Sadie sitting in the last row of the gallery.

She looked good.

She looks just like she always does, an irritated voice in his head snapped. She's got her hair scrapped back like an onion and a damn black suit on in the middle of summer. Don't be an idiot, Baxter. She's not your type.

She was, in fact, as far from his type as the moon was from the South Pole, but that didn't seem to change the fact that he was pleased to see her. Or that he liked the idea of her sitting in the gallery, watching him while he worked.

You really are losing it, man. And after just one kiss. For God's sake, she didn't even kiss you back! What's gotten into you? This is Hanging Judge Thompson you're drooling over. Hello? Is anybody home? She's an iceberg, dammit! Just ask her ex.

That should have sent him running for cover, but when he started walking again, he headed right for the lady. Later, he'd have to give some serious thought as to why she intrigued the hell out of him, but for now, she obviously had come looking for him and he intended to find out the reason.

"Howdy, Your Judgeship," he drawled, grinning crookedly. "You having a slow day or what? Surely you can find something better to sit in on than this."

She didn't smile as he had hoped. Instead, she said, "You took a hit with that last witness, but you handled it well. I hope your client realizes that he's lucky you're on his side."

Surprised, he teasingly clutched at his heart. "My God, a compliment! Help me. I think it's the big one!"

"Don't let it go to your head, Counselor," she said dryly, her lips twitching. "You're good, but I've seen better."

"And here I thought I was God's gift to jurisprudence. There goes the ego, shot down again." Comfortably sprawled sideways on the bench seat in front of her, he stretched his arm out along the back and arched a brow at her. "Since you didn't hunt me down to marvel at my legal skills, you must have had another reason for seeking me out. To what do I owe the pleasure of your company, Your Honor?"

Right before his eyes, the confident, self-possessed judge melted into a shy, hesitant, woman who wasn't quite sure of herself. "I..." She swallowed, then blurted out, "I wanted to thank you for the rose. You didn't have to go to so much trouble, but I appreciate the gesture. And accept your apology."

Heat stained her cheeks, and in spite of all his best intentions, his eyes lingered on the soft, seductive curve of her mouth. There was passion there in the full bottom lip and the bow of the top—any man with eyes could see it. Yet she seemed totally unaware of it, and he couldn't help but wonder what would have happened when he'd kissed her if she'd kissed him back.

Impulsively, ignoring the voice in his head that warned him he needed to steer clear of this woman, he said, "Then have lunch with me. There's a little place a couple of blocks over that makes great fajitas."

Yes. The word rose to her tongue with a

swiftness that shook her to the core even as her common sense demanded to know if she'd lost her mind. What was she doing? Had she already forgotten what happened when she let herself get tangled up with a man? Even something as innocent as lunch? When she'd first started dating David, it had started out innocently, too. Then, before it was over, he'd taken half of everything of value she had. That wasn't a mistake she intended to repeat, and the best way to do that was to nip things in the bud now.

"It sounds great," she said with true regret as she pushed to her feet. "But I can't. I never socialize with lawyers. It's just not a smart thing to do when you could end up representing someone in my courtroom."

It was a practical excuse, but she only had to look in his eyes to see that he knew as well as she did that other judges and lawyers socialized all the time. He was enough of a gentleman, however, not to point that out. With a wry twist of his mouth, he, too, stood. "Then I guess we'll have to keep meeting in courtrooms and elevators. See you around, Your Judgeship."

Giving her a mocking salute, he strolled out of the now-empty courtroom, leaving her alone, fighting the need to call him back.

Chapter 4

"And now for the local news. Louis Humphrey, the state's star witness in the Dominic Dominguez Mexican mafia trial, was killed in a car accident early this morning at the intersection of San Pedro and Oblate. Witnesses say Humphrey, traveling at a high rate of speed, ran the traffic light and plowed into a black van. He was killed instantly. The driver of the van, who sustained only minor injuries, was treated and released at the scene. At this point, there seems to be no connection between the accident and threats allegedly made against Humphrey by members of the drug cartel for turning state's evidence, but the police are still investigating the cause of the accident. Stay tuned for the news at noon for more on this story. Now for the weather..."

Disturbed, Sadie turned off the small portable television in her bedroom and frowned at herself in the mirror as she checked her appearance one last time before leaving for work. Pretrial motions in the Dominguez trial were scheduled to be heard before her that morning in court, and the loss of the state's main witness couldn't have come at a better time for the defendant. A smart defense attorney would already be celebrating a victory for his client, and Dominguez had hired nothing but the best. To say that the day was going to be interesting was putting it mildly.

Not surprisingly, Ethan Kingston, Dominguez's attorney, took the offensive the second court was called into session. A tall, stout man with a flowing white mane of hair, he stood with a grace that was surprising for such a big man, and when he spoke with that booming voice of his, everyone in the room sat up straighter.

"Your Honor, in light of the sudden, regrettable death of the state's main witness, there is very little evidence against my client. The state only had conjecture and supposition to begin with, and now, there isn't even that. Due to a glaring lack of evidence, I therefore request that all charges against Mr. Dominguez be dropped immediately and my client be allowed to get on with the rest of his life.''

Infuriated, the prosecutor jumped to his feet. "Your Honor, this is outrageous!" Young and fresh-faced, Michael Dunn didn't present nearly as imposing a figure as Kingston, but he had a sharp, quick legal mind and wasn't often out-flanked. "I'm not surprised that Mr. Kingston would try to take advantage of Mr. Humphrey's sudden, tragic death, but for him to stand there and tell this court that the state has no evidence is reprehensible. We have the murder weapon, which belongs to the defendant, and witnesses that can attest that Mr. Dominguez not only had motive, but the opportunity to commit the crime. If that's not enough, I've just learned that the police have discovered that Mr. Humphrey's brakes were tampered with, which makes his death a murder, not an accident. And the one person who had the most to gain from his unexpected demise was the defendant. Under no circumstances should the charges against him be dropped.''

Wounded, Kingston slapped a hand over his

chest as if he'd just been stabbed in the heart. "Your Honor, Mr. Dunn does my client an injustice. He's obviously a desperate man who will say anything to prejudice this court—"

Insulted, Sadie gave him a look that stopped him cold. "I would suggest you stop right there, Counselor. I have no intention of being prejudiced one way or the other in this case, but I know a just cause when I hear it. Your request that charges be dropped is denied and your objection duly noted. Now that that's settled, I suggest you proceed with any other pretrial motions you wish to enter at this time."

A smart man, Kingston knew better than to beat a dead horse. Opening his briefcase, he withdrew the motions he wanted rulings on before the actual jury trial began and approached the bench to present them to Sadie for consideration. And all the while, his client watched Sadie with dark, cold eyes.

It didn't take a genius to figure out that he didn't like her, didn't like the idea of a woman controlling his destiny. But that was his problem, not hers, and she had no intention of letting him intimidate her. Ignoring him, she accepted motions from both Kingston and Michael Dunn, glanced through them, then nodded. ''Everything appears to be in order. I'll look them over and make my rulings when we reconvene here on June 14 at 10 a.m. Until then, we are adjourned.''

All business, she dismissed them with the bang of her gavel and let out a silent sigh of relief as the next case on the court's docket was called. There was the usual shuffle of people in the courtroom as attorneys and their clients from the previous case made room for the lawyers and prosecutors handling the next. Kingston and his client headed for the exit, and Sadie silently admitted to herself that she was glad to have a two-week breather before she had to deal with either one of them again. There was something about Dominguez that gave her the willies.

As if reading her thoughts, the mafia boss stopped at the double doors that led to the corridor and turned to face her. He didn't say a word, didn't so much as blink. He just stood there, staring at her with a menace that chilled her to the bone, before he finally turned and walked out.

Long after the doors swung shut behind him, Sadie felt as if he'd somehow managed to step on her grave. Shaken, she shivered and told herself her imagination was just playing tricks on her. The threat she'd thought she'd seen in the man's eyes was just due to the uneven lighting by the door. It had to be. Only a fool would chance antagonizing a judge who had the power to send him to prison for the rest of his life. And whatever else Dominic Dominguez was, he was no fool.

She had a full docket of plea bargains to keep her busy after that, but the incident with Dominguez had cast a shadow on the morning and set the tone for the day. A defendant charged with armed robbery forgot to take his antidepressant medication and flipped out right there in the courtroom. Another one decided he didn't want the plea bargain after all and got in a shouting match with his own lawyer. By the time she called for the noon recess, she felt like she'd spent the morning at the zoo.

"Go on to lunch," she told Betty, her clerk, as she headed for her chambers. "I lost my appetite when the last defendant started talking about killing chickens on his grandmother's farm, so I'll just catch up on some paperwork—"

"Oh, but you can't!"

"Believe me, it's not going to hurt me to

miss a meal or two,'' she said with a laugh as she pushed open the door to her private chambers. ''And it's not like I haven't had anything to eat today—''

She stepped into her office, took one look at her desk, and that was as far as she got. Her eyes wide with surprise, she could do nothing but stare at the picnic lunch, complete with red gingham tablecloth, that someone had spread out on her desk. There was everything from deviled eggs to barbecued chicken to pecan pie.

Stunned, she glanced at Betty in bewilderment. ''Who…?''

She didn't see Noah standing back out of sight near the door until he stepped forward. When she gasped softly, Betty said worriedly, ''I'm sorry, Judge. I shouldn't have let Mr. Baxter in here without checking with you first, but he said he was your neighbor and he wanted to surprise you.…''

He had done that, all right. He'd stolen the breath right out of her lungs, and she didn't know why. He knew her history, knew she didn't date lawyers—or anyone else, for that matter—so why was he being so persistent? Her eyes searching his, she told her clerk, ''It's okay, Betty. He really is my neighbor. You can go on to lunch. I'll deal with Mr. Baxter.''

The other woman didn't need to be told twice. Quietly letting herself out, she shut the door behind her, leaving the two of them alone in Sadie's chambers. In the abrupt silence left behind by her leave-taking, expectation seemed to hum. What did he want from her? Staring up at him, she frowned in confusion. ''I don't know what to say. Why did you do this?''

''Damned if I know,'' he replied honestly. ''I guess because we got off to a bad start and every time we run into each other, something seems to go wrong. I thought it was time we declared a truce. I guess my timing was off, huh? Did I hear you say something about some-body killing chickens?''

Shuddering, she grimaced. ''Believe me, you don't want to go down that road. I already lost my appetite—there's no sense in you losing yours. Especially after you went to so much trouble. Please…go ahead and eat.''

''Only if you'll try a bite of something. Just one,'' he coaxed, urging her around her desk to her chair. ''What can it hurt?''

''It seems to me that Eve said the same thing to Adam about an apple,'' she remarked dryly, grinning. "You're tempting me and I have to wonder why. Just what are you up to, Mr. Baxter?"

He could, when he chose, look as innocent as a three-year-old. Widening his eyes guilelessly, he said, "*Moi?* You wound me, Judge. It's just lunch. It's harmless—*I'm* harmless. So whaddaya say? Try just one bite, and if you still don't want to eat, then I'll get out of here and leave you in peace."

Hesitating, Sadie knew she shouldn't let herself get to know him any better than she already did. Noah Baxter was about as harmless as the devil himself, and she'd do well to remember that. But Lord, the man was charming! She should have sent him packing immediately. The least she could do was taste whatever it was that smelled so good.

"All right," she said, giving in. "A bite— but *not* chicken! I don't think I could handle that right now."

"Fair enough," he agreed, grinning. "Now, first things first. How about some pie?"

"Pie?" She laughed, surprised. "You want to start with dessert?"

"Life's too short to start with anything *but* dessert," he said simply. "Wait till you taste this. I guarantee it's the best thing you ever put your mouth to. Here, try some.''

She would have sworn that she wasn't hungry, but the second she took a bite of the pecan pie, she couldn't help but groan. ''Oh, God, that's wonderful! Where did you get that?''

''My secretary's mother-in-law owns a restaurant. Sure you don't want to try the chicken? I swear to God, it melts in your mouth.''

She didn't, but that didn't stop him from filling a plate for her with a sample of everything. Then, acting like the big brother she'd never had, he joked and teased and told her some outrageous stories that made her laugh till she cried. And without even realizing it, she began to eat. Before she knew it, she'd eaten everything on her plate.

Narrowing her eyes, she tried to frown at him and failed miserably. ''I underestimated you, Mr. Baxter. You're sneakier than I thought. Do you realize that between the two of us, we've eaten enough to feed a small army?''

Not the least repentant, he only grinned. ''I noticed that you particularly liked the chicken once you tasted it.''

She had, in fact, loved it, and he knew it, the rat. ''How'm I going to work after this?'' she demanded. "Niles Haskel is appearing before me in a little over an hour to defend a bank robber, and you know how he has a tendency to talk in a monotone. I'll never be able to stay awake."

"Knowing Haskel, he'll never notice if you don't," he retorted, his blue eyes twinkling as he helped her clean off her desk. "He likes to hear himself talk. As long as you let him drone on, he'll be happy as a clam at high tide."

"Thanks just the same, but I'd just as soon not encourage him. The man already thinks he's Clarence Darrow." Glancing at the clock on the wall, she gasped and jumped to her feet. "God, where did the time go? Court starts in ten minutes! I have to talk to Betty about the rest of the afternoon's agenda, find a robe that's not wrinkled, check my hair...."

Noah had never seen her quite so frantic, especially about her appearance, and he had to admit that he liked her best when she was shaken out of that calm, cool demeanor of hers. She seldom let anyone else catch a glimpse of the real woman behind the unbending Judge Thompson, and when she did, he was, against all his better judgment, fascinated.

He should have gotten out of there—they

both had work to get back to and he'd been thinking about the lady too much lately. But when he moved, it wasn't toward the door. Instead, he stepped in front of her, blocking her path, when she turned to the mirror that hung on the back of a closet door.

Caught off guard, she ran full tilt into the hard wall of his chest. His hands snapped up, latching onto her upper arms to steady her before him, but she hardly noticed. Flustered, she gasped. "Noah! What are you doing? I have to get ready—"

"Your hair looks just fine," he assured her. "Though you might want to change your robe."

She immediately looked down at herself, frowning. "It's wrinkled, isn't it? I was afraid of that."

"It isn't yet, but it could be in a minute."

"In a minute? What are you talking—"

He would have sworn he never intended to kiss her. Not again. Not after the last time, when she stirred things up in him that days later he still couldn't understand. But she was so damn close that he could smell the subtle, maddening fresh scent of her, and all he could think about was that soft, tempting mouth of hers.

Just a kiss, he told himself. That was all he wanted. One simple, uncomplicated kiss to see if she tasted half as good as he remembered. What could it hurt?

His hands tightened on her arms, and something of his intent must have shown in his face. Her eyes wide, she immediately planted her palms against his chest. ''Noah, don't!''

''I know this is crazy,'' he murmured huskily. ''But there's something about your mouth. I just have to kiss you. Just once. Please...''

Her heart fluttering like a trapped dove, she watched his mouth draw slowly, inexorably closer, and braced herself for the same hard kiss he'd given her before. But when his lips settled on hers, he didn't force her, didn't try to dominate her with his overpowering strength. Instead, his touch as light as a feather, he simply caressed her mouth with his with a gentleness that caught her completely off guard.

Her heart suddenly pounding, she trembled as heat slowly drizzled through her, tempting her to melt against him, to open her mouth to his, to invite the feel of his arms around her, hard and strong. Just this once, she thought longingly. She wasn't crazy enough to wish for anything else—she wanted nothing to do with promises from any man—but just this once, she wanted to know why songwriters wrote love songs.

But even as she started to relax, to soften, she remembered David. And her own inadequacies. Between one heartbeat and the next, her blood turned cold.

She knew he felt the change—how could he not? She was stiff as a board in his arms, cringing from his touch. A sob rising in her throat, she dreaded the moment when he pulled back. Every hateful rumor he'd ever heard about her would be there in his eyes, and if he'd ever wondered if they were true, now he would know. But there, for just a minute, when he'd kissed her so sweetly, she'd been so close to…something. Then it was gone and the loss made her want to cry.

"Sadie? What is it?"

A coward would have ducked her head, come up with some kind of mumbled excuse and gotten the hell out of there, but whatever she was, she didn't like to think she was a coward. Sick at heart, she stepped back and looked him right in the eye. "I'm sorry, Noah. I'm just not any good at this type of thing—"

"Says who?"

"My ex. You don't have to pretend you haven't heard," she said bitterly. "Everyone has."

He didn't deny it. A deaf man couldn't have missed the trash David Lincoln had spread about her. And like everyone else, he'd believed it. But that was before he'd held her in his arms, before he'd felt, just for a second, the way she'd trembled from the most innocent of kisses. He was beginning to think the lady was far from cold, and he'd have liked nothing more than to prove it to her. But that would take time, time neither of them had at the moment.

"From what I heard, your ex was a jerk," he said softly, reaching out to trail a finger across her bottom lip. "So if it's all the same to you, I'll just consider the source and make up my own mind."

"But—"

"No buts, Your Judgeship. We don't have time for them. Or did you forget that we both have to work this afternoon?"

He watched dismay bloom in her eyes and grinned. The always punctual, eminently responsible Judge Thompson *had* forgotten that she had a case to try. That had to be a first.

"Oh, God, I've got to go!" she cried. "I'm late!"

Her cheeks flushed, her robe flying out behind her, she grabbed the briefs she'd meant to go over during lunch, glanced wildly around to make sure she hadn't forgotten anything, then rushed out. Chuckling, Noah followed her out of her chambers and didn't mind admitting that he liked shaking her out of her usual reserve. If she was this flustered after what was hardly more than a brush of his lips against hers, he couldn't help but wonder what she would be like after a full-fledged, mouth-to-mouth, tongue-teasing smooch.

"'Regarding the charge of murder, we, the jury, find the defendant, Jonathan Taylor, not guilty....'"

The courtroom erupted in chaos. Family and friends of the victim jumped to their feet, yelling in outrage. Furious, Judge Quincy banged his gavel. "Order!" he roared. "We will have order or I'll clear this courtroom. Do I make myself clear? Shut the hell up!"

Silence fell, thick and tense. Scowling, Quincy nodded to the jury foreman to proceed reading the verdict. Clearing his throat, the man obediently continued: '''Regarding the charge of manslaughter, we, the jury, find the defendant, Jonathan Taylor, not guilty....''''

Stunned, unable to believe his ears, Noah hardly heard the judge thank the jurors for their time and effort. Then Taylor was slapping him on the back, his tight smile smug and triumphant. "Son of a bitch, you did it, man! Can you believe it? I thought my butt was fried. *Not guilty*—damn, that sounds good! And I owe it all to you. You earned your money and a bonus on top of that. Here, let me pay you, then let's go out and celebrate. I know this great little place—"

"I can't," Noah lied without batting an eye. "I figured the jury would come back with a verdict pretty quick and had my secretary book appointments for this afternoon. I need to get back to the office."

"Cancel them," the other man said arrogantly as he wrote out the check and handed it to him. "With the bonus I'm paying you, you don't need those penny-ante cases anyway."

Noah took one look at the amount of the check and felt like throwing up. Thirty grand. Without a moment's hesitation, the bastard had given him a twenty-thousand-dollar bonus above and beyond the fee they'd agreed on when Taylor had first come to him as a client. Blood money. That's all it was. His mother was dead by his own hand, her money now in his control, and all he had to do was write out a check, add enough zeros to the total, and that was supposed to make everything all right.

Sickened, Noah cursed himself for being too damn good at what he did. He didn't want the money, didn't want anything to do with it, but if he didn't accept the check, Taylor really would get off scot-free. And he'd be damned if he'd let him do that.

He took the check and shoved it into his pocket, then loaded his paperwork and notes into his briefcase. Making no attempt to hide his distaste, he said flatly, ''I'm not canceling anything, Taylor. You hired me to do a job, and I did it better than I wanted to. End of story. If you want to go celebrate killing your mother and getting away with it, go do it with someone else. I've got better things to do with my time.''

An ugly sneer on his face, Taylor cursed him, but he couldn't damn him any worse than Noah damned himself. Snatching up his briefcase, he turned his back on Taylor and walked out. But he didn't go back to the office. He couldn't.

He'd had his fill of clients and criminals. To hell with all of them. He was taking the afternoon off.

But first he had a check to take care of.

He drove to the nearest children's shelter, introduced himself to the nun who ran the place and presented her the endorsed check. Pleased, she started to thank him, then noticed the amount. Her mouth fell open.

"Mr. Baxter, this is for thirty thousand dollars!"

"Yes, ma'am, it is."

"But...*thirty thousand!* Good Lord, it's a small fortune. Are you sure you want to donate all of this to the shelter?"

"Believe me, I'm sure," he replied dryly. "Use it for whatever you want. New playground equipment, clothes for the kids. Take them all to Disneyland if you want. Just don't ask me to take it back, Sister. I don't want anything to do with it."

There was no doubting his sincerity. Her eyes searching his, the nun laughed and cried and impulsively hugged him. "Oh, Mr. Baxter, you don't know what an angel you are! We had some unexpected expenses last week with a leaky roof, and just this morning, I was going over the budget and wondering how we were going to get through the month. Then God sent you to us. Thank you so much!''

He wasn't an angel by any stretch of the imagination, but he was glad she could use the money. ''You're more than welcome, Sister. Use it in good health.''

She blessed him and asked God to look out for him, and Noah didn't have the heart to tell her that the man upstairs probably wasn't looking down on him too favorably right now. And he couldn't say he blamed Him. Not when he'd just helped a murderer walk.

The Sister's praise ringing in his ears, he left the children's shelter feeling like a hypocrite. He should have gone back to his office—he had plenty of work to keep him busy the rest of the day—but he wasn't fit for human company and just wanted to be left alone. Without making a conscious decision, he went home.

At that time of day, the Lone Star Social Club was deserted and quiet as a tomb. Alice was holed up in her apartment watching soap operas, and the rest of the tenants were all working. He quietly let himself into his apartment, shut the door and headed straight for the bottle of scotch in the cabinet in the kitchen.

Sometimes a man just needed a drink to wash a foul taste from his mouth.

The news of Jonathan Taylor's acquittal spread through the courthouse like wildfire. Shocked that the jury had so blatantly ignored the evidence, Sadie thought first of Noah. She'd been in his shoes and knew what it was like to defend someone you knew in your heart was guilty as sin. She'd never done less than her best for such clients because that was her job, but that was a part of practicing law that she'd never been completely comfortable with. Considering his distaste for his client, she had to think Noah was the same way. In spite of the fact that it was a feather in any lawyer's hat to pull off an acquittal in the face of such overwhelming evidence, that had to have been the last thing he wanted.

A lawyer who was only in the profession for the money and the number of wins he could rack up would be celebrating right now, but her gut told her Noah wasn't doing anything close to that. If she hadn't been stuck in court herself, she would have gone looking for him. Instead, she had to content herself with calling his office during the afternoon recess. When his secretary informed her that she hadn't seen or heard from him since that morning and that he normally checked in throughout the day, she didn't like the sound of that at all. Where the devil was he?

He was a grown man and not about to do anything stupid, but that didn't stop her from growing more and more concerned as the afternoon dragged by. His secretary had promised to call if he showed up, but though Sadie kept asking her clerk, there were no messages. For all practical purposes, Noah had dropped off the face of the earth, and by the time five o'clock finally rolled around, she was really starting to worry. He was certainly under no obligation to check in with her, she acknowledged, but after the picnic lunch they'd shared in her chambers, she liked to think they were friends of a sort. If the man was going to disappear for most of the day, it was just common courtesy to let someone know where you were. And the second she saw him, she was going to tell him so!

Fuming, she walked home and immediately stormed up the stairs to his apartment. The place was quiet, but that didn't stop her from pounding on the door. When there was no an-swer, she automatically checked the door handle to see if it was locked. With a faint click, it turned easily in her hand.

"Noah?"

Her hesitant call echoed unchecked through the apartment, and for a moment, she thought he'd just forgotten to lock up before he left. Then she heard what sounded like the clink of glass coming from the rear of the apartment. Cautiously pushing the door open farther, she peeked inside. "Noah? It's Sadie. I hope you're decent, because I'm coming in."

"Hell, no, I'm not decent," he growled. "Haven't you heard? I'm the boy wonder, the legal eagle who can even get cold-blooded killers off. Hire me, and you get a Get Out Of Jail Free card. Doesn't matter what the evidence is, just call Noah Baxter. He'll charm the jury right out of their socks."

She followed his voice to the kitchen and found him at the old-fashioned chrome dinette, making serious inroads on a bottle of scotch. Sometime over the course of the afternoon, he'd shed his coat and tie and rolled back the cuffs of his shirt. His hair was disheveled, his mouth flat with self-disgust, and as she watched, he carefully poured himself an impressive snifter of scotch.

He didn't spill a drop, but he had to concentrate on the task more than he should have. Arching a brow at him, she nodded at the half-full bottle of liquor. ''Just how much of that have you had?''

''Not enough,'' he retorted. Deliberately swallowing a gulp, he grimaced in distaste. ''It's not my favorite drink, but it's great stuff if you want to get drunk.'' Holding out the bottle to her, he surveyed her through eyes that were more than a little bleary. ''Want some?''

Amusement curling the edges of her mouth, she shook her head. ''I don't have much of a head for alcohol,'' she admitted as she took the chair across from him at the table. ''Have you had anything to eat today?''

''Not that I can remember.'' Turning up the snifter, he drained it, then sat the empty glass back on the table with a snap. ''I guess you heard about the verdict.''

She nodded, wincing as he reached for the bottle again. ''Just about everyone was talking about it.''

''Yeah, I imagine they were,'' he retorted bitterly as he poured himself another drink. ''I really made a name for myself this time. Noah Baxter will defend the lowest of the low as long as they've got money to burn. And Taylor certainly has plenty of the green stuff. The son of a bitch wrote me out a check for thirty thousand big ones without batting an eye. God, am I good or what?''

She'd never seen a man look so miserable. Sympathy welled in her, the need to hug him so fierce it stunned her. She shouldn't be here, she thought, panicking. He was just a neighbor, a colleague. His peace of mind wasn't her concern. Pushing back from the table, she rose to her feet, but instead of getting out of there as fast as her legs would carry her, she found herself reaching for the bottle of scotch.

Surprised, he grinned crookedly up at her. ''You gonna tie one on with me, Your Honorableness?''

''No, just putting it away before you fall flat on your face. You need to eat something.''

''Aw, c'mon, Judge—''

''Don't *Judge* me. I don't know what you're all upset about anyway,'' she scolded as she checked the contents of his refrigerator and found nothing but eggs and a moldy piece of cheese. God, what did the man live on? She'd have to call out for pizza. Shutting the door on the refrigerator, she surveyed him ruefully. He had no right to look so darn attractive when she knew he had to be half-lit! ''I can't believe I'm admitting this, but you're good, Counselor. Why else do you think Taylor called you when he was in trouble? He needed the best and he was willing to pay for it. So why are you beating yourself up for doing the job you were hired to do?''

''You want a list? Dammit, Sadie, because of me a damn killer got away with murder! Then he had the nerve to give me a bonus, damn his lying hide!''

She could see how that would irritate a man with principles, but he was looking at the situation all wrong. ''The jury let him get away with murder, not you,'' she stated reasonably. ''Just from the little bit I heard, the evidence was overwhelming. He should have been convicted. It's not your fault that he wasn't. The jury ignored the evidence. It happens, Noah. Not often, thank God, but nobody ever said the system was perfect.''

''Today it stunk. God, you should have seen him,'' he told her bitterly, pushing away what was left of his glass of scotch in sudden distaste. ''He was so damn smug when he handed me that check that I wanted to cram it down his throat.''

Her lips twitched at the image that brought to mind. ''Now, that's something I would have liked to see—Taylor choking on his own money.''

''If I hadn't thought he'd press charges against me for assault, I might have done it. Can you believe it? The bastard thought I'd celebrate with him. He couldn't seem to get it through his thick head that I didn't want anything to do with him or his stinking money.''

Shocked, she sputtered, ''You gave him his check back? Darn it, Noah, you earned that money—''

''I thought about burning it,'' he confided. ''But it seemed such a waste. If money was the only way I could make the jerk accountable, then by God, I was going to make him pay. So I gave it to St. Joseph's Children Shelter.''

''All of it?'' she squeaked. ''You gave all thirty thousand of it to the shelter?''

One side of his mouth curling up into a wicked grin, he nodded. ''The Sisters were thrilled to get it. Seems their cash flow is— *was*—a little short this month. It's not now.''

He was serious. He'd given away what

amounted to a small fortune, and hours later, when most men would have been kicking themselves for doing something so impulsive, he was damn proud of himself. Stunned, she laughed. "Lord, I don't think you could have found a better way of letting people know what you think of him, and you didn't have to say a word. I've got to admit, Counselor, sometimes you surprise me."

"One can only try," he replied modestly, grinning. Sprawled in his chair, his legs stretched out under the table and crossed at the ankles, he cocked a brow at her. "So what exactly are you doing here anyway, Ms. Chief Justice? Don't tell me you were worried about me?"

Teasing humor glinted in his blue eyes, along with something else, something that made her mouth go dry and her heart stumble into the craziest rhythm. Blushing, she shrugged. "I might have been a little concerned. Your secretary didn't know where you were all afternoon and..."

Too late, she realized what she'd just admitted to and quickly tried to backtrack. "I mean I—"

"You checked up on me!"

"No, I didn't," she fibbed. "I just…"

When she floundered, searching for words, he pressed. "Go on. Admit it. You were worried about me and went to the trouble of trying to track me down." Slapping his hand over his heart, he grinned. "I'm touched."

"What you are is half-lit," she retorted. Stepping around the table, she reached for the phone on the counter behind him. "I'm going to call and order a pizza."

The second his hand snapped out and snagged her wrist, she knew she'd made a tactical mistake coming anywhere within touching distance of the man. Tugging her closer, he sent her tumbling onto his lap. "Noah! What are you doing?"

"What does it look like I'm doing?" He laughed, nuzzling her neck. "I'm seducing you."

Confused by the way he could make her heart thunder with just a touch, she clutched at him, flustered. "But we already had this discussion. I told you I'm not any good at this."

"Wanna bet?" he teased, and deliberately pressed his thumb to the pulse racing in her wrist. When she gasped, he smiled down into her startled eyes and gently turned the gesture into a caress, slowly rubbing his thumb back and forth across her sensitive skin. ''I don't know about you, sweetheart,'' he murmured, ''but that doesn't feel like indifference to me. Kiss me.''

''No! I— Noah, this isn't smart.''

''I'm going to have to disagree with you there, Your Judgeship. This is just about the smartest thing I've done all day.'' Drawing her closer, he brushed her mouth with his, whisper soft. ''Nothing hot and heavy's going to happen here,'' he promised her quietly. ''Just a few kisses, a little petting, a man and woman enjoying themselves. Nothing to get all stiff and nervous about. No one's going to judge you or analyze your every move. Okay?''

Caught in the warmth of his eyes, the feel of his arms strong and sure around her, she longed to believe him. But after the nightmare of her marriage, the countless times she'd disappointed not only herself but her husband, he was asking more of her than she could give. ''I can't,'' she whispered, tears welling in her eyes. ''I just can't.''

''Then let me,'' he said huskily, and covered her mouth with his.

He kissed her as if they had all the time in

the world, as if nothing else mattered but pleasuring her, savoring her, sweetly, softly devouring her. His voice a husky growl that did strange things to her stomach, he murmured reassurances to her, trailing kisses over the curve of her cheek and brow before always coming patiently back to her mouth.

"Open your mouth, sweetheart," he coaxed softly against her lips. "Let me in."

She shouldn't. Somewhere in her spinning head, a voice warned her she was asking for trouble, that she was only setting herself up for the same heartbreaking disappointment she'd suffered time and time again in the past, but she was powerless to resist his rough, seducing words. Her heart pounding, she slowly, hesitantly, parted her lips.

At the first touch of his tongue, heat jolted through her like a bolt of electricity, setting nerve endings she hadn't known she had tingling. Whimpering, awash in strange new feelings that stunned and delighted and frightened her with their strength, she quivered in his arms, torn by conflicting emotions that urged her to run for cover and melt against him at one and the same time.

Noah felt the battle going on inside her, the

needs she was afraid to trust, and it was all he could do not to crush her mouth under his and give in to the desire burning in his blood. But she was as shy and hesitant as a virgin, and that was one sure way to make her bolt. And scaring the enticing Judge Thompson off, he was discovering to his consternation, was the last thing he wanted. God, she made him ache! He had to touch her—just once—feel the womanly curves of her that were normally hidden beneath the black, concealing folds of her judicial robes. Giving in to the need even as his tongue teased and flirted with hers, he slipped his hand under the jacket of the very proper business suit she wore and unerringly found the soft, enticing fullness of her breast.

It was a mistake. He knew it the second he felt her stiffen in alarm. A split second later, her cheeks hot and her breathing ragged, she was pushing out of his arms and scrambling to her feet, putting half the distance of the kitchen between them in the time it took for him to blink. Instinctively, he reached for her.

"No!" She took a quick step back. "I'm sorry. Please. I can't do this—"

Amazed that she would think such a thing after he'd felt the passion in her, he said,

"Sweetheart, I don't know what kind of head games your ex played with you, but trust me, there's nothing wrong with you. Come here and let's talk about it. You know I'm not going to hurt you."

She wanted to—he could see the longing in her eyes—but there was also fear there, and it was the stronger of the two emotions. "I can't," she said, and before he could stop her, she turned and ran as if the devil himself was after her. Swearing, there was nothing Noah could do but let her go.

Chapter 5

The antique grandfather clock downstairs in the entrance hall struck midnight, the deep, sonorous tones echoing softly through the dark, silent rooms of the social club. Standing at his bedroom window gazing out at the thinning crowd of tourists who still partied on the River Walk, the faint light streaming through the window carving his face in harsh shadows, Noah knew he needed to go to bed. But what was the point? He wouldn't sleep. Not when every time he closed his eyes, he saw Sadie's pale face as she'd practically run out of his apartment.

He never should have touched her. She'd told him herself that she was no good at sex, and he damn well should have kept his hands to himself. He wasn't a masochist—he didn't need that kind of frustration. But he'd had too much to drink—not that that was any excuse—and he couldn't forget how good she felt in his arms. Reaching for her had been as natural as breathing.

He'd scared her.

Something twisted in his gut at the thought of her being afraid of anything, especially him. Dammit, he'd grown up in a family of women! He loved women, liked everything about them, and the last thing he'd do was scare one. Especially Sadie. Despite the tough-judge image she presented to the rest of the world, she had an underlying vulnerability that stirred his protective instincts, and all he wanted to do was wrap her tight in his arms and promise her nothing would ever hurt her again.

But she wasn't about to let him get that close, and he didn't know if that was a blessing or a curse. He just knew he couldn't sleep for the woman. She was intruding more and more on his thoughts, making him crazy, when he hadn't let a woman do that to him in years. And he didn't even know how the hell it had happened. It wasn't as if they were dating or really even seeing each other. She wasn't the kind of woman looking for a casual affair, and at this point in his life, with his family responsibilities, he couldn't afford to let himself get involved in anything else—

The sudden shrill ringing of the phone shattered his thoughts and the quiet of the night, and with a muttered curse, he turned from the window and stalked over to the bed in the dark to snatch up the phone on the nightstand. At that hour of the night, he knew it had to be a client in trouble, wanting him to bail him out of jail.

"Yeah? This is Baxter."

"I'm at the police station. Get over here and get me the hell out of here."

There was no greeting, no identification of the caller, but none was really needed. He didn't know anyone who could match Jonathan Taylor for arrogance. "What have you done this time, Taylor? You already killed your mother and your father's dead. You start on the rest of your relatives or what?"

"When I want your wisecracks, I'll ask for them, Counselor," the other man said coldly. "I didn't do anything but stop by a bar for a drink, and a wiseass of a bartender refused to serve me. The jerk said I was a murderer, and I hit him over the head with a bar stool."

"Did you kill him?"

"No. But the jackass has a bad ticker, and now he's in the hospital, and the police think he might not make it. They're trying to hang an attempted-murder rap on me."

Noah couldn't think of a person who deserved it more. "How many witnesses were there?"

"The damn bar was packed," he snapped impatiently. "What has that got to do with anything now, dammit? I need you to get me out of here."

"I just want to make sure there're enough witnesses to put you away for good this time," Noah said coldly. "Call somebody else, Taylor. I'm not interested."

"The hell I will! You're my lawyer, damn you!"

"Correction," he said silkily. "I *was* your lawyer. I resigned that position this morning when the jury came back with its verdict and you paid me. You may have more money than God, but you're still an amoral piece of trash, and I want nothing more to do with you."

Amused, the bastard sneered, "That's what this is about? You don't like my character? Tell it to someone who cares, Baxter. Until I say differently, you're still my attorney, and if you don't get your butt down here ASAP, I'll ruin you. All I have to do is make a few calls. By the time I get through with you, you'll be lucky if you've got a handful of clients left.''

Unimpressed, Noah laughed. ''Are you kidding? Thanks to you, Taylor, I can write my own ticket. I'm so good I got a goddamn murderer acquitted. So talk all you want. You couldn't hurt my reputation if you tried.''

Without another word, he hung up, ending the one phone call Taylor was allowed to make for an attorney. He would, in all likelihood, have to spend the rest of the night in jail. As far as justice went, it wasn't much, but it was more than Noah had hoped for earlier in the day.

His mood considerably lighter, he switched on the light, checked Sadie's number in the phone book and impulsively called her. It wasn't until he heard her sleepy ''Hello'' in his ear that he remembered it was after midnight. ''Damn,'' he said huskily, ''I'm sorry. I guess I woke you, didn't I?''

''Noah?'' The drowsiness abruptly clearing from her head when she squinted at the clock, Sadie pushed herself upright and snapped on the bedside light. "What is it? Why are you calling so late?"

"Because, like an idiot, I didn't look at the clock. It's nothing that won't keep. Go back to bed, Your Judgeship. We'll talk tomorrow."

There was something about the way he said *Your Judgeship* that sounded like an endearment. With his voice alone, he reached out and stroked her, and it took no imagination whatsoever to feel his hands moving over her, slowly rekindling the fires that he'd lit when he'd pulled her onto his lap hours earlier in his apartment.

Her heart thumping, she knew she was in no shape to deal with him tonight, even if it was over the phone, but instead of agreeing to postpone the conversation until another time, she heard herself say, "I'll only lie awake wondering what the problem is if you don't tell me now, so just spit it out. What's wrong?"

"You're not going to let this go, are you?" he teased. "All right, have it your way. I just thought you might want to know Jonathan Taylor called a few minutes ago. He's been arrested."

"You're kidding! For what?"

"Attempted murder." He gave her the particulars of the assault, then added smugly, "This time I think he's cooked his goose for good. There was a whole bar full of witnesses, and unless he's somehow able to buy them all off, this is one rap he's not going to be able to walk away from."

Settling back against the headboard, she said flatly, "It's no more than he deserves. How did he react to the news that he's looking at jail this time?"

"We didn't get around to that. I told him to call somebody else. I was no longer his lawyer. That's when he threatened to ruin me."

Indignant, she sputtered, "Are you kidding me? Talk about arrogance. The man's incredible! I hope you laughed in his face."

"I sure did." He chuckled. "It felt damn good. That's why I called. I thought you might want to come up for a little drink to celebrate justice. It does exist after all."

Just a drink. Just a little toast between friends to cap off a day that had ended better than it had begun. He made it sound so simple, but they weren't friends and never could be. He made her want things she couldn't have, ache for something that she'd accepted with the end of her marriage was quite simply beyond her reach.

She'd thought of nothing but him from the moment she'd run out of his apartment earlier, and as much as she hated it, she'd known she couldn't see him anymore. Every time they were in touching distance lately, she seemed to end up in his arms, and it had to stop. Because if it didn't, one day soon, when she couldn't give him what he wanted, he would draw back from her with the same look of anger and resentment she'd seen on David's face on their wedding night and every other night of their brief marriage that he'd made love to her. And that was something she didn't think she would be able to bear. Not from Noah. So she had to end it now, before she got hurt and he ended up despising her.

"I can't." Pain lancing her heart, she felt tears sting her eyes and never knew how she kept her voice steady when she said quietly, "In fact, I think it would be better if we didn't see each other again. Trust me, it's for the best."

"Says who? Dammit, Sadie—"

"I'm sorry, but it has to be this way. Good night."

He was swearing when she hung up. When the phone rang again almost immediately, she reached over and unplugged it. Silence fell like a stone, cold and hard. She half expected him to come rushing down the stairs to force a confrontation, but seconds, then minutes, passed, and there was no sound of any movement from his apartment. She should have been relieved—he was going to be reasonable. But ten minutes later, when she switched off the bedside lamp and lay back down, it wasn't relief that painfully squeezed her heart.

A wise man would have accepted her decision and let it go. But he wasn't used to getting the brush-off from a woman. Especially from one he knew damn well was attracted to him, whether she wanted to admit it or not. He didn't like it, dammit! He didn't like it at all, and by God, he wasn't going to let her get away with it!

Storming into the outer office of Sadie's chambers the next morning before court started, he scowled at her clerk. "Is she in?"

"Yes, but..." Alarmed when he headed purposefully toward the door to Sadie's office, Betty jumped up from her desk and moved to intercept him. "Mr. Baxter, you can't go in there!"

"The hell I can't," he said, stepping around her. "If she doesn't want to see me, she's going to have to damn well tell me to my face."

He shoved open the door and strode into Sadie's private chambers like he owned the place, his gaze immediately zeroing in on her at her desk. "We need to talk, sweetheart," he began.

That was as far as he got. Too late, he realized that she wasn't alone. Fred Hollingsworth and Melinda Carter, two of the biggest gossips in the San Antonio legal community, were seated in chairs in front of her desk, their eyes wide with shock as they looked from him to Sadie and back again. His greeting to Sadie humming on the suddenly tense air, he could already hear the gossip:

Have you heard the latest? Noah Baxter and Judge Thompson. Can you believe it? He walked right into her office and called her "sweetheart"!

Swearing under his breath, Noah wanted to tell them not to read anything into a casual endearment. He called everyone from his landlady to the female sheriff deputies "sweetheart." He didn't mean anything by it except affection. But nobody called Sadie Thompson anything but "Judge."

Anger flashing in his eyes at the thought of anyone talking about her, he racked his brain for a reason for being there and could come up with nothing but a lie. "I apologize for interrupting, Your Honor," he said gruffly. "But I need to talk to you about that restraining order you slapped on Robert Barnes."

At her blank look, he prodded, "You know, the construction worker who got into a fight with his boss and hit him over the head with a two-by-four. Remember?"

She didn't, of course. There was no such person, but he saw from the way her eyes glinted that she knew the only restraining order he wanted to talk about was the one she'd slapped on the two of them last night. And she didn't want to discuss it. But she could hardly say that with Carter and Hollingsworth sitting right there, blatantly taking in every word.

"Of course," she fibbed stiffly. "I remember very well, Mr. Baxter. The matter is settled, but if you insist on talking about it, come back in fifteen minutes. I can give you a few minutes before court starts."

What he had to say would take a heck of a

lot longer than a few minutes, but he'd have to be satisfied with what he could get. Nodding curtly, he headed for the door.

Left to deal with Hollingsworth and Carter on her own, Sadie would have liked nothing more than to send them both packing. They were the worst kind of gossips, malicious and unconcerned about who they hurt with the tales they carried, and she wanted nothing to do with either one of them. Hiding her distaste, she quickly wrapped up the discussion they'd been having about a case that was being tried in her courtroom later that week. She was afraid they would linger until Noah returned and grill her about their relationship, but she should have known better. They were more interested in a good, juicy story than the truth, and as soon as they'd concluded their business with her, they rushed out like a couple of reporters trying to beat each other out of the scoop of the century.

They'd hardly disappeared before Noah stepped quietly into her chambers and shut the door behind them. When she just looked at him, making no attempt to hide her irritation, he said, ''Go ahead and say it. That was a stupid thing to do. I should have made sure you were alone before I came barging in.''

"No, you shouldn't have come barging in at all,'' she retorted, rising to her feet to confront him. ''I told you last night that I can't see you anymore, and I meant it. There's nothing left to say.''

"So the judge has made her decision and I'm just supposed to accept it, no questions asked?'' he shot back, stung. ''I don't think so, sweetheart. We were friends, dammit! Do you make a habit of kicking friends out of your life without bothering to tell them why?''

"No, of course not!''

"Well, then, what the hell's going on? What'd I do that has you running scared?''

"I'm not running scared,'' she snapped, struggling for patience. ''I just decided that it would be better if we didn't see each other anymore. If I misled you into thinking I was interested in you, I'm sorry, but I'm not. It's nothing personal.''

It was the wrong thing to say to a man who loved a challenge and knew women as well as he did. "So you're not interested, are you?'' he said silkily as he started toward her. "Prove it.

I dare you. Let me kiss you and we'll see just how interested you are.''

She swore she wasn't going to let him chase her around her office, but the second he took a step toward her, her heart jumped into her throat and she skittered away like a shy doe. When he only laughed and came after her, she put her desk between them and glared at him. ''Dammit, Noah, this isn't a game!''

He didn't even bother to answer. Feinting left, he suddenly moved right when she darted in the opposite direction, and without quite knowing how it happened, she plowed right into his chest. ''Gotcha,'' he purred.

The second his arms closed around her, Sadie felt as if she'd come home. She wanted to melt against him and pretend, just for a moment, that she was just like any other woman caught close against the man she was attracted to. Her breathing was ragged, her heartbeat frantic, her body already softening against his. She wanted him to kiss her…and was terrified that when he did, she would stiffen like a poker and feel nothing but coldness.

Sudden tears flooding her eyes, she buried her face against his chest. ''Please, Noah,'' she said thickly, ''I'm not any good at this. You've got to believe me.''

''I scared you off when I kissed you yesterday, didn't I?'' he murmured, gathering her closer against him.

She couldn't deny it. ''You terrified me,'' she whispered. ''Every time you come near me, I end up in your arms, and it's got to stop. Before you want more. I can't do...that. You'll only be disappointed and I'll be miserable.''

Staring down at her, Noah didn't pretend to misunderstand. She was telling him she was frigid, and if he was smart, he'd thank her for the warning and leave her to deal with her problems alone. But dammit, she didn't feel frigid in his arms! She was soft and warm, and he knew it only took one kiss from her to push every other woman he'd ever kissed from his mind. He was asking for trouble, but he couldn't walk away from her. Not yet.

''I appreciate the warning, honey,'' he told her huskily, ''but it'd take a hell of a lot for you to disappointment me. I think you're short-changing yourself.''

''No, I'm not. You don't know. David—''

He didn't want to talk about her loser of an ex-husband, didn't want to think about her in bed with Lincoln and the pain and humiliation she must have suffered at his hands. Not when he had her in his arms and all he wanted to do was kiss her the way a man kisses a woman who's driving him absolutely nuts. Hotly, passionately, completely. But he couldn't, not without being just as big a jerk as Lincoln. She was more fragile than a virgin, and if he didn't want to shatter what was left of her self-confidence, he was going to have to be very, very careful.

Resigned to just hugging her, he said roughly, "I don't know what kind of guilt trip your ex laid on you, but you're not frigid. That's not a problem a woman takes the blame for alone. You had a husband, sweetheart. He was experienced. Unless he was a selfish clod, he should have been able to please you."

He watched her eyes widen in surprise and said softly, "Think about it. Think about what you're denying yourself, denying *us,* just because David Lincoln was an insensitive bastard who was more concerned with his own pleasure than his wife's. He messed with your head and your faith in yourself as a woman when you were married and he's still doing it today. It doesn't have to be that way, honey. *You* can change everything just by giving yourself a chance.''

She wanted to believe him—he could see the need in her eyes—but there were doubts there, too, doubts that had sunk their claws into her long before he'd come into her life. They wouldn't let go of her easily.

Reluctantly, he made himself release her. ''Think about it,'' he said again. ''If you change your mind or just want to talk, you know where to find me.''

Left alone with her thoughts, Sadie didn't want to think about David, didn't want to think about a marriage that had gone wrong right from the start. The nights she'd lain awake staring at the ceiling and feeling all alone even though David was right there in the bed beside her were too painful to remember, too numerous to count. But all that day and the next, memories kept intruding, forcing their way into her thoughts, refusing to be ignored. And as much as she tried to pretend that none of it had ever happened, she couldn't.

A week passed. One long miserable week in which she had too much time to think about the mistakes she'd made, the first of which was not listening to her mother. Over and over again as she was growing up, her mother had warned her to never trust a man, to never let her guard down with one because he would only use her, then walk away. She'd been raised to protect her heart at all cost, and she hadn't. It wasn't a mistake she intended to make again.

She told herself she was happy with her life just as it was. She didn't need Noah. She didn't need any man. But everywhere she looked, there were lovers, whispering with their heads together, laughing softly at some private joke, kissing. Only she was alone, just as it seemed she'd always been.

And it hurt. She had her work and the crowds of people that invariably filled the courthouse to distract her from her solitary existence during the day, but it was after work, when she returned to her empty apartment, that was the most difficult. She was lonely, and how she stood the silence of her own company for so long, she never knew. But on the eighth day, she stepped into her empty apartment after a particularly difficult day at work and knew she couldn't take it a second longer. Whirling, she escaped to the back veranda of the social club just as the shadows of the slowly approaching night were starting to gather.

Lights sprang on along the River Walk, drenching it in romance, and somewhere down-stream, a woman laughed softly and a man murmured in reply. It was a quiet, intimate sound, a private moment shared between lovers, and something stirred deep inside Sadie. She told herself she didn't envy the unseen couple their relationship—she truly believed that some people weren't meant to go two-by-two through life and she was one of them. But there were times, especially lately, when a yearning she couldn't dismiss lodged right beneath her heart. She knew it was just a basic human need for physical contact and told herself it would pass. So far, though, it hadn't, and she was beginning to think it wouldn't until she did something about it.

''Oh, there you are, dear! I didn't see you sitting in the dark.''

Looking up from her thoughts to find her landlady standing before her, she blinked away her melancholy and smiled. ''Hello, Alice. It's a nice evening, isn't it? Would you like to join me?''

The older lady's quick smile flashed in the darkness. ''It has been a while since we've had a chance to talk,'' she said as she sank onto a wicker settee that was angled next to the rocker Sadie occupied. "I've been meaning to come across the hall for a visit, but the older I get, the more time just seems to get away from me. So how are you doing, dear? Working hard, as usual?"

Not one to dump her troubles on others, Sadie nodded and started to tell her she was just fine, when she found herself confiding, instead, "Actually, I was sitting here thinking I needed to make some changes in my life."

Alarmed, Alice peered at her in the darkness. "Changes? You're not thinking of moving, are you? You just moved in!"

"No," Sadie assured her, smiling. "I love it here. In fact, I can't imagine living anywhere else. No, I just need to change..." She floundered, searching for the right words. "I just feel like there's something missing, you know?" she finally said. "And I'm not talking about things—I have everything I need. But there are times like tonight, when I sit here in the shadows and watch couples strolling on the River Walk, that I feel so...alone."

Beside her, Alice reached out to pat her hand reassuringly. "It hasn't been that long since you divorced, dear. Give yourself some time. You'll find someone.''

"I'm not saying I want to get married again,'' she said quickly, horrified at the thought. "God forbid! No, I've been there and done that, and once was enough. I don't ever intend to be emotionally involved with anyone again. Not after David and the hell he put me through. But I've got to find a way to make peace with the past, and lately, I've been wondering if the only way to do that is with another man.''

Confused, Alice frowned. "But you just said—''

"That I didn't want to get emotionally involved,'' Sadie finished for her. "Yes, I know, but that doesn't necessarily mean I can't have a physical relationship with someone, does it?''

Slightly shocked, Alice blinked. "Well, no, I suppose not. Men don't need to engage their emotions to have sex, but women are a different breed, don't you think? We're the caregivers, and I would think it would take a very cold, highly disciplined woman to go to bed with a man without letting her feelings come into play. And I'm sorry, my dear, but you don't strike me that way at all. I'd hate to see you get hurt.

Please think about this before you do anything impulsive.''

Considering that she was the least impulsive person she knew, Sadie had to smile. ''You don't have to worry about that. I've never done an impulsive thing in my life.''

But long after the summer mosquitoes drove the two of them inside and Sadie retired to her own apartment for the night, she couldn't forget her conversation with Alice. She wasn't surprised that Alice would advise against a loveless relationship—she was an incurable romantic who believed every woman secretly longed for a husband and 2.2 kids. She would never understand why anyone would ever settle for anything less than happily ever after.

It wasn't, Sadie admitted to herself, a solution that would work for everyone. But she had never been like everyone else. She'd learned the valuable lesson her mother had spent years trying to instill in her and wouldn't risk her heart again, but why couldn't she have a physical relationship with a caring man who had the patience to show her what she had been missing all these years? Was that too much to ask for?

The thought nagged at her all night, tempting her, seducing her with the possibilities. By the time her alarm went off the next morning, she knew she was going to do it. *Please think about this before you do anything impulsive.* Alice's words of caution echoed in her head, but she'd already made the decision, and she couldn't believe it was the wrong one. Quickly dressing in a power suit for work, she only took time to twist her hair up before letting herself out of her apartment and hurrying upstairs.

Standing in his kitchen in his bare feet, his hair still wet from his shower, Noah glared at his coffeemaker and willed the damn thing to hurry up. He needed caffeine and lots of it. Even on a good day, he didn't operate on all cylinders until he'd had two cups of coffee, and it was going to take at least that much this morning just to get his eyes open. A client had gotten him out of bed at two to bail him out of a drunk-driving charge, and he hadn't gotten back home until four. It seemed his head had barely touched the pillow before the alarm had gone off. If he hadn't had to be in court at ten, he would have already gone back to bed.

Coffee finally drizzled down into the pot, dark and rich and strong enough to put hair on his chest. Stirring to life, he reached for the biggest mug in the cabinet just as there was a brisk knock at his front door. Surprised, he glanced at the clock and lifted a brow. Seventhirty. Nobody but his sisters had the nerve to come calling on him at that hour of the morning, and not even they dared that on a week morning without checking first to see if he had to be in court.

Frowning, he stepped into the living room, checked the peephole—and almost dropped his coffee at the sight of Sadie standing somewhat impatiently outside his door. Staying away from her for more than a week had been much more difficult than he'd anticipated. Every time he'd stepped into the courthouse, he'd had to fight the need to slip into her courtroom just to get a look at her. He wouldn't pressure her, he'd told himself. He'd told her to come to him if she needed to talk. The last thing he'd expected was for her to actually do it.

Pulling open the door, he had to hook a thumb in the pocket of his jeans to keep from reaching for her. No woman had a right to look so tempting in a black suit that was nononsense and practical, without a single frill. But she'd left the white silk blouse she wore open at the throat and sprinkled on some kind of light, teasing perfume that was guaranteed to drive a man out of his mind. And she'd forgotten her shoes.

His mouth twitching, he stared pointedly at her bare feet. ''Don't look now, Your Honor, but you seem to be missing a vital part of your wardrobe. Were you in a hurry to see me or what?''

Her eyes roaming over him, Sadie hardly heard him. He hadn't dressed for work yet and wore only a faded pair of jeans that he'd obviously dragged on after a shower. His hair was still damp, his jaw freshly shaved, his bare chest tempting. She took one look and felt her heart clench. He was a walking, talking ad for sex.

For the first time since making her decision, she had to wonder if she was out of her mind. He was a virile man who was so far out of her league that he wasn't even in the same universe. But she couldn't bring herself to back down now. She was tired of being ruled by her own doubts, tired of living on the outside of life looking in.

Gathering her courage, she said, ''Actually, I was,'' and had the satisfaction of surprising him. "May I come in? I need to talk to you, but I'd rather not do it out here in the hall."

Opening the door wider, he motioned her inside. "Can I get you some coffee? Or tea? I think I've got some around here somewhere."

Her stomach lurched at the thought of putting anything into it, and she quickly shook her head. "No, thank you. I really don't have time. I just wanted to tell you..." Not sure how to proceed, she hesitated, the words she'd so carefully rehearsed in her head suddenly sounding brazen.

If he hadn't been blocking the door, she might have bolted right then. Trapped, she blurted out, "I don't want a relationship. Or a commitment. I had that with David, and it blew up in my face. I couldn't be what he wanted, and the harder I tried to please him, the more I disappointed him and myself. I won't do that again. I won't lay my heart on the line for a man."

If she expected an argument from him, she didn't get one. "Okay. I can understand that," he said quietly. "You don't want a relationship. So what do you want?"

"I'm getting to that." Unable to stand there and look him in the eye while she baldly admitted that she just wanted sex from him, she turned to restlessly prowl around the living room. "I've been thinking a lot about what you said, and I realized that you were right. I have been missing a lot in life because of what happened with David, and I don't have to. Just because I don't want a relationship doesn't mean I can't have a man in my life when I need one. So...I thought..."

Floundering, she cast a quick look over her shoulder and found him watching her like a hawk.

"What?" he asked, frowning. "That I might be available whenever you felt the need to call?"

Put like that, she had to admit that it sounded horribly presumptuous. "We're two reasonable adults," she said, blushing hotly. "I enjoy your company. And your kisses. I thought we could explore that further."

She couldn't quite bring herself to admit that she just wanted a physical relationship, no strings attached, but he had no such trouble. "You're talking about sex," he said flatly. "You want sex. With me." When she nodded, he added, "With no emotional entanglements. Right?"

Her heart pounding, she couldn't deny it. "I know it sounds outrageous—"

"You're damn right it does. You're covering your butt, aren't you, sweetheart? You want to make sure that if we have the same troubles you and your ex had, you can walk away without getting hurt."

He was angry, and she couldn't say she blamed him. But she wasn't completely selfish. "The arrangement works both ways," she said huskily. "Everything you've heard about me is true. This could turn out to be as much of a disaster for you as it could for me. If it does, I would expect you to say so and we would end it right there with no hard feelings."

"I'm not David Lincoln," he growled. "It wouldn't be a disaster."

His eyes fierce, he dropped his gaze to her mouth, her breasts, and just that easily sent heat coiling through her. No, she thought, shaken, she didn't think either one of them would be disappointed, but she'd ended too many nights in tears to be optimistic. "At this point, we can't be sure of anything," she said quietly. "And although I don't want or expect a commitment, I would expect you to be intimate exclusively with me for the time we would be involved, just as I would be with you. For health reasons, of course.''

''Of course,'' he said tersely.

It was, she thought, an eminently practical arrangement, one in which she'd tried to work out all possible contingencies. He should have at least appreciated the thought she'd given to the arrangement, but she'd never seen a man less appreciative. He did, in fact, look like he was about to blow a gasket. She watched his color deepen, his eyes flash with what seemed to be fury, and had a sinking feeling he was going to turn her down flat.

Before he could, she said hurriedly, ''Don't give me an answer now. I know I just sprang this on you from out of the blue, and I imagine you'd like some time to think about it. You can call me later and let me know your decision.'' Not giving him time to so much as sputter a protest, she flew out the door and down the stairs, half expecting him to stop her any second. He didn't.

Chapter 6

Standing at the back of Sadie's courtroom, Noah watched grim-faced as she questioned a defendant who had wisely decided to accept a plea bargain. How, he wondered furiously, could the no-nonsense judge who sat there in her austere black robes with every hair twisted up in a nice, neat knot on the back of her head be the same woman who had sought him out in his apartment just that morning and propositioned him?

He couldn't think of the last woman who had knocked his legs out from under him so easily, and he'd been fuming about it ever since. Just sex. That was all she wanted. And just to make sure they could part friends when she no longer had any further need of his sexual expertise, she didn't plan to get emotionally involved and didn't want him to, either.

Lord, he wanted to shake her! Did she have any idea how insulting her little proposal was? Or how little she was willing to settle for? Damn her, he should, just on sheer principle, tan her hide for selling herself so short, then turn her down flat. It was no more than she deserved.

But as much as he knew he should, he wasn't there to do that. Not when he was the reason she'd suggested such an outrageous proposal to begin with. Thanks to David Lincoln, she'd been completely turned off men since her divorce—until *he* gave her a small taste of what passion was all about. He'd given her a sample of what she'd been missing and now she'd decided she wanted more. If he didn't agree to her crazy proposal, she'd probably go looking for someone else who would. And just the thought of any other man touching her, kissing her, making love to her, made him want to throw something.

No, he thought grimly, striding toward the front of the courtroom as one case was dismissed and another was called. It wasn't going to happen. If she thought she was ready for sex, then by God, she didn't need to go looking for a partner. He was her man. Her only man.

"Your Honor, I realize I'm interrupting the proceedings," he said as the prosecutor and defense lawyer took their places at the appropriate counsel tables, "but may I approach the bench? I need to speak with you a moment."

In the process of reviewing paperwork, Sadie glanced up sharply at the first sound of his voice. She didn't so much as blink, but Noah didn't miss the surprise she quickly hid behind narrowed eyes. Frowning at him over the top of her reading glasses, she said sternly, "This is most unusual, Mr. Baxter. Make it quick."

He could have picked a less public place to tell her, but he'd been too ticked at the time he'd come looking for her to think of that. Now, however, he had no intention of announcing something so private to a roomful of curious spectators. Nodding at the microphone sitting in front of her, he said quietly, "I suggest you cover that thing."

Lightning quick, she slapped her hand over it. "Dammit, Noah," she told him in a low whisper that didn't carry beyond his ears, "I don't know what this is all about, but surely it can wait until later. We're trying to have court here!''

''This'll just take a second,'' he promised. ''I just wanted you to know that I've considered your proposal and I've decided to accept it. I thought you'd want to know.''

He saw in a glance that not only had he floored her, but that she had all the symptoms of shock. Becoming color flooded her cheeks, and she couldn't seem to find her voice. He seemed to remember having the same problem when she'd dropped that damn proposal on him without warning. Good, he thought in satisfaction as he saluted her goodbye and headed for the nearest exit. Now she knew what it felt like.

How she got through the rest of the day, Sadie never knew. She couldn't concentrate, couldn't think of anything but Noah and her own proposal, which, now that she'd had time to reflect, sounded more and more insulting. What could she have been thinking of? she wondered, appalled at her own daring. And what had Noah been thinking of to ever agree to such a thing? They both must have been working too hard!

She would have to find a way to convince

him she'd made a mistake, of course. Not, she felt sure, that he would be that hard to convince. He had to know that they couldn't possibly go through with such a ridiculous plan. She would talk to him, explain that she'd reconsidered, and he would no doubt be relieved. She would lose him as a lover, but keep him as a friend, and that was far more important to her than going to bed with him.

Satisfied that the problem could be solved so easily, she spent the afternoon working out what she was going to say to him. But when he called her at home after work, he didn't give her time to do much more than tell him hello. ''I'll be down in fifteen minutes to take you to dinner,'' he said by way of a greeting. ''Wear something casual.''

''But—''

''Fifteen minutes,'' he repeated, and hung up.

Frustrated, she glared down at the phone and almost called him back, only to decide that maybe it would be better if she told him about her change of heart someplace other than her apartment. Then if for some crazy reason he tried to talk her into sticking to their agreement,

the discussion wouldn't get too heated—or personal—in a public place.

Changing into a comfortable summer dress
and sandals, she was determined to be cool and
self-possessed when she opened the door to him
fifteen minutes later. He didn't make it easy for
her. There was something about the man in
jeans that just made her mouth go dry. And then
there was that glint in his eyes, the one that was
dark and intimate and private and made her go
breathless with just one long, heated look. Convinced he must be able to hear the hammering
of her heart, she wondered wildly whatever had
possessed her to think, even for a second, that
she could handle him in her bed. This was a
man who knew his way around women. She
should have seen that, should have realized
what a risk getting involved with him could be.
If she made the mistake of letting him make
love to her, she'd be outmanned, overwhelmed,
ravaged by the experience. And she'd never be
able to keep her emotions at bay. It would be
nothing but a disaster.

"Ready?" he asked huskily.

She nodded stiffly and grabbed her purse.
"Where are we going?"

"A little place on the edge of town," he said

as she preceded him out into the hall. ''One of my sisters told me about it. I thought you might like it.''

The Texas Bar and Grill was located just north of the city limits in an old rock-and-log building that looked like it had been standing there since the beginning of time. The food was reported to be great, but that wasn't the reason Noah had decided to bring Sadie there. He hadn't forgotten how protective she was of her reputation, and the Texas Bar and Grill was a long way from the courthouse. Off the beaten path and a watering hole for ranchers and cowboys, it wasn't the kind of place they were likely to meet anyone they knew.

Pulling into the parking lot, which was full of pickups of every color and description, he saw her surprise and grinned. She'd been as wary as a virgin ever since she'd opened her door to him, and he could just imagine what was going on in her head. She no doubt expected him to wine and dine her at some fancy restaurant, then rush her back home to bed the first chance he got, but the lady wasn't even close to being ready for that. She might think she wanted a blatant affair right now, but he knew better. She was too skittish, her opinion of her own sex appeal too low. He needed to find a way to build her confidence and make her comfortable with his touch so that when he finally did take her to bed, she would be just as eager for him as he was for her.

And that could take weeks, maybe months.

He stifled a groan at the thought and wondered, not for the first time, if he'd been some kind of a masochist to ever agree to such a crazy arrangement. Only someone who enjoyed self-inflicted torture would set himself up for the kind of frustration that could make a normally mild-mannered man chew glass. And that wasn't him. He liked easy, uncomplicated relationships in which nobody got hurt, and if he had any sense, he'd call the whole thing off right now.

But that, he knew, wasn't going to happen. Not when he still wanted Sadie so badly that he ached.

Escorting her inside, he saw that the restaurant was just as his sister had described. The decor was rustic, the music being played by the band in the corner country-and-western, the drink of choice more often than not beer instead of wine or hard liquor. Most of the tables were full, the bar was all but deserted and the dance floor was crowded with slow-moving cowboys who seemed content just to hold their women and sway to the music.

It was, he decided, the kind of place where Sadie should have been able to relax and let down her guard, but if anything, she seemed more nervous than ever. The second they were seated and the hostess left them with their menus, she straightened her shoulders as if bracing herself for something and lifted her chin. "We need to talk," she said in her best judge's voice.

She was going to call it off. She didn't say the words, but she didn't have to—second thoughts were written all over her face. And he wasn't going to let her get away with it. One corner of his mouth crooking up into a wicked grin, he teased, "I just love it when you talk like a judge, Your Honor. Are you going to find me in contempt?"

She tried to frown, but he surprised a laugh out of her and the effect was ruined. "I'm trying to be serious here," she scolded.

"Then why are you smiling?"

"I'm not!"

"Yes, you are." Reaching across the table, he dared to trace the corner of her mouth.

"Right here," he said huskily. "It's very becoming. There's just something about your mouth—"

In a flash, her fingers closed around his, trapping his hand against her flushed cheeks. "Noah, please—"

"I'm trying, honey," he teased, turning his hand to capture hers in his, "but this isn't exactly the place for that kind of thing. No matter what you may have heard about me, I'm not an exhibitionist."

She gasped, blushing, but before she could sputter a response, their waitress arrived. Scowling at him, Sadie shot him a silent warning to behave himself, but he had no intention of doing any such thing, not as long as he could distract her so easily from breaking things off. Giving her an innocent look, he grinned. "Tell the lady your order, sweetheart. We can stare into each other's eyes later."

She wanted to kill him. And laugh. She couldn't let him do this to her, but she couldn't seem to stop him. As soon as the waitress took their orders and left them alone, he flirted and teased and made it impossible for her to even think about trying to carry on a serious conversation. Before she knew it, the waitress was back with their food.

Later, she couldn't have said what they talked about as they ate, but she couldn't remember when she had enjoyed a meal more. He made her laugh and relax, and time just seemed to fly by. Before she knew it, she'd eaten over half of her steak and was sure he'd have to roll her out of the restaurant just to get her to his truck. But instead of leaving when they both finished eating, he pulled her out on the dance floor.

Startled, she remembered too late that the only reason he'd invited her out to dinner in the first place was that he probably planned to take her back home and have sex afterward, and she wanted to kick herself for not insisting on telling him earlier that she'd changed her mind. Now he wanted to get romantic, and she had nobody to blame but herself.

Her heart suddenly racing, she stiffened as his arms came around her, but if he noticed, he didn't seem to care. Chuckling, he just gathered her close and began to sway with her just like every other couple packed onto the dance floor.

Stunned by the strength of the need to melt against him, she held herself rigid against him and tried not to notice how safe he made her feel. But with every beat of the music, she fought a losing battle. The world shrank until nothing existed but Noah...the heat and strength and hardness of him against her. In the corner, the band changed gears and shifted into the more upbeat tempo of country rock, but she hardly noticed. Without a word, Noah steered her out of the main flow of more energetic dancers and continued to sway with her, content just to hold her.

The clean, male scent of him wrapping around her as surely as his arms, she could have stayed just that way for hours and never needed anything else. But she couldn't. She couldn't let him go on thinking they had an arrangement when she was going to back out at her front door.

Gathering her courage, she drew back as far as his encircling arms would allow. "Noah, please, we have to talk."

"I hear you, sweetheart," he murmured, pulling her close again to nip at her ear. "You want to retract your proposal."

"Yes!" Relieved that he understood and wasn't going to give her a hard time about it, she said, "I know you must think I'm the most

wishy-washy woman you've ever had the misfortune to deal with, but I really don't know
what I was thinking of this morning when I
came to your place. Any other man would have
laughed in my face and sent me packing, which
was probably no more than I deserved, but you
listened to me—''

''Honey, I was in shock,'' he said, laughing
softly. ''You propositioned me!''

''God, don't remind me!'' she groaned, burying her face against his chest. ''I've never done
anything so outrageous in my life. I still can't
believe I did it. And God only knows how I got
through court this afternoon. I couldn't concentrate to save my life. The more I thought about
it, the more I realized that there was no way
this was going to work and I didn't know how
I was going to tell you.''

''Hey, I'm a reasonable kind of guy—you
should know that by now. You can tell me anything. Anyway, there's nothing to panic
about,'' he added. ''It'll work. Trust me.''

Cradled against him, swaying in time to the
music, she didn't register his words for several
long seconds. Then, alarmed, she drew back
and frowned up at him in confusion. ''What do

you mean…*it'll work?* Didn't you hear what I just said?''

"Of course I did," he retorted easily. "I just don't agree with you. The only way I can see that we could have a problem is if we weren't attracted to each other. Is that what you're trying to say? That you're not attracted to me?''

Flustered, she blushed. "Well, no, but—''

"Then we're okay. And it isn't as if I'm going to sweep you off to bed like some caveman the first chance I get. I know you're not ready for that. So relax," he said softly, tugging her back against him. "We're going to take it nice and slow, and then when you're ready, all you have to do is say the word, and I'll take care of the rest. What's there to be afraid of?''

She should have been able to think of plenty, but the man had the most amazing effect on her. With his arms around her and his heart beating sure and steady against hers, her fears seemed very far away and she couldn't think of another reason to object. Later, she knew she was probably going to regret that, but for now, she'd never felt safer in her life. Giving in to what they both wanted, she relaxed.

The nerves were back, however, hours later when they walked into the Lone Star Social

Club. It was nearly midnight, and the old house was quiet, the lights in the hall dim. Aware of his closeness as he followed her to her front door, Sadie fumbled in her purse for her keys and reminded herself there was no reason to act like a ninny. He'd promised her nothing was going to happen.

But the evening had been one of the most romantic of her life, and after dancing one dance after another with him cheek to cheek, she couldn't help but be slightly apprehensive. From what David had taught her about men, this was where he forgot all the pretty words and pressed for what he wanted. Unable to stop herself, she tensed.

But as he took her keys from her and unlocked her door for her, it quickly became apparent she had nothing to worry about. Handing her keys back to her, he made no effort to take her into his arms or talk his way into her apartment. His eyes never leaving hers, he closed her fingers around her keys, then slowly lifted her hand to his mouth.

She hadn't expected such a courtly gesture from him, and her heart stuttered in anticipation. In the suddenly hushed silence, she found herself rushing to thank him for the evening. "I had a wonderful time tonight,'' she began huskily.

That was as far as she got. Giving her an old-fashioned kiss on the back of the hand, he made her tremble with nothing more than the flick of his tongue.

''So did I,'' he rasped. ''Especially the dancing. I like holding you in my arms. We'll do it again. Soon. But not tonight.'' With that, he reluctantly released her and pushed open her front door. ''Good night, Your Judgeship. Go on inside. I'll head on upstairs when I hear your dead bolt.''

She wanted to protest, to reach for him and the kiss she suddenly realized she desperately needed. But he had made her a promise and he was sticking to it. Unless she wanted him to think she was ready for a more physical relationship after just one evening of dancing, she had to let him go.

Murmuring a quiet good-night, she stepped into her apartment, shut the door and shot the dead bolt. On the other side of the door, she heard Noah make his way through the sleeping house to the central staircase. Long after his footsteps faded away upstairs, she still stood there, listening to the thunder of her own heart.

*   *   *

Nice and slow. When Noah had told her that their *arrangement* would proceed nice and slow, she'd taken that to mean that there would be more nights out, more evenings of dinner and dancing and getting to know each other. It never entered her head that it meant he would drop off the face of the earth without a word for the next three days. Not that he was required to check in and report his activities to her, she reminded herself. After all, it wasn't as if they had any emotional involvement. They weren't having a flaming affair; there was no commitment between them at all. Just sex. She'd made it clear that was what she wanted, and she had no right to complain just because he'd apparently taken her at her word.

Still, she found herself sitting around her apartment after work, waiting for the phone to ring and listening for the sound of his footsteps overhead, signaling that he was home. And it horrified her. What was she doing? She'd never had a problem with being alone before; she didn't need a man to keep her entertained. She had friends, hobbies—a life, for God's sake!— and that wasn't going to change just because she planned to eventually have sex with Noah Baxter.

Deciding it had been too long since she'd seen her friends, she called Nancy and Jane and invited them to go shopping with her at River Center Mall on the river. She'd barely talked to either one of them since they'd helped her move into the social club, and they were only too eager to catch up on the latest gossip. They all agreed to meet at the food court, and five minutes later, she hit the streets, deciding to walk since it was such a nice evening.

Three hours later, she returned to the social club feeling like a new woman. Urged on by Nancy and Jane, who'd immediately sensed she was down, she'd bought an outrageous number of new clothes in the hottest new colors of the summer. She wasn't one to keep up with the latest fads, but as she tried on one outfit after another in bright, carefree colors, she was amazed at the difference in herself. She looked younger, prettier, happier.

Thrilled that she was finally getting away from dark suits and power clothes, Nancy tried to talk her into a makeover, complete with a new hairstyle, but she'd drawn the line at that. She still had a reputation to uphold, and as the youngest judge in the state, she was already scrutinized more than the other judges. If she walked into the courthouse with a short, sassy new haircut that totally destroyed the staid image of Hanging Judge Thompson, she'd set the legal community on its ear. So she'd just bought the clothes, but passed on the do. Then, however, she needed accessories. Before she knew it, she'd almost bought out the mall and had so many packages that Jane had to give her a ride home.

Weighted down with bags, she waved from the porch as her friend drove off, then punched in the security code to the house's impressive leaded-glass front door. She never even saw Noah until she pulled open the door and plowed right into him. "Oh!"

"Whoa, there, Your Honorableness," he told her with a laugh when she instinctively started to pull back. "Not so fast. I just love it when you throw yourself at me. Did you miss me?"

With his arms tight around her and her packages and her heart thumping madly, she almost told him that the days had seemed unbearably long. But his grin was cocky and a little too sure, and she was just the woman to bring him down a notch or two.

"Miss you?" she repeated innocently, her

eyes wide as she gazed up at him. "I didn't even know you were gone."

"Little liar," he told her, chuckling. "I had to take care of an emergency in Austin. I just got back into town today, and it's been crazy. All my appointments had to be rescheduled, and I can see already that it's going to take me at least a week, bare minimum, to get back on schedule. That doesn't mean I've forgotten our arrangement," he assured her quickly. "It's just that I'm going to have to juggle some things. What are you doing Saturday evening? I should be able to get away by then. Why don't we take in a movie and sit at the back and neck?"

He was teasing—she thought—but it didn't matter if he wasn't. She was booked. Regretfully, she shook her head. "Sorry, but I can't. The Safe Haven Children's Ranch is having their annual fund-raising dance that night and I'm on the decorating committee. I'm going to be busy the whole day."

"Hell!" Glancing at his watch, he swore again. "I've got to meet with a client out by Sea World in twenty minutes. I've got to go, dammit!"

He sounded so aggrieved that Sadie couldn't

help but laugh. "So what's stopping you, Counselor?"

"You are!" he retorted. "I missed you." Shaking his head as if he couldn't figure out how that had happened, he took a step back, then another one. "I may not get back to you for a couple of days, but that doesn't mean I've forgotten you," he assured her huskily. "I'm just up to my ears in work right now. As soon as I get it all sorted out, I'll call you."

Another glance at his watch drew a muttered curse from him, and with a rueful grimace, he turned and hurried out. For the first time in three days, Sadie walked into her apartment smiling.

When two days came and went and he didn't call her as he'd promised to, Sadie wasn't really surprised. Noah was one of those rare breed of lawyers who had chosen to work for himself rather than a big law firm, and she knew what that was like. When you were on your own, *you* had to scramble for clients, *you* had to do the legwork, *you* had to take the calls in the middle of the night when a client needed you to get him out of jail. And even when you were a success, as Noah was, you could never take that success for granted. Because if you got sick or hurt or even just wanted to take a day off once in a while, you couldn't let up, couldn't relax. Because there was no one to take your place.

Knowing why he was busy, however, didn't make her any less restless. When Friday morning rolled around, she was wide-awake a full hour and a half before her alarm was programmed to go off. Knowing it was useless to try to go back to sleep, she groaned and rolled out of bed. If she was up, she decided, then she might as well go into her office. The security guard would let her in, and she could get some work done. The Dominguez trial started Monday, and she still had pretrial motions to study and make a final ruling on.

Twenty minutes later, dressed in a simple yellow skirt and a white tailored blouse instead of her usual suit, she quietly slipped out of the social club and walked to the courthouse four blocks away just as the sun was peeking over the horizon. It was a beautiful morning, clear and cool, and the birds were singing like mad. The city was just starting to come to life, and if she hadn't had so much work to do, she would have gone down to one of the cafés on the River Walk and had breakfast. Instead, she stopped by Heavenly Scents, a bakery that was just across the river and a block over from the social club, and bought a lemon-filled doughnut and a cup of coffee to have at her desk. The mouthwatering scent teased her all the way to the courthouse.

As usual, Lloyd Mallory, the security guard who manned the metal detectors at the employee entrance, was working the early shift. ''Mornin', Judge,'' he drawled, nodding at her with a smile. ''You're in early. Gotta big trial starting today?''

''Not this morning,'' she replied. ''But Monday's going to be a circus. We begin jury selection for the Dominguez trial, and the place is going to be crawling with the press.''

''Oh, yeah,'' he said, interest sparking in his eyes. ''That's that guy who has connections with the Mexican mafia, isn't it? He killed Henry Bingham.''

''Allegedly,'' she stressed. ''Until the state proves otherwise, he's an innocent man.'' Unable to discuss the case any more than that, she deliberately changed the subject. ''So how're those twin granddaughters of yours? Still getting into mischief?''

She knew Lloyd, knew how much he loved

talking about the three-year-olds, and not surprisingly, he immediately launched into a tale about their latest run-in with the family cat. Sadie was still chuckling when she left him a few minutes later and went upstairs to her office.

Juggling her breakfast and briefcase and keys, she finally got the door to her private chambers unlocked without dropping anything, but when she tried to push it open with her shoulder, it only moved a couple of inches. Frowning, she tried again, but with her hands full, the door held fast.

''Well, for heaven's sake!''

Something was obviously blocking it, but she couldn't for the life of her imagine what it was, unless the cleaning lady had moved the furniture out of the way to clean, then forgot to put it back before she let herself out through the door that opened into Sadie's clerk's office. The woman had never done such a thing before, but Sadie supposed there was a first time for everything. Grumbling, she set her things on the floor to free her hands, braced her feet and shoved with all her might.

Inside, something shifted, and suddenly, without warning, the door flew open. Off balance, she gasped, stumbling headlong into her office. If she hadn't managed to catch herself by grabbing onto the door handle at the last moment, she would have fallen flat on her face.

Muttering a curse, she straightened, only to gasp as she got her first good look at her chambers. Chaos. There was no other word to describe it. The place had been trashed. Someone had pried open the locked drawers of her file cabinets and desk and dumped the contents all over the floor, then swept every book from the bookshelves that lined the walls. Chairs had been overturned—that was what had blocked the door—and framed pictures and her diplomas torn from the walls.

But it was the damage done to her law books that struck her right in the heart. She'd gone into debt up to her ears to buy them the first year out of law school, and she treasured them more than anything else she owned. Now they lay like fallen soldiers in the dirt. Spines had been broken, pages torn out, then ground underfoot. If someone had wanted to show her their total disrespect for her and the law, they couldn't have found a better way.

Tears stung her eyes, but before she could even blink them away, the anger hit her, hot and fierce. They weren't going to get away with this! Whoever did this would pay! Suddenly furious, she started toward her desk to call security and the police, only to stop in her tracks when she realized she was about to contaminate a crime scene. Whirling, she ran for the stairs and Lloyd.

An hour later, Detective Sam Kelly met with her in her clerk's office. A tall, lean man with kind, but watchful eyes, he had gone over every inch of her chambers with the evidence team, collecting fingerprints, then left to check with security about the security cameras that were strategically placed throughout the building. If they were lucky, he'd told her, they'd have a nice head shot of whoever had done this to her and wouldn't have to rely on fingerprints, but now, judging from the unsmiling set of his mouth, they'd hit nothing but a brick wall.

Her spine ramrod straight, she faced him unflinchingly. "There wasn't anything on the tapes, was there?"

"Actually, there was," he replied, surprising her, "but it's not very helpful. The camera caught him coming through the window by the fire escape at the end of the hall—"

"Then you know what he looks like—"

"No," he said regretfully. "He had on a ski mask. But he wasn't wearing gloves. With all the prints we collected, we're bound to have gotten a few good ones that belong to him. If his prints are on record, we've got him."

"But surely they are if he makes a habit of doing this kind of thing."

"You would think so," he agreed, "but his motive doesn't appear to have been robbery since nothing's missing. I don't know about you, but that seems damn odd to me. He took a hell of a risk just to trash the place, and I've got to ask myself why." His midnight-blue eyes sharpening on her face, he said, "Looks like it's up to you, Your Honor, to help us make sense of this. You know anyone who's got it in for you?"

"Just every two-bit punk who's found guilty in my courtroom," she retorted. "You really think this was personal?"

"I think it has to be," he replied. "Why else would this guy pick on you? No other offices in the courthouse were touched."

Listening to the entire conversation from her desk, Sadie's clerk, Betty, said, "It's because of the trial."

Sam shot her a sharp glance. "What trial?"

"The Dominic Dominguez trial," she said. "It starts Monday, and somebody doesn't want Judge Thompson trying it. She got a threatening letter about it."

"I'm sure that doesn't have anything to do with this," Sadie said, frowning at the younger woman. "Every judge gets those kind of things occasionally. They're harmless."

"Maybe, maybe not," Sam said. "Depends on just how threatening it is. Did you happen to keep it?"

"No."

"Yes," Betty said quickly.

Surprised, Sadie lifted a brow at her. "I thought you threw it away."

"I did, but something told me it could be important, so I pulled it out of the trash and filed it." Opening the lower drawer of her desk, she removed a folder and handed it to Detective Kelly. "I kept the envelope, too. It probably has a lot of different fingerprints on it, but the letter only has mine and the judge's...and hopefully whoever wrote it."

Sadie had thought the detective's expression was somber before, but now, as he opened the file and read the unsigned letter, he looked positively grim. He checked the postmark on the envelope and swore. The letter had been mailed in San Antonio. ''If the trial on Monday involved anybody but Dominguez, this letter would probably be just a bluff. But he's a vindictive son of a—gun,'' he substituted, remembering just in time who he was talking to. ''He's capable of anything, and if he thought intimidating you would cause a mistrial, then he wouldn't hesitate.''

Sadie snorted at that as she watched him place the entire file in an evidence bag. ''He's wasting his time, Detective. It would take a lot more than an unsigned letter and the trashing of my office to make me back away from this trial. And if Dominguez doesn't know that by now, then he'll certainly know it on Monday when I walk into the courtroom. I don't scare easily.''

He nodded approvingly, liking her spunk. ''I'm glad to hear it. But that doesn't change the fact that the man might not stop with just trying to scare you. For your own safety, I'm going to increase security around you while you're here in the courthouse and beef up the patrols in your neighborhood until we know for sure this newest stunt isn't connected with the trial. Where do you live?''

"The Lone Star Social Club. It's on—"

"I know where it is," he said with a slow, rueful smile. "I used to live there myself—a couple of years ago. Did anyone warn you about the place before you moved in?"

"You mean the legend?" At his nod, a faint blush tinged her cheeks. "Alice mentioned something about it, but I didn't really take her seriously. I don't believe in that sort of thing."

Amusement dancing in his eyes, he said dryly, "Neither did I...until I got married. Trust me, you don't need to believe in it for it to work."

Chapter 7

"God, Sadie, are you sure you're all right?" Jane demanded worriedly. "I've been trying to call you ever since yesterday morning, but your line's always busy."

"I know," she said with a grimace. "It's been crazy. The phone's been ringing off the wall with calls from reporters, and I finally unplugged it. I'm sorry I didn't think to call you. It's just that everything's been so hectic."

"From the news reports, it's been a circus," Bob retorted. "Did Dominguez really put a contract out on you?"

Sadie rolled her eyes at that, not surprised that such speculation was circulating on the gossip mill. The media had been grossly irresponsible and jumped to all sorts of ridiculous conclusions about who had trashed her office and why. "No," she said firmly. "There's no contract. In fact, Dominguez wasn't even involved. Apparently, the police were able to identify some of the prints at the scene and link the break-in to a habitual thief named Osgood I sent to Huntsville three years ago. He just got out and wanted revenge. Detective Kelly called a little over an hour ago to tell me they'd already arrested him. So there's nothing to worry about. I'm fine."

"Just the same, I don't like the sound of this," Tommy said grimly. "He could get out on bond. Maybe you should come and stay with me and Nancy for a while. I know the police have been keeping an eye on you, but that's not the same thing as having friends around you."

Touched, Sadie laughed and gave him a fierce hug. "I appreciate the offer, but it's not necessary. Really," she insisted when her friends still looked skeptical. "C'mon, guys, will you stop it! Kelly assured me Osgood's locked up nice and tight, with no possibility of bail. And just as soon as the paperwork is done and his parole's revoked, he'll be going back to Huntsville. So lighten up, okay? Kelly wouldn't have scaled back on the police protection if I was in any danger.''

They weren't completely convinced, but they let the subject drop, and for a little while, Sadie was able to talk and laugh with them and forget the nightmare of the last thirty-six hours. Sam Kelly had tried to keep a lid on the story, but he'd have had an easier time making the San Antonio River change direction and run upstream. By the time the police finished investigating the crime scene, the courthouse was teeming with people and the story had spread like wildfire. It had been the main topic of conversation ever since.

She'd hoped that by the time she arrived at the fund-raising dinner and dance for the Safe Haven Children's Ranch, the gossip would have run its course and everyone would just let it go. But whenever she drifted away from her immediate circle of friends, she was either bombarded with questions or praised for her bravery. Uncomfortable at the idea of being labeled some kind of heroine, she was trying to get back to Jane and Nancy and the guys when she found herself cornered by the Safe Haven board of directors, who had questions of their own. Forcing a smile, she tried to hang on to her sense of humor, but it wasn't easy.

"I don't know how you could be so brave. I would have been scared to death!"

"Was a threatening note really carved in the top of your desk?"

"I heard you have twenty-four-hour police protection now because Dominguez put a contract out on you. That must be awful. Do you have any privacy at all?"

Amazed by what people were willing to believe, she explained again that Dominguez had nothing to do with the vandalism of her office, then said patiently, "I was more angry than afraid. And I don't know how all these rumors got started, but most of them are pure fabrication. Nothing was carved in my desk, and the police never did put me under twenty-four-hour guard."

"What about the contract Dominguez put out on you?" the president of the board asked. "Jeez, Sadie, I don't know how you're so calm. If I were you, I think I'd just disappear off the face of the earth until it was safe to come out again."

"First of all, there is no contract. And if there was, when would it be safe to come out again?'' she asked logically. ''When he's convicted? *If* he's convicted? If he really wanted to eliminate me, it wouldn't matter where I went or how long I laid low. People with the kind of connections Dominguez has have a long reach. I'd never be completely safe, so why bother?''

''But aren't you terrified?''

''Of Dominguez?'' she asked, surprised. ''No, I wouldn't say that I am. Cautious, yes, but only because of who he is and the group he's connected with. But he hasn't made any threats against me directly—at least none that I know of—and until he does, I can't go around being afraid all the time.''

Thoroughly sick of the subject, she said, ''Please, can we just forget it for now? This is supposed to be a fun night, and we're here to raise money for the kids and the ranch, not talk about me. How are ticket sales going so far? It looks like we've got a good crowd.''

Someone produced the latest numbers, and from there, the conversation shifted to the caterer and the amount of food ordered for the evening. Relieved to no longer be the center of attention, Sadie checked to make sure the decorations were holding up, then went in search of the table where all the board members were supposed to sit.

Not for the first time, she wondered why she'd come. It wasn't as if she enjoyed this type of occasion. Small talk wasn't her thing, and she wasn't a very good dancer. Not that she had to worry about beating off men with a stick, she admitted ruefully. Her reputation preceded her, and the man who worked up the nerve to approach her was a rare breed indeed.

"Has anyone told you yet that you look good enough to eat, sweetheart?" a rough voice murmured in her ear. "Why don't we blow this popstand and go somewhere we can be alone?"

Startled, Sadie whirled, only to gasp at the sight of Noah standing before her looking like he'd just stepped out of the pages of *GQ*. Dressed in a tux, his dark, wavy hair slicked back and nearly tamed, wicked amusement dancing in his eyes, he was, to put it quite simply, gorgeous.

"You're staring, beautiful," he teased, appraising her as thoroughly as she did him. "Like what you see?"

He knew she did, but she had no intention of pandering to his ego any more than she already had. "It's not bad for a rented suit," she said with a shrug, and was rewarded with a shout of laughter that drew more than one appreciative female look from across the room. Pleased with herself, she arched a brow at him. "What are you doing here, anyway? I thought you didn't go to these kinds of things."

What she'd heard, in fact, was that while he supported numerous charities around the city, he didn't dress up in a monkey suit for anyone. Then it hit her. "It's because of what happened yesterday in my office, isn't it?" she guessed. "That's why you're here. You think I'm still in danger, and you're playing watchdog."

She'd hit the nail on the head and he didn't bother to deny it. She was damn right he was there to watch over her. The second he'd heard about the vandalism, his first instinct had been to drop everything and go running up to her office to make sure she really was okay. But he'd had back-to-back court appointments all day that he couldn't get out of, so he'd had to content himself with calling her, instead. It wasn't until he'd heard her voice on the phone that he'd realized just how worried about her he was.

She'd assured him she was fine, that it was just a random act of violence, but he hadn't bought any of it. She wasn't fine—no one could see her things viciously destroyed without being affected by it. And although he'd heard that there was an arrest in the case of a perp that had no connections to Dominguez, everything tied up just a little too neatly for him. He didn't believe that anything like this was just random or that the timing of the attack was in any way coincidental.

Which was why he was trussed up like a gorilla in an ill-fitting tux and had paid an outrageous fee to drink lukewarm champagne and eat cold chicken. Until he knew for sure that she really wasn't in danger, he was sticking close whenever he could, so the lady would just have to get used to having him around. He knew, however, better than to tell her that. She wore her independence like a badge and didn't think she needed anyone. If he made the mistake of admitting that he intended to watch over her like a hawk, she wouldn't let him anywhere near her.

"I'm here because we have an arrangement and I heard they were going to have dancing here tonight," he replied in a murmur that was for her ears only. "You know how well we fit together, honey. Where else would I be?"

Heat bloomed in her cheeks, just as he'd known it would, and he knew the exact second when she remembered that they were in a very public setting, in full view of many of the same people who had been only too eager to titter and whisper over the malicious things her ex had said about her. She paled and went as stiff as a board, and it was all he could do not to pull her into his arms and really give the tattle-mongers something to wag their tongues about.

That's all it would take to show the blabber-mouths that not only did she not give a damn about what they thought of her, but they didn't know what they were talking about, he thought angrily, cursing the judgmental jerks who had put that look in her eyes. One hot, passionate kiss in front of the biggest gossips in town and she would shut them all up for good.

But she'd never go for it, and neither would he, he realized. The next time he had her in his arms, he didn't want any spectators. "On second thought, I think I'm going to have to ask for a rain check on any dancing," he rasped softly as his eyes hungrily roamed over the green silk dress that molded her body like a lover's hands. "I'm afraid if I touched you while you were wearing that dress, I just might not be able to let you go.''

''Noah—''

''I know,'' he said with a rueful grimace. ''This isn't the place to talk about how I want to make love to you. There's just something about you that makes me hotter than a randy teenager. But we're not going to discuss that now or I just might embarrass us both. Go circulate, Your Honor, or whatever it is that you have to do at this shindig. I'll catch up with you later.''

Her cheeks fiery and her heart hammering against her ribs, Sadie couldn't think of a single other person in the room she wanted to leave him to talk to. But he was easily the most eligible bachelor there and if she lingered by his side too long, she would end up looking like an old maid hanging on his every word. Then the comments would really start flying. So she let him go and tried not to watch him too closely as he moved through the crowd, greeting the movers and shakers of city government with the ease of a man who was completely at home in his surroundings.

Distracted by his mere presence, Sadie couldn't have said who she talked to or what subjects were discussed as she circulated before dinner was served. Then it was time for them to take their places at the round tables set up around the room, and suddenly Noah was casually asking her if the seat next to her was taken. Before she could stutter anything but a no, he was sitting beside her, his long legs stretched out next to hers under the table.

If others thought it was the least unusual that the playboy of south central Texas deliberately chose to sit next to Hanging Judge Thompson, they gave no sign of it, but Sadie was a nervous wreck. She'd been talked about enough for one evening, and the last thing she wanted was the gossips to remember all the talk about her and Noah in the courthouse elevator. Hurriedly, she turned in self-defense to the man on the other side of her. A local businessman who not only contributed his money to the children's ranch on a regular basis, but also his time, Austin Sennet was a good man who was crazy about his family. Sadie knew his wife, who was currently visiting her sick mother in Austin, and had been to their home on several occasions. She only had to ask about his children to get him talking.

Relieved, she appeared totally engrossed in a

tale about his three-year-old daughter, but she'd never felt like such a fraud in her life. All her senses were attuned to Noah. She heard him strike up a conversation with the woman on his right, knew every time that he glanced back at her. Her heart pounding and her palms damp, she sent up a silent prayer of thanks that she really wasn't required to think in her conversation with Austin or she would have been in real trouble.

Despite that, she might have gotten through the evening without any problems if Noah hadn't chosen that moment to rub his leg along hers under the table. Startled, she jumped.

Arching a brow at her, Austin studied her in concern. "Are you okay? You look a little flushed all of a sudden."

Sudden hysteria bubbled in her throat. Flushed? she thought wildly, almost choking on a giggle of nervousness. Oh, yeah, she was definitely that. What woman wouldn't be when Noah Baxter was playing footsies with her under the table and enjoying every minute of it?!

She was going to kill him, she decided when she shot him a glance and found him smiling at her innocently. Oh, he was enjoying this! Deliberately teasing her, he managed to get his shoe off, then slowly rubbed his sock-clad foot along her instep. All around them, people laughed and talked as waiters scurried to deliver food to the guests before it grew cold, and no one had a clue that right in front of them, he was boldly trying to seduce her.

And coming awfully close to succeeding.

"Sadie? Are you sure you're all right? Your color keeps coming and going. Would you like me to find a doctor? I know Janice Creswell and Kurt Ringer are here somewhere. Just say the word and I'll find one of them for you."

"No!" Jerking her gaze away from Noah's, she turned back to Austin, blushing furiously as Noah continued to tease her under the table. "It's n-nothing," she assured him shakily. "It's j-just a little warm in here, don't you think? I'll be fine once I get something cold to drink."

As if on cue, the two waiters assigned to their table arrived then, and while one placed steaming plates of roast chicken before each of the eight guests seated at the round table, the other filled the wineglasses with a sparkling Chardonnay. Sadie took one sip and knew she needed to keep a clear head, but it was already too late for that. It had been from the moment

Noah touched her. She was trembling, her thoughts scattered, and all he'd done was play with her toes. Tightening her fingers around the stem of her wineglass, she took a fortifying gulp and prayed that it would steady her nerves. If it didn't, she was going to be a basket case by the end of the evening.

The speeches started then, and the toasts. Achingly aware of Noah's every move, Sadie hardly noticed how many times the waiter refilled her glass. When the dancing began and the men at the table started asking the women to dance, Austin politely asked her to join him on the dance floor. Normally, she would have declined with the excuse that she had two left feet, which wasn't far from the truth, but the wine had relaxed her inhibitions and her head was pleasantly fuzzy. With a smile, she rose to her feet.

The song was a slow one, thank God, or her head would have been reeling and she would have been in real trouble. A perfect gentleman, Austin held her at just the right distance and thankfully wasn't any more creative when it came to dancing than she was. They'd barely circled the floor once, however, when Noah tapped him on the shoulder.

"Mind if I cut in?"

He directed the question at Austin, but his eyes were on hers, dark and challenging, daring her to protest. And just that quickly, electricity sparked in the air between them. Sadie stiffened—she couldn't help it—her heart already pounding, and knew Austin had to feel the sudden tension she couldn't hide. But while his eyes were speculative as he glanced down at her, then to Noah and back again, he was too much of a gentleman to ask what was going on between the two of them.

Instead, he said easily, "Not at all. Another few minutes and she probably would have been begging someone to rescue her anyway. I hadn't stepped on her toes yet, but it was only a matter of time."

"I thought you did just fine," Sadie said with a shaky smile. "You made me feel very comfortable. In case you couldn't tell, I'm not much of a dancer, either."

"I don't know that I agree with that," he retorted with a grin. "Anyone who can get around the entire dance floor without running into my big feet has to be pretty darn good. Have a good time, you two. I think I'm going to cut and run. I want to call Karen before it gets too late.''

Then, before Sadie was ready for it, she found herself surrounded by dancers, yet somehow alone with Noah. He reached for her, and the only protest she could make was a pitifully weak and unintentionally provocative one. ''This probably isn't a smart thing to do, but I can't seem to help myself.'' She'd longed to feel his arms around her from the moment she'd turned to find him smiling down at her in his tux. Without another word, she walked into his arms.

The second he touched her, he knew he never should have followed her out onto the dance floor. Not after he'd just spent the last hour driving himself crazy playing with her foot under the table and imagining all the other parts of her he wanted to get his hands on. If he was smart, he'd come up with an excuse to leave, then get the hell out of there. Now! But he hadn't liked seeing her in another man's arms, even one as mild mannered and nonthreatening as Austin Sennet. As long as she wanted to dance, he wasn't going anywhere.

But, God, this was torture! Clenching his teeth on a groan, he fought the need to pull her full against him. No, dammit! He could just imagine the kind of talk that would generate, the eyebrows it would raise, and that was the one thing he was determined to spare her. Especially tonight, when she'd finally relaxed her guard with him a little. If he didn't want to blow that, he'd damn well keep her at a politically correct distance and be thankful for it.

It should have been easy. He wasn't an animal—his mother had raised him to be a gentleman and he knew how to treat a lady. He certainly could control his baser instincts. Or at least, he told himself, he would have if the lady had cooperated. But somewhere between his good intentions and the path to hell, Sadie took matters into her own hands. One second he held her a nice, safe twelve inches away, and the next she was draped all over him like a heat rash.

She couldn't have shocked him more if she'd dragged his mouth down to hers and given him a French kiss right there in front of God and everyone. Swearing softly under his breath, he immediately tried to put her from him and found his hands full of a stubborn woman who had a mind of her own. With a murmur of protest, she eluded his every move and found a spot on his shoulder for her cheek that met with her approval. Sighing with contentment, she closed her eyes and snuggled against him.

"Dammit, Sadie, what are you doing?" he growled in her ear.

"Isn't it obvious?" she murmured, chuckling. "I'm dancing, silly. And it feels wonderful. *You* feel wonderful."

If they'd been anywhere else but where they were, he would have shown her right then and there just how good wonderful could feel. But they were in a highly public place, and Judge Sadie Thompson didn't do things like this. Already they were starting to draw interested looks and she didn't even seem to be aware of it. What the devil was going on?

He started to ask her, only to suddenly remember the number of times the waiter had made the circle around their table refilling wineglasses. The man had stopped at Sadie's chair just as often as he had everyone else's, but he'd merely thought the waiter was topping off the glass she just seemed to be sipping at.

Drawing back slightly, he frowned down at her searchingly and groaned at the sight of her slightly flushed face and dreamy smile. "Oh, God, you're smashed!"

"Oh, I don't think so," she replied primly, then spoiled the effect by frowning slightly in confusion. "Things do look a little fuzzy."

In spite of himself, he couldn't help but grin. Considering the amount of wine she had downed, she was lucky she could even open her eyes. Seeing straight would, no doubt, be beyond her capabilities for quite some time to come. "I imagine they do," he said dryly, chuckling as he kept an arm around her waist and steered her off the dance floor. "C'mon, Your Honor, I think I'd better take you home."

"But it's still early."

"Trust me, sweetheart, you're going to thank me for this tomorrow—if you remember it. Did you park your car in the hotel garage?"

She looked around vaguely. "My car? No. I didn't want to bother with finding a parking place so I took a cab."

"Good." Escorting her straight out into the hallway outside the ballroom, he leaned her against the solid support of a wall. "I'm going to get your purse," he told her when she blinked up at him owlishly. "Stay right here."

He doubted if she could have moved under her own power if her life had depended on it, but he wasn't taking any chances. Quickly retrieving her small clutch purse from the table, he stuffed it into his pocket and rushed back to find her right where he'd left her, still propping up the wall.

The second she saw him, she gave him a slow, inviting smile that sent heat spilling into his loins. He reached for her, slipping an arm around her waist to pull her into his side, and didn't have a clue what kind of trouble he was in until she confided softly, "I've given it some serious thought, and I want you to make love to me tonight."

Just that easily, she'd taken the wind right out of his sails. Stunned, he stopped in his tracks. "What?"

Undaunted, she repeated dutifully, "I want you to make love to me. You told me to let you know when I was ready, so I am. I want to do it tonight."

With need forming a tight fist in his gut, Noah stared down at her and reminded himself that she was soused. She didn't know what she was saying, what she was asking for. Hell, she'd probably never had that much wine in her life, and he had no intention of taking advantage of her in that condition. He didn't doubt that they'd make love one day soon, but when they did, she'd know what she was doing every step of the way.

"We'll talk about it when I get you home," he rasped. "C'mon. My truck's in the garage."

Five minutes later, convinced he had everything under control, he had her strapped in the passenger seat of his Explorer. Then, as he pulled out of the garage, she reached out and trailed the fingers of her left hand over his thigh. He almost wrecked the truck right there and then. "Dammit, Sadie, stop that!"

She only laughed softly and teased him again. Cursing, he covered her hand with his own, dragged it farther down his leg to his knee and trapped it there. "Behave yourself," he growled sternly.

He might as well have asked the wind not to blow. Her inhibitions destroyed by the wine, she was feeling pretty cocky. Under his hand, her fingers stroked tantalizing circles. If she'd wanted to drive him slowly out of his mind, she couldn't have found a better way. Sweat breaking out on his brow, he hit the accelerator and raced toward the social club.

How he got them home without having a wreck, he never knew. He ran one stop sign and almost cruised through another before he realized what he was doing and slammed on the brakes. Thankfully, he'd taken a shortcut through the narrow, winding streets that had once been cow paths to the river during the days of the Alamo, and at that time of night, there was virtually no traffic.

Later, he told himself, he was going to laugh over her timing, but he didn't feel much like laughing when he got Sadie into her apartment and she was still feeling amorous. Reminding himself he was going to be a gentleman if it killed him, he caught her hands before she could slide her arms around him. But, God, he ached for her! If he could just kiss her, just once...

Clenching his jaw on an oath, he put the brakes to that thought immediately. No! He wanted her too much. If he so much as touched her, he'd have her flat on her back in bed before either one of them knew what happened, and tomorrow she wouldn't even remember it.

"How about some coffee?" he suggested hurriedly, stepping around her and heading for the kitchen. "Something strong and black. Where do you keep it?"

For someone who had just consumed enough wine to float a battleship, she was damn quick on her feet. In the time it took for him to take a single step toward the galley-style kitchen that was identical to his own, she was standing in front of him, blocking his path, taking his hand with a slow smile that made his insides curl. "No coffee," she said softly. "Not to-night."

He groaned, wondering if she knew just how much of a temptress she was. "Sweetheart, it's late. You need to be in bed."

"I agree," she said huskily. "So what's taking you so long?"

The little witch was baiting him, flirting with him, and enjoying every minute of it. "Alone," he said firmly, frowning sternly. "You're snockered, honey. Smashed, okay? I know you usually know your own mind, but not when it's pickled with wine. You're in no shape to make any decisions tonight, so it's into bed with you and I'm out of here. We'll talk tomorrow."

He should have left right then, but she had ahold of his hand, and when he turned to go, she simply refused to let go. Glancing back over his shoulder at her, he warned, "This isn't smart, Your Honor. C'mon and let go before we both do something we could regret."

"Stay with me," she said huskily, her brown

eyes pleading. ''Just until I fall asleep. That's all I ask.''

He shouldn't have. Not when just the feel of her hand on his was enough to warm his blood. Staying with her, watching her fall asleep, would rip him apart. He was only so strong, dammit! A man could resist only so much temptation. But he couldn't leave her, not when she was looking up at him with such longing in her eyes.

''Just until you fall asleep,'' he agreed hoarsely. ''I'll wait here until you change.''

A smile like liquid sunshine broke across her face. Impulsively, she stretched up on tiptoe and brushed a feather-light kiss to his cheek. ''It won't take me a second. I'll be right back.''

With a smile and a rustle of silk, she was gone, leaving behind a tantalizing, slightly sweet, slightly spicy all-woman scent that he knew would haunt him in his dreams. How he was going to get through the next forty or fifty minutes, he didn't know, and that's probably what it would take for her to change and relax enough to fall asleep. God, what had he set himself up for?

Ten minutes later, his worst fears were realized. She appeared at the doorway dressed for bed, and his heart stopped dead in his chest. Cotton. She wore a simple, white cotton summer gown. Long and modest, it had a round neck and short sleeves and covered her all the way to her bare toes. It wasn't in any way, shape or form the least bit provocative, but there was something about it and the way her toes peeked out from underneath the ruffled hem that just destroyed him.

With her hair down around her shoulders, she looked innocent, virginal, sexy as hell. A wise man wouldn't have gotten anywhere close to touching distance, and when it came to women, he'd always considered himself smarter than most. Where this particular one was concerned, however, he didn't have the brains God gave a flea. One second, half the length of the living room was between them, and the next, he was standing right in front of her and he didn't have a clue how he'd gotten there.

God, she was beautiful! He wanted to touch her, to run his hands over her gown and her skin and kiss her until they were both dizzy with need. But as much as he knew that that was what she wanted, too, he couldn't. Not when he knew that there was no way in hell that she'd be standing before him now in nothing but a nightgown if she hadn't had way too much to drink.

Regret thickening his voice, he said, "Honey, I don't think this is a very good idea."

She didn't argue, didn't try to change his mind, didn't, in fact, say anything. Instead, she just took his hand and pulled him after her into the dark, private, intimate shadows of her bedroom so he could hold her until she fell asleep.

He would have sworn he couldn't do it. Not tonight. Not when she wore only a thin gown that could tempt the devil himself. He didn't have that kind of self-control. But when she crawled into her old-fashioned poster bed and turned to smile at him in the darkness, nothing short of an earthquake could have stopped him from joining her.

Tugging off his shoes, he slid in beside her and told himself nothing was going to get out of hand as long as he kept his clothes on, and he had no intention of taking them off. Then Sadie snuggled up against him, spoon fashion, her bottom nestling against his loins, and all he could think about was getting her and himself naked. Now!

Before he could so much as move, however, Sadie pulled the arm he'd draped around her waist closer, found just the right spot for her head on his shoulder and sighed in contentment as she closed her eyes. Almost immediately, her body went totally slack against his. In the time it took to draw her next breath, she was asleep.

Stunned, Noah stared down at her suspiciously, unable to believe she could fall asleep so fast. She had to be teasing him. But her breathing was slow and easy, her body totally boneless, the expression on her face in the shadowy light relaxed and at peace. If she was faking, then she should have been in Hollywood.

Stay with me. Just until I fall asleep. That's all I ask.

He'd done as she'd asked; there was no longer any reason to stay, he told himself. Except for the woman in his arms. When she woke up in the morning, the tipsy little seductress who had shed her inhibitions on the dance floor and boldly told him she wanted him to take her to bed would, in all likelihood, be gone. In her place would be the straitlaced, always proper Judge Sadie Thompson, who fascinated him every bit as much as the sleeping beauty in his arms. It was just that he didn't see the flirty side of her very often, and he wasn't ready to let her go. Not yet. He'd stay, just for a while. What could it hurt?

Chapter 8

It was the feel of Noah's hands on her, stroking her, caressing her, that slowly brought her from a dead sleep to heart-pounding consciousness. Disoriented, her blood heating and her head thick, she blinked her eyes open to discover him in bed with her, fully clothed, his long legs tangled with hers as he leaned over her, pressing her down into the mattress. And she didn't have a clue how he had gotten there.

Confused, her heart tripping over itself, she caught his hand and clung tight. "Noah? How…"

When she couldn't finish the question, a slow smile curled one corner of his mouth. "If you're trying to ask how I ended up in your bed, you invited me in," he said in a husky

voice still rough with sleep. "Don't you remember?"

Her eyes wide and searching his, she started
to tell him she was sure she had done no such
thing, when fuzzy images of the night before
swam up from the cloudy depths of her memory. "Oh, God!"

"You had quite a bit to drink," he said quietly, lifting a hand to her hair to tenderly push
it back from her face. "How's your head this
morning?"

It wasn't her head she was worried about.
She hadn't just asked him into her bed—she'd
asked him to make love to her! She remembered it clearly now and cringed in mortification. Dear God, how could she have done such
a thing? Talk about brazen! She didn't remember much of what happened after they reached
her apartment, but she remembered enough to
know that he hadn't done anything more than
hold her, and then only reluctantly. She was the
one who had insisted.

Hot color firing her cheeks, she'd never been
so embarrassed in her life. "I'm fine," she assured him stiffly. "Embarrassed to death, but
fine. I'm sorry if I put you in an uncomfortable
position. I never meant to, but I just couldn't

seem to help myself. Obviously, I don't handle wine very well.''

''Are you sober now? Your head's clear?''

''Yes, of course. But—''

''Good,'' he murmured, and gently covered her mouth with his.

Her body still soft and warm from sleep, she'd slept with the feel of his arms around her all night, holding her close against the hard strength of his body, and she'd never felt so safe. He wouldn't hurt her. She knew that, and with a quiet sound of pleasure, she gave herself up to the wonder of his kiss.

There'd never been any doubt that he was a man who knew how to kiss, but of all the times he'd kissed her, he'd never kissed her quite the way he did then. Slowly, languidly, as if she were some beautiful, exotic creature that had totally entranced him, and he couldn't seem to get enough of her. His mouth warm and tempting, he tasted and nibbled and savored her like a man who planned to do nothing else for the rest of the morning.

When he finally let her up for air, her guard was down and she was floating. Her eyes as dark as a fawn's, she looked up at him dazedly. ''Noah—''

"Easy," he murmured, trailing kisses along her jaw. "We're going to do this nice and easy. No pressure, no rush, just slow and natural, at our own pace. You did tell me last night that you wanted me to make love to you." Drawing back slightly, he frowned. "You do remember, don't you?"

Caught in the trap of his heated gaze, her heart thumping madly, every nerve in her body tingling with awareness, she should have, for her own protection, told him that she couldn't recall anything from last night, especially that. But she couldn't lie to him or herself, not when he was this close and the one clear memory she had of the previous evening was when she'd asked him to make love to her. She'd wanted him so badly she'd ached. She still did.

But her brain wasn't pickled with wine now, and the inadequacies that never failed to make her feel like she'd been born into the wrong time period clutched at her heart, and just that easily, doubt crept in to cool her blood. She stiffened; she couldn't help it.

"Some things are better off forgotten," she hedged. "The wine went to my head."

She knew the second the words left her tongue that he wasn't going to let her get away with that. His gaze sharp, peering right into her soul, he growled, ''Are you saying that you didn't want me?''

''No. I mean yes!'' Flushed, she said, ''I wasn't exactly in top form, if I remember correctly. In fact, you told me I was soused!''

''You were, but that doesn't mean you didn't know what you were doing. The wine just lowered your inhibitions. If you'll just give me a little time, I can do the same thing.''

''No!''

Panicking, she lifted a hand to hold him at bay, but he only caught it and pressed a tender kiss into her palm. ''Five minutes,'' he murmured against the sensitive skin of her palm. ''Just give me five minutes. If you still want to stop after that, all you have to do is say so. You know I would never hurt you.''

''It's not me I'm worried about,'' she whispered, blinking back stupid tears. ''It's you.''

''Me?'' he repeated, stunned. ''You're worried about hurting *me?* For God's sake, how?''

''By disappointing you,'' she said simply, starkly. ''It's going to happen. It always does.''

''Hush,'' he ordered huskily, kissing her softly. ''Don't even think about going there. That's the past and it has nothing to do with now. With us. Come here,'' he coaxed, rolling to his side and taking her with him. ''Let me show you.''

''Noah—''

He silenced her with a kiss. A simple, soft, teasing brush of his lips that didn't demand anything of her. Once. Twice. With infinite patience, his mouth came back to hers again and again, like a butterfly dancing back to the honeyed petals of a flower, lingering only long enough to sip the nectar from her lips before taking flight once more. And every time he returned, the kiss was warmer, sweeter, richer.

Her heart tripping, she closed her eyes with a sigh and never knew that the next time their lips met, she was the one who lifted her mouth to his. Murmuring her name, he took the kiss deeper, teasing her with his tongue, and just that easily, magic rained down on them like a burst of stardust from the Milky Way. Her senses swimming, Sadie moaned and crowded closer.

He turned her bones to water and pulled emotions from her she wasn't even aware that she'd had, all without doing anything but kissing her. And she loved it. She loved the taste and feel and heat of him, the tenderness he gave to her so effortlessly. She curled into him; she couldn't help herself, the need to be heart to heart with him more than she could resist. Nothing had ever felt so perfect in her life.

He sensed it—she should have known that he would. He was an experienced man and he knew when a woman was ready and willing to respond to him with all her heart and soul. For a moment that seemed to spin out into eternity, his arms tightened around her and his kiss turned fierce and hot and possessive. Lightning sparked between them, setting the very air sizzling.

She was sinking fast, when Noah abruptly jerked his mouth from hers. His breathing as ragged as hers, he told her all the things he wanted to do to her, all the ways he wanted to make love to her, how he wanted to make her fly apart and come undone in his arms. He made it sound wonderful and earthy and horribly, horribly intimate, and all the while he talked, his hands roamed over her, under her nightgown, touching, caressing, enticing.

She should have been apprehensive—any second now, he was going to go too far, touch her too intimately, and something in her would just freeze. But her blood didn't cool; her body didn't brace in trepidation. Not when Noah was kissing her like there was no tomorrow. And when his fingers moved to the buttons of her gown and undid them one by one with painstaking slowness, her heart jumped, but not with dread. Never with that.

She loved the way he made her feel when he touched her, and when his hand tenderly cupped her breast and he swept his thumb over her already beaded nipple, she thought nothing had ever felt so good. Then, with a murmur of need, he leaned down and replaced his thumb with his mouth. Lightning streaked through her, straight to her loins. Startled, she arched up off the mattress with a jagged cry, reaching for him.

Noah almost lost it then. God, she was sweet! And so damn responsive when she let herself go. He wanted her so badly his teeth ached, and if she'd been any other woman, he would have long since given in to the needs driving him. But this was Sadie, innocent in all the ways that counted, and his gut twisted just at the thought of her tightening up on him.

He wouldn't do that to her, he vowed silently. He wouldn't be a selfish jackass like her ex and take his own satisfaction at the expense of hers. She deserved a hell of a lot more than that and by God, she was going to get it—even if it killed him.

It nearly did. Where he found the strength to hang on to his self-control, he never knew. Her skin was like satin, her breasts full and plump and so pretty that all he could think of was getting her out of her gown so he could see all of her. Murmuring reassurances to her, kissing her until they were both breathless and almost past reason, he slowly, carefully, undressed her, then tore off his own clothes. His heart pounding as he took her naked body against his, he knew this was the moment of truth. If ever she was going to bolt, it would be now.

But instead of going all stiff on him, she turned to him trustingly and pressed close from breast to thigh. Before he could do anything but groan, the fire raging in his loins heated to flash point. Control, what he had left of it, balanced on a razor's edge.

His jaw rigid, he struggled to get a grip, but he was fighting a losing battle. His blood was hot, his hands shaking, and he couldn't hold back any longer. He kissed her hungrily and pulled her under him, and to his delight, she came willingly, eagerly. Her hands roamed shyly over him and almost destroyed him. Wrenching his mouth from hers, he groaned, "This is the point of no return, sweetheart. If you want me to stop, you've got to tell me now."

"No!" she whimpered, clutching at him when he made a slight move to withdraw. "Don't stop! I couldn't stand it. Please..."

Restless, she moved against him, telling him without words of the ache that had lodged low in her belly, and he understood perfectly. The same fire burned him from the inside out. Murmuring soothingly, he slid his hand down over her stomach to the nestling of curls between her thighs and gently stroked her silken folds. Hot and wet, she cried out, shuddering wildly. "Noah!"

"I know, honey," he murmured, dropping kisses onto her mouth as his fingers continued to caress her delicate, intimate flesh. "God, you're sensitive! That's it, sweetheart. Don't fight it. Just go with it."

With soft words and the sure, steady rhythm of his stroking fingers, he built the tension in her until she was writhing and half out of her mind with need. Her hips lifting urgently to his and her eyes dark with passion, she was wild and beautiful, and just watching her gave him a fierce satisfaction. From the first time he'd kissed her, he'd wanted to strip away the prim and proper facade she presented to the rest of the world to reveal the very real, very passionate woman he'd suspected was underneath. He'd thought he'd known what to expect, but nothing could have prepared him for the way she gave herself to him. She quite simply took his breath away.

This first time was for her. Nothing was as important to him as her pleasure, and given the chance, he would have taken her right to the edge and over with his hand alone. But she would have none of it. "No!" she cried. "Not like this. I want you. Now!"

He might have been able to resist his own needs, but never hers. Not when she knew what she wanted and was so sweetly fierce about it. Reaching for him, she explored the hot, hard length of him, and something in him just seemed to snap. With a rough growl, he endured the exquisite pleasure of her touch for all of ten seconds, then settled himself between her thighs, his arousal hot and hard against her.

Outside, a mockingbird greeted the morning sun with a happy trill, but inside, their eyes locked and the only sound was that of hushed expectancy. Watching every nuance of her expression, he slowly began to enter her. If he'd seen so much as a twinge of doubt, he would have found a way to stop immediately, but the light in her eyes was anything but fear. She smiled, and his heart turned over. Slowly, inexorably, he filled her until he was seeded deep inside her. Wonder shimmered between them, then he was moving and her hips were lifting to his and suddenly they were both caught up in a staggering vortex of heat and tension and unbearable need.

Madness. It took her like a storm, stunning her, delighting her, destroying her. She cried out, startled, pleasure rippling through her in waves. Shuddering, she heard Noah murmuring to her, praising her, holding her as she slowly floated back down to earth; then he was moving over her, his thrusts wild and fierce, and her senses took over again. This time when she shattered, however, he was right there with her, her name a hoarse cry on his lips as he took her with him over the very edge of reason.

Boneless, too shaken by what they had just shared to move, Sadie cradled Noah in her arms long after their thundering hearts quieted and silence settled down around them. David had told her often enough that she wasn't a passionate woman, and over the course of their short-lived marriage, she'd never had any reason to think differently. After all, her faults had been glaringly obvious. She was the one who'd lain stiff and unmoving in the night, unable to unbend enough to enjoy making love with her own husband. She'd never come close to losing control, never been anything but uptight and frigid and totally lacking as a woman. Angry and frustrated, David never failed to make it clear that she was the one with the problem.

And she'd believed him. All this time, she'd been wrong.

How could she have known? She'd had no experience with men until David came along and swept her off her feet so quickly that she forgot all the warnings her mother had drilled into her head from the time she was old enough to understand the difference between right and wrong. A virgin and in love with love for the first time in her life, she'd blamed her inexperience when she'd felt only the mildest response to David's hurried kisses and rough caresses. Once she had the security of knowing they were married and she felt free to let herself go, she convinced herself that things would be better. They weren't.

She hadn't had a clue what was missing until now. Chemistry. She hadn't had a clue that it packed such a punch, and even now, didn't know how to deal with it...or Noah. He'd made her want and ache and shudder and shown her a side of herself she hadn't known existed. She'd been married; she should have known what to expect. But somehow everything had become much more complicated, much more *intimate,* and too late, she realized she was in way over her head. And it scared her to death.

In desperate need of some time to herself to think, she would have bolted then, but Noah must have sensed the emotions churning in her like a storm, because before she could move so much as a muscle, he rolled off her and gathered her close against his side.

"You're awfully quiet," he murmured, drawing back slightly to get a good look at her. Lifting a hand to the dark cloud of her hair, he pushed it back and studied her solemnly. "Are you okay? I didn't hurt you, did I?"

She blushed crimson and looked anywhere

but at him. ''No, of course not,'' she said huskily. ''You were very...careful with me.''

He had, in fact, been gentle and tender and made the whole experience wonderful for her. But that wasn't something she was prepared to discuss with him yet, not when her emotions were still in a spin and she was naked in his arms, with nothing but a sheet to cover her. Deliberately changing the subject, she asked, ''Exactly how much did I have to drink last night?''

A crooked grin propped up one corner of his mouth. ''I lost count after six glasses. How's your head?''

''A little thick,'' she replied, rubbing at the headache that had lodged itself in her temple. ''I guess this is what a hangover feels like.''

She didn't look hungover. With her hair wild and free, her skin flushed and her eyes still languorous with passion, she looked fantastic. He would have liked nothing more than to make love to her again and lose himself in her, but it was too soon. She wasn't ready for that, and if the truth were to be told, he probably wasn't, either. Their arrangement was for *just sex,* and that was a long way from what they'd just shared. Alarm bells should have been going off all over the place, and the fact that they weren't told him all too clearly that things might be getting out of hand. He needed some distance to think about that, deal with it, decide where, if anywhere, they were going from here.

But he didn't want to leave her, dammit. She was so quiet he could almost feel her withdrawing from him, and it frustrated him no end. He wanted to know what was going on in her head, to kiss her until she melted against him again so she wouldn't get caught up in thinking too much and call off their arrangement. Not yet, dammit! He wanted more time with her.

Impulsively, he said, ''You just need some food in you and a little fresh air to clear your head. Why don't we get dressed and go down on the River Walk for breakfast? Then later, you can go with me to my sister's softball game. Her team's playing for the intramural championship, and I'm coaching them. I can't sit with you, but my mother and the rest of my sisters will be there. They'll keep you entertained.''

He wanted her to meet his family. Caught off guard, Sadie was stunned by the need to say yes. What in the world was wrong with her? she wondered wildly. They had an unemotional, practical agreement, nothing more. That meant no friendship, no dates, no confidences exchanged in the dark. And *definitely* no family. She'd made it clear from the beginning that she didn't want a relationship, didn't want to be involved with him any other way. She'd set the rules and was sure she would never be tempted to so much as bend them, let alone break them. But now, after making love with him just once, she was tempted to do just that. How had he gotten to her so fast?

Clutching the sheet to her breast, she grabbed her robe from the end of the bed and quickly slipped into it. "I don't think that's a very good idea," she said stiffly as she rose to her feet and turned to face him. "If we start getting involved in each other's lives, things could get complicated."

"And you don't want that."

It wasn't a question, but a flat statement of fact in a tone that was more than a little irritated. Surprised, she went perfectly still and said cautiously, "I didn't think you did, either. If I misunderstood—"

"No, you didn't," he said curtly. "You didn't misunderstand a damn thing. I like my life just the way it is, and the last thing I want

is complications with a woman.'' Rising from
the bed splendidly nude, he snatched up his
clothes from where he'd tossed them and
dragged them on. ''If you change your mind
about the game, it's at Butler Field at three
o'clock. If you don't show, I guess you'll call
me the next time you want sex.''

His jaw set in granite, he stalked into the
living room and out the front door to her apartment, shutting it with a decided snap. Stunned,
Sadie stood in the silence of his abrupt depar-
ture and couldn't for the life of her figure out
what he was so upset about. She was just sticking to the terms of their original agreement.
Wasn't that what he wanted?

It was a perfect day for the championship
game. The humidity was low, the breeze light,
the temperature in the low nineties. The bleachers were packed with fans for both teams, and
there was an excitement in the air that was almost visible. As the girls warmed up, Noah
laughed and joked with his sister Natalie and
the rest of the team just as he always did, but
his eyes kept drifting to the stands. His mother
was up there, along with Alex, Rachel and
Kelly, but it was Sadie he was looking for and

he knew it. He wanted her there, dammit, and she was nowhere to be found.

And he had nobody to blame but himself. He knew how gun-shy she was, how leery she was of getting involved, and what had he done? Invited her to meet his family. Talk about stupid! He'd just wanted to spend the day with her, and instead, he'd scared her away. After the way she'd shattered in his arms, he should have known she'd be vulnerable and given her the space she needed to deal with it. Instead, he'd pushed her, and now he'd be lucky if she let him anywhere near her ever again.

Swearing, he turned his back on the crowd and sighed in relief as the pitcher for the opposing team finished her warm-up and everyone got into position for the game to begin. All business, he grabbed his sister Natalie, who just happened to be his lead-off batter, before she exited the dugout to face the pitcher at home plate. ''Remember what I told you about the lady's slider,'' he said, reminding her of the phenomenal pitch the opposing pitcher had developed that no one else in softball could throw. ''She's still perfecting it and might not chance throwing it in a big game, but just in case she does, I want you to be ready. It's going to come in fast, with no spin on it, and if you can get under it, it's going to be one–zip before the lady knows what hit her. Go get her, tiger.''

Flashing her dimples, her eyes alight with the competitive spirit that flourished in all the women of his family, Nat grinned cockily. ''She's toast—she just doesn't know it yet.''

With his sister at the plate and the championship on the line, concentrating should have been easy. They were playing a tough team, and if he was going to help Natalie and the team win, he had to put Sadie out of his mind and focus on the game. But as he prowled the dugout and stared out at the field, the only woman he saw was Sadie. He knew she wasn't coming, but he couldn't get the feel and taste of her out of his head. He'd foolishly thought that if he could ever get her in bed, just once, he would finally get past his craving for her, but nothing could have been further from the truth. Even now, he wanted her, and for a heck of a lot more than one or two or even a dozen nights. For the first time in his life, he was thinking long-term, and he didn't even know how the hell it had happened.

The crack of the bat as it connected with the ball, then the roar of the crowd, jerked him back from his thoughts in time to see Natalie racing around first base and heading for second for all she was worth. In the outfield, the center fielder was backing up all the way to the fence with her glove raised, ready to catch the ball as it began to drop, and Noah's heart plummeted like a stone.

"No, no," he muttered. "Dammit, drop it!"

As if she heard him over the screaming and yelling of the fans, the center fielder shifted her raised glove a mere fraction of an inch to block the sun from her eyes, but it was a fraction of an inch too much. The sun hit her right in the eyes, and in the next instant, the ball dropped, missing her glove by mere centimeters, and hit the ground. As the crowd gasped, it rolled harmlessly away.

Behind him, Noah could hear his mother and sisters going nuts, along with the rest of Lady Legal Eagle supporters, but he couldn't take his eyes off Natalie. Long-legged and beautiful, she was in her first year of law school and planned to set up practice with him when she graduated. Studious and idealistic, she could, when she wanted to, look as prim and proper as Sadie. But this wasn't one of those times. Her ponytail trailing out behind her, her face fierce with concentration, she came around third base like Joe DiMaggio at his best, and God help anyone who got in her way. The catcher for the Heart Attacks thought about it for all of two seconds, then wisely decided discretion was the better part of valor. Never breaking stride, Natalie hit home plate dead center with her foot, scoring a home run, then ran into the arms of her cheering teammates, who poured out of the dugout to congratulate her.

As soon as hugs and high fives were traded, she grinned triumphantly and launched herself into Noah's arms. "Like I said," she told him with a laugh, "she's toast!"

"She damn sure is!" Chuckling, Noah gave her a bear hug and whirled her around, only to stop in surprise as he suddenly spied Sadie in the stands. She'd come, he thought, dazed. After the way he'd left her earlier, he'd wondered more than once over the course of the day if he'd ever see her again. And now she was here, and he couldn't help but wonder why. What was she trying to tell him?

"Hey, big brother, you okay?" his sister teased, punching him lightly in the chest. "You look like you just got hit in the head with the ball."

Jerking his attention back to Nat, he pulled her ponytail teasingly. ''It isn't every day I see my baby sister run the bases for an in-the-park home run. You did good, kid. We got 'em on the ropes. Now let's see if we can put them away. Tanya, you're up. Everybody else, back in the dugout.''

Sadie watched him disappear into the dugout with the rest of the team and wondered what had ever possessed her to come. She had no business going anywhere near the man, not after the loving they'd shared. And especially not after she'd opened the morning paper and found a picture of the two of them spread across the society page. The photographer had caught them when they were dancing close, and she'd taken one look at the picture and groaned. She'd been smiling up at Noah with her heart in her eyes, there for anyone to see, and just thinking about what the legal community was no doubt already saying about the two of them made her want to cringe.

She should have stayed home and worked. After all, it wasn't as if she had nothing to do. She had one of the biggest trials of her career to prepare for. The Dominguez trial started Monday and it would take her the rest of the weekend to get ready for it. But when she'd pulled her briefcase out and tried to buckle down to work, all she'd been able to see was Noah's face when he'd invited her to the game. He'd really wanted her to come.

She'd told herself she couldn't. She shouldn't. So what the devil was she doing here? Where was her backbone? Her spine? She'd never intended to leave her apartment, but then she'd noticed that she was out of bread and milk. She headed for the grocery store, and the next thing she knew, she was pulling into the ball-field parking lot. She didn't even know how she'd gotten there, for heaven's sake! And now, Noah had seen her. He would think… God, she didn't want to think about what he would think. She should just slip away while she still could.

But in the end, her curiosity wouldn't let her. His mother was there, and his sisters, and she found herself scanning the crowd for them, wondering what they looked like. Then the game caught her attention, and before she knew it, it was the bottom of the ninth inning and the game was tied. There was a runner at third, just waiting for the chance to steal home, and the same long-legged blonde who had started the game was up to bat. A hushed expectancy fell over the crowd as she took her stance in the batter's box.

"C'mon, Nat," the woman in front of Sadie yelled suddenly, startling her. "Knock it over the fence!"

Glancing over her shoulder, the batter found the woman in the crowd and grinned cockily. "Whatever you say, Mom." Winking, she turned back to the pitcher and took the first pitch. With stunning ease, she knocked it out of the park. In the time it took to swing the bat, the game was over.

The crowd went wild. The winning team came running out of the dugout, laughing and screaming, to hug the third-base runner and the girl named Nat as they each came across home plate, and then the fans in the stands were pouring out of the bleachers. Caught up in the tide of excitement, Sadie didn't stand a chance. Laughing, she hurried down the steps and suddenly found herself face to face with Noah.

People surged around them, but Sadie had eyes for no one but him. He was grinning, his blue eyes sparkling with something that stopped her heart in midbeat. Before she could guess his intentions, he grabbed her and kissed her.

"Gosh, Mom," a feminine voice drawled behind them, "d'you think he knows her or did he just grab the first woman he saw?"

"Of course he knows her," a slightly more mature voice replied knowingly. "Do you think he just goes around grabbing women off the street?"

"I don't think he's that desperate yet," a third woman confided, adding her two cents. "Of course, there was that circus woman who wanted to get him up on her trapeze."

"Rachel!"

"Behave yourself, girls," their mother chided, chuckling. "Can't you see your brother's busy?"

Dazed, her knees threatening to buckle any second, Sadie felt laughter ripple through Noah; then he was lifting his head and turning to face his family. Blushing crimson, Sadie would have liked nothing better than to disappear into the woodwork, but he never gave her the chance. Anticipating her need to bolt, he pressed his hand firmly at the back of her waist to keep her close.

"Don't go running scared, Your Honor," he murmured under his breath, then proceeded to introduce her to his mother and four sisters.

Short and plump with laughing brown eyes and dark curly hair that held barely a trace of gray, Gillian Baxter hardly looked old enough to be the mother of the brood that all towered over her like giants. Sadie liked her immediately, as she did Noah's sisters, and realized as she shook hands all the way around, that the entire gang—except for Natalie and Noah, of course—had sat right in front of her during the game. Gillian Baxter, in fact, had been the one who had loudly advised her daughter to knock one out of the park.

"You must be very special if Noah's willing to bring you around the family," his mother confided with a grin. "He doesn't usually bring anyone around, and I don't know why. It's not like we're going to give him the third degree or something."

"At least not until we get him alone," Kelly drawled, flashing dimples that were identical to Noah's. A doctor in her first year of residency, she added dryly, "We may act like a bunch of hoydens sometimes, but we do have some manners."

"So you can come celebrate with us without worrying about us embarrassing you," Alex, the youngest, said. "We're going to Pizza Warehouse. You'll come, won't you?"

The other sisters immediately seconded the invitation, and Sadie suddenly found herself the focus of all eyes, including Noah's. He didn't press her to accept, but he didn't have to. He'd already asked her once today to meet his family, and she only had to look in his eyes to see that it was important to him for some reason that she get to know his mother and sisters.

Once, that would have terrified her. Now, it was her own need to say yes that scared the living daylights out of her. What in the world was wrong with her? This wasn't what they'd agreed to; it wasn't what she wanted. She couldn't. Because as long as all they shared was sex, she couldn't get hurt.

"No, I—I can't," she said, panicking. Sliding free of Noah's touch, she took a quick step back. "It's nice of you to include me, but I just…can't. I shouldn't have come. I'm sorry." Tears flooding her eyes, she turned and fled.

Chapter 9

She spent the rest of the weekend totally and completely alone. Noah didn't call or drop by or force his company on her in any way. He gave her the space she wanted, and she should have been relieved. The apartment was peaceful and quiet, the phone didn't ring once and she had time to finish all the pretrial motions she'd brought home with her for the Dominguez trial and do a little housework, as well.

She'd never been more miserable in her life.

She lost track of the number of times she picked up the phone to call him just to hear the sound of his voice, only to realize at the last moment what she was doing and slam it back down again. She didn't need the sound of a man's voice to make her day complete; she never had. She'd always been self-sufficient and independent, and she wasn't about to change just because she'd gone to bed with the man. She readily admitted that he'd made her feel things she'd never dreamed existed, but that didn't mean she needed him. She didn't *need* anyone. She had her friends, a wonderful, rewarding career and a full life. That was more than enough for any woman.

By the time Sunday evening rolled around, she'd firmly convinced herself that she wasn't the least bit lonely. Then she dreamed of nothing but Noah all night long. She reached for him too many times in the night and always came up empty-handed. When her alarm finally went off Monday morning, she was restless and achy and furious with him. She pulled herself out of bed and stumbled into the bathroom, took one look in the mirror and groaned at the sight of the darkened circles under her eyes. How had he managed to do this to her after just one night of sex?

Squinting at herself in the mirror, she would have liked nothing better than to go back to bed, but that was a luxury she didn't have—not with the Dominguez trial scheduled to get under way in a matter of hours. So she shuffled into the kitchen, instead, and put on a pot of coffee. She was going to need at least a gallon of it just to get her eyes open.

It took considerable effort on her part, but when court convened at nine, she looked nothing like the woman who had rolled tiredly out of bed two hours before. All business, without so much as a single wrinkle in her black judicial robes, she was starched and ironed and had every hair neatly confined in a twist at the back of her head. Her reading glasses perched on her nose, she didn't smile at either the D.A. or the defense attorney as she took her seat at the bench and greeted them, but then again, she seldom did in court. Both sides were always looking for something to use against each other, and she didn't want to be accused of playing favorites.

Not surprisingly, the courtroom was packed, every seat in the gallery taken. Anticipation of the trial had been building for weeks, and the death of the state's key witness had only fueled interest in the proceedings. Guilty or innocent, Dominic Dominguez was a man who stirred people's passions, and she expected a full courtroom for the duration of the trial. She had no intention, however, of letting the situation turn into a circus. No cameras were allowed inside, and the press was restricted to a small area. Spectators would behave or she'd have them removed immediately.

Banging her gavel, she called the courtroom to order and greeted Michael Dunn, the prosecutor, and Ethan Kingston, Dominguez's attorney. ''Before I rule on the pretrial motions and we begin jury selection, I want to make it clear, gentlemen, that there will be no histrionics in this courtroom. You will conduct yourself in a professional manner or you'll answer to me. That goes for the spectators, too,'' she added, glancing sharply at a couple in the back who had their heads together and were whispering loudly. ''This is a murder trial, not some kind of sporting event in which everyone chooses up sides. I will not allow outbursts or vocal responses to testimony or my rulings from the gallery, so if anyone has a problem with that, you will remove yourself now, please. Otherwise, we can begin.''

When no one moved, she nodded, satisfied, and reached for the pretrial motions both lawyers had submitted several weeks ago. Most of them had to do with the rules of evidence, and as Sadie informed both parties of her decision on each motion, she made no apology for leaning toward the prosecution in such matters. She firmly believed in protecting the rights of the innocent, but at the same time, she refused to dismiss any evidence because of what amounted to very minor technicalities.

"As to your motions to deny the admission of evidence collected from the defendant's car and home, Mr. Kingston, both motions are denied," she concluded. "The officer on the scene acted properly and had sufficient reason to be suspicious of Mr. Dominguez when he stopped him for the broken taillight and the defendant was combative."

From the defense table, Dominic Dominguez glared at her with cold, black eyes that promised retribution. Chilled, Sadie ignored him and called for jury selection to begin. At the most routine trial, it was a tedious procedure. In a murder trial of such magnitude, it could take days to seat an acceptable jury. Resigned, Sadie sat back and waited for the bailiff to bring in the first group of jurors from the jury room downstairs.

Once questioning started, she hurried things along as much as possible, but the process was slow. Nearly everyone had heard about the case and formed an opinion about the defendant's guilt or innocence, so finding jurors who were unbiased wasn't easy. By the end of the day, six stood out, though one of them had expressed reservations about sitting on any jury that would take him away from his work for longer than a few days. With so much negative publicity about the trial already, the last thing either side wanted was to pick someone who would lose his job for doing his civic duty, so for all practical purposes, after seven hours of questioning, they had five potential jurors. It was going to be a long trial.

Afraid jury selection was going to drag out all week, Sadie kept everyone until nearly six before adjourning for the day. Instructing everyone to be back there the following morning at nine, she'd barely banged her gavel before reporters, anxious to get in sound bites for the six o'clock news, hurried out. The lawyers for both sides strolled out at a more leisurely pace, along with the spectators in the gallery, and within minutes, the courtroom was empty.

With a headache starting to throb in her temple, Sadie would have liked nothing better than to call it a day, but she had some research to do and she didn't want to cart a dozen or more law books home on a day when she'd walked to work. So she retired to her chambers, instead, slipped out of her shoes and made herself a glass of iced tea. Normally, Betty stayed as long she did, but she let her go home early. Silence settled over the office, and with a sigh of relief, she dug out the books she would need, propped her stocking feet on her desk, crossed them at the ankles and began to read.

She never intended to fall asleep. But it had been a long, tense day, and she'd slept little the night before. Exhaustion came from out of nowhere to weight her lids, and it just seemed easier to close them. Just five minutes, she told herself sleepily. She'd just rest her eyes for five minutes, then get back to her reading.

Five minutes stretched into a half hour and more, and she never noticed. Outside, the city traffic quieted and the sun dropped lower in the sky. Shadows grew long and thickened in density, and she never noticed. Then, in the hallway right outside the private entrance to her chambers, a vacuum cleaner roared to life as the cleaning crew invaded that area of the courthouse.

Startled, Sadie jerked awake to find herself sitting in near darkness in her chambers. The book she had been reading had long since fallen out of her hands to the carpeted floor, and her glasses were halfway down her nose. Pushing them up, she squinted down at her watch and nearly fell out of her chair. It was almost eight o'clock!

"Oh, my God!" Swinging her feet off her desk, she hurriedly started to gather up her things. She still had to walk home, and although it was only four blocks, she preferred not to do it in total darkness.

"That was dumb, Sadie," she grumbled as she returned the stack of law books to their proper places in the stacked bookcases that lined her chambers, then quickly cleared the rest of her desk and locked the file cabinets. "Real dumb. Next time you want to take a nap, go home first."

The cleaning lady opened her office door and gasped in surprise at the sight of her. "I'm sorry, Your Honor. I didn't know you were still here. Would you like me to come back later?"

"No, that's okay," Sadie said easily, slinging her purse over her shoulder as she lifted her briefcase. "Actually, I fell asleep and lost track of time. Come on in. I was just leaving. Good night."

"Oh, but shouldn't you call security and have someone take you to the front door?" the older woman asked worriedly, stopping her before she could walk out the door. "There's not supposed to be anybody in the building, but what if that man found a way to get back in, the one who trashed your office the other night?"

"Oh, but the police caught him," she assured her. "Didn't you hear? He just got out of prison and wanted to get back at me for sending him there. He's in jail without bail."

Sadie was sure there was nothing to be concerned about, but the older woman still didn't appear convinced. Humoring her, Sadie agreed to call security. "You're probably right. The building is pretty deserted, and there's no sense taking chances."

Five minutes later, Vince Fowler escorted her to the east side entrance of the courthouse and unlocked the door for her. Looking out at the deepening twilight, he frowned. "It's getting pretty dark out there, Your Honor. You shouldn't be walking around by yourself. Is your car in the garage across the street? I'll walk you over."

Touched, she smiled. "Actually, I didn't

bring my car this morning—I usually don't unless it's raining. I live at the Lone Star Social Club and it's only four blocks away."

"You're gonna walk?!"

He sounded so shocked that she would even consider doing such a thing that she couldn't help but laugh. "That's the plan. It's not far. And there are plenty of people out and about, especially near the River Walk. I'll be perfectly safe."

From the disapproving look on his face, he obviously didn't agree, but he only said gruffly, "If it's all the same to you, I'll stand here and watch you until you turn the corner. If you run into trouble between here and there, I can be there in ten seconds flat."

She didn't, of course. The courthouse was well lit and she made it across the street to the opposite corner without seeing a soul. Smiling, she waved to Vince, then turned the corner and headed east toward the Lone Star Social Club. It was a beautiful night for a walk, warm and breezy, and as she neared the River Walk, the sound of music on the air turned the evening festive. Smiling, she saw tourists strolling hand in hand two blocks ahead of her and made a mental note to track down Vince tomorrow to tell him there were people in sight the entire way home. She'd have to thank him, too, for being so concerned. It was comforting to know that the security personnel were so conscientious.

Lost in her thoughts, she passed the entrance to a narrow alley and never saw the man waiting there for her in the shadows. Lightning quick, a dirty, tattooed arm reached out of the darkness and whipped around her throat. Startled, she grabbed desperately at the arm that was like a lead pipe against her windpipe and tried to scream, but the only sound that came out was a muffled whimper.

Two blocks away, tourists still strolled hand in hand, but they were headed in the same direction she was, and no one saw her being dragged in the alley. Horrified, she fought wildly. This couldn't be happening! Not right in the middle of downtown at eight o'clock in the evening. Someone would see…hear…

But no one did.

There was no cry of alarm, no shout to stop. Muttering curses in her ear as she struggled violently against his hold, her abductor jerked her farther back into the alley, away from the reach of the streetlights, away from help, into a black abyss of shadows that were darker than the bowels of hell. There, he could do whatever he wanted to her and no one would know until it was too late.

"No! Please..." she croaked.

Blind with terror, she kicked and clawed at him, but she was gasping for air, and her efforts were pitifully ineffective. Growing weaker by the moment, she was just seconds away from blacking out completely and her attacker knew it. Controlling her easily, he laughed sinisterly.

"You're not so tough now, are you, Judge?" he sneered. "It's just me and you, with no fancy deputies or cops to watch over you, and I can do anything I want to you before I snap that stiff neck of yours. So what do you think I should do first, huh? Find out what makes you scream?"

"No—"

"I can, you know," he whispered silkily. "I can make you scream and scream until you think you'll never stop. Want to know how?" Murmuring in her ear, he told her all the sick, evil ways a psychopath could torture a woman. "Some women really get off on pain. Do you? It won't take me a second to find out."

He was tormenting her, pushing her buttons,

playing with her mind. She knew that, but still, she couldn't prevent herself from whimpering and trying to shrink away from him.

Pleased, he laughed wickedly. ''You know, I got a feeling you and me are going to get along just fine. And everybody told me you were real hard to work with. Why, I bet if I asked you to go back and change all those pretrial motion things you made in court today, you'd do it in a heartbeat, wouldn't you?''

That's what this was about? The Dominguez trial? Horrified, knowing she was going to die, she could do nothing but gasp, ''I—I can't!''

It was the wrong thing to say. The arm pressed against her windpipe tightened and his tone turned cold. ''Then maybe I'd better give you a taste of what you're going to get next time if you don't.''

''No!''

Sobbing, she fought against his hold, but he was bigger and stronger, and with grim purpose, he grabbed her left arm and jerked it up behind her. An instant later, she felt the sting of a hypodermic needle as it was jabbed into her upper arm.

''No!'' she tried to scream again, but there was barely any air in her lungs and the word was nothing but a soundless whisper. Then, with no warning, her attacker released her and shoved her violently away from him, sending her to her hands and knees on the rough pavement. She cried out in terror, her bruised throat protesting painfully, and flinched, waiting for the next blow, but it never came. Dazed, gasping as she dragged in deep, gulping breaths, she heard the sound of footsteps running away from her and tried to glance back over her shoulder as her attacker took off back down the alley, but she suddenly seemed to have lost control of her body. Her arms and legs grew heavy, refusing to do her bidding, and try though she might, she couldn't find the strength to get up.

Confused, she frowned down at her hands in the darkness and blinked owlishly as her fingers seemed to blur right before her eyes. Something was…wrong. Whimpering, she tried to clear her head, but a fog had descended over her from out of nowhere, and suddenly the darkness that surrounded her was closing in on her, swamping her, threatening to drag her under. She couldn't think, couldn't move, couldn't remember where she was or how she had gotten there.

Frightened, her blood roaring in her ears, she

tried to scream for help, but she barely managed a weak cry before the blackness came down on her like a ton of bricks. The night consumed her, and with nothing more than a faint whimper, she collapsed facedown in the alley.

He'd never wanted to call a woman so badly in his life.

How he'd gotten through the rest of the weekend and all day Monday without picking up the phone, Noah never knew. He hadn't been able to think of anything but her face as she'd hurried away from him and his family after the softball game. She'd been running scared, and it was all his fault. He shouldn't have asked her to the game, shouldn't have kissed her right in front of his family when he knew she was afraid of any further involvement with him.

And then there was that damn picture in the newspaper.

The moment he'd opened the paper Sunday morning and seen the picture of her dancing with him, her smile dreamy, he'd known the two of them were going to be the talk of the courthouse Monday morning. And he hadn't been wrong. The second he stepped through the front doors, he'd heard the whispers, the gossip, the hateful innuendos that couldn't hurt his thick hide but would no doubt wound Sadie deeply if she heard them. And he didn't doubt for a second that she had. How could she not? People stood around in the hallways and in the restrooms, openly talking about the two of them, speculating about what he could possibly see in a woman whose own husband said she was stiff as a board in bed.

And it infuriated him. He'd been in a rage all day thinking about what this was going to do to her. They'd had one damn night together. One, dammit! One fantastic, wonderful night. She'd been so sweet, so responsive, and when she'd come undone in his arms, she'd turned him inside out. But her confidence in her sexual attractiveness was still fragile, and it would take a lot more than one night of loving to repair the self-esteem David Lincoln had so viciously crushed. After today's snide remarks, she was probably questioning herself and her response to him and wondering if he'd just been amusing himself with her. He'd be damn lucky if she ever let him come near her again.

That thought nagged at him all day, demanding that he go to her and tell her not to let petty gossips dirty the incredible loving they'd shared. But the Dominguez trial had started that morning, and he'd known she'd have her hands full dealing with that. He was a distraction she didn't need, so he'd bided his time and waited until he got home to call her.

She wasn't there, however, and all he got was her machine. Leaving a message for her to call him, he glanced at the clock and realized that it was just barely five and she might not be home for at least another hour, not when it was the first day of a big trial and she had jury selection to get through. Curbing his impatience, he resigned himself to a long wait.

How he waited until six to call her again, he never knew. Once more, her answering machine picked up the call, and he left a terse message for her to call him. She didn't. When six-thirty came and went without any word from her, he told himself there was no reason for concern. By seven, he was pacing the floor and leaving messages for her every fifteen minutes.

He was, he told himself, going to tell her off when she finally got home. He didn't have any rights where she was concerned, and she would probably be real quick to tell him that she didn't answer to anyone but herself, but it was common courtesy to let someone know where you were when you'd had an especially bad day. He was concerned about her, dammit, and if she didn't like it, that was tough.

When eight o'clock rolled past and there was still no word from her, he readily admitted that he was a hell of a lot more than concerned. Where the devil was she? She should have been home hours ago. She could have gone out with friends directly from work, of course, or stopped at one of the cafés along the River Walk for a quiet dinner alone on the way home, but he didn't think so. Not after the day she'd had. She was a proud, private woman who hated having her affairs talked about in public, and if he knew her the way he was beginning to think he did, he'd bet money that she'd have headed home the first chance work was over. So what had happened to her between the court-house and the social club? It was only four blocks, dammit!

Making a snap decision, he headed for the door, intending to go out and look for her, when the phone suddenly rang shrilly. "Thank God!" he muttered. "It's about damn time!"

But when he strode quickly back across the living room and snatched up the phone, it wasn't Sadie on the other end. Instead, he recognized Sam Kelly's voice and felt his heart stop dead in his chest. He'd taken over Sam's lease when he got married and moved into the apartment located over Heavenly Scents, the bakery his wife owned and operated just across the river and a block west on Commerce. He'd run into the detective a few times at the courthouse and they'd become friends, but the man had never called him at home.

"What's wrong?" he demanded sharply. "It's Sadie, isn't it? Something's happened to her."

Sam, knowing better than to sugarcoat the truth, gave it to him straight. "She was found unconscious in an alley halfway between the courthouse and the social club."

"Oh, God! How is she? What happened?"

"I don't know yet. She was taken to University Hospital, and the last I heard, she was still unconscious. I'm on my way out there now, but I saw the picture of the two of you in Sunday's paper and figured you'd want to know."

Something squeezed Noah's heart at the thought of her being hurt. "Thanks, man," he said gruffly. "I owe you one. I'll see you there.'' He hung up, grabbed his keys and rushed out the door.

She was sick as a dog.

For an hour after she regained consciousness, she retched miserably every time she tried to sit up. There was nothing left in her stomach, but that didn't seem to matter. Her head swam, she broke out in a cold sweat and the nausea took her in waves. By the time it passed, she was so weak she could barely lift her head. Still, she forced herself to sit up, then held herself perfectly quiet until the nausea subsided. She had to get out of there and get home so she could rest, because there was no way in hell she was letting the lowlife who had dragged her into the alley best her. Tomorrow, she was residing over the Dominguez trial even if she had to be carried into the courtroom on a stretcher.

The emergency room doctor was young— barely out of medical school—and clearly out of his element when it came to bullheaded women. Flustered, he obviously thought she was nuts, though he struggled not to show it. ''Please, Judge Thompson...Sadie...I know you want to get out of here, but you can't. The drug is still in your system and could cause you problems for the next twelve hours. Let me admit you,'' he pleaded. ''Just for observation until tomorrow morning. You've been through a nasty ordeal and have no business being alone just yet.''

Stubbornly, she shook her head, only to groan in regret as her stomach roiled. ''You don't understand,'' she said weakly, closing her eyes so the room would stop spinning. ''I have to be in court in the morning. Nothing can interfere with that, so just give me something for this nausea and let me out of here. I'll be fine.''

''And what if you have a more adverse reaction to the drug?'' he demanded in growing frustration. ''You live alone, don't you? What would you do then? You're too weak to help yourself. If you weren't able to get to the phone and call for help, you could be in serious trouble.''

Stirring herself, she forced open her eyes. ''The phone's right by my bed,'' she began tiredly, only to completely forget what she was going to say next when there was a knock at the door of the small examining room they'd placed her in and Sam Kelly strode in with Noah right on his heels.

Up until that moment, she'd told herself she

was holding up well. She'd been through a nightmare, but she wasn't seriously hurt and she'd be back to her old self in no time. She just needed some peace and quiet to regroup. Then Noah walked in the door and the tears she hadn't even realized she was fighting were suddenly there in her eyes, flooding them. How had he known she needed him when she hadn't known it herself?

"Noah."

That was all she could manage to choke out, then he was there, right in front of her, his eyes fierce as he ignored everyone else in the room and reached for her. "Are you all right?"

She started to nod, remembered why she couldn't, and said thickly, "Yes. H-he didn't hurt me that m-much—just scared m-me."

The doctor frowned at that. "He did a lot more than that," he said disapprovingly. "Besides badly bruising her throat, he also injected her with some kind of street drug that knocked her out, then made her violently ill. She needs to be admitted for observation the rest of the night, but she refuses. Maybe one of you gentlemen can change her mind."

He sailed out without another word, leaving Noah and Sam frowning at her in concern. "I really am all right,'' she said defensively. ''I just want to go home.''

''Obviously, that's something we're going to have to talk about,'' Noah said.

She would have been okay if he hadn't reached for her then. His arms closed around her, sure and strong, cradling her against him as carefully as if she were made of spun glass, and for the first time in what seemed like hours, she felt safe. It was then that her control broke. She turned her face against the hard wall of his chest, and suddenly she was sobbing. Hard, racking sobs that hurt her bruised throat and stomach muscles that were still sore from being sick. Another time, she would have been mortified at the thought of breaking down like that, especially in front of Sam Kelly, but right then, she didn't have the strength to care. Clinging to Noah as though she would never let him go, she cried until there were no more tears left in her.

His arms tight around her, his heart breaking at the sound of her sobs, Noah bent his head to hers and cradled her against him, the rage seething in him just barely controlled as he murmured reassurances to her. Whoever had done this to her would pay, he promised himself grimly. He didn't know how or when, but by God, the monster would pay. He would see to it personally.

Her sobs gradually quieted, leaving her spent against his chest, and still he held her, not sure if he could ever let her go again. Why hadn't he noticed before how small she was? How fragile? Whoever dragged her into that alley could have broken her in two with his bare hands and there wouldn't have been a damn thing she could have done to stop him.

"I'm s-sorry," she sniffed against his chest.

"For what?" he growled. "Crying? Don't be ridiculous. You just went through hell. I'd be worried about you if you weren't crying."

"Can you give us the details?" Sam asked quietly. "How did you end up in that alley? If a tourist hadn't heard you cry out and flagged down a bicycle cop, you might still be there. What happened?"

She stiffened in Noah's arms, and for a second, he didn't think she was going to be able to talk about it. He should have known, however, that Her Judgeship was made of sterner stuff than that. He felt her draw in a bracing breath, then she was pulling back to face Sam, and Noah couldn't help but admire her. God, she was something! Her face was blotchy from crying, her eyes slightly swollen, her skin as pale as cream, but she sat as regally as a Supreme Court justice, her emotions once again firmly in check.

In a voice that was still rough from the abuse her throat had taken, she told them how she had fallen asleep in her office and slept to nearly eight. "By the time I got my things together and started walking home, it was almost dark, but I wasn't scared or anything. There were still quite a few people on the streets, especially as I got closer to the River Walk, which is why I was so surprised when somebody grabbed me when I passed the alley. There were at least three couples just two blocks away."

"And they didn't come running when you screamed?" Noah demanded, outraged. "They must have heard you."

"I didn't scream," she said hoarsely. "I couldn't. He had me by the throat."

He swore, damning her assailant to hell and back, while Sam jotted down notes. "Did you get a look at him?" the detective asked. "I know it was dark, but—"

"He grabbed me from behind and made sure I didn't see anything," she said regretfully.

''Not even his hands. He wanted me to reverse the rulings I made on motions in the Dominguez trial today.''

For a second, neither man blinked. Then the import of her words hit and they exploded, both of them talking at once.

''What the hell!''

''The son of a bitch!''

''*Dominguez* was behind the attack? Are you sure?''

''I need you to tell me word for word what this jerk said, Sadie,'' Sam said curtly. ''Did he actually admit that Dominguez hired him to rough you up?''

She shook her head and immediately regretted it as her stomach turned over. Sucking in a sharp breath, she reached out a hand for Noah to steady herself. When his fingers closed around hers and her stomach finally quit heaving, she said faintly, ''He never said Dominguez sent him. He just told me to reverse the decisions I had made in the Dominguez trial. When I told him I couldn't, he said he was going to give me a taste of what would happen to me next time if I didn't. Then he shot me up with the drug.''

Noah swore, the curses that rolled off his

tongue ones that Sadie had never actually heard anyone say out loud before.

Equally grim-faced, Sam said, "You realize that the trashing of your office wasn't a coincidence, don't you? Somebody in Dominguez's organization probably got to Osgood and paid him big money to make it look like he wanted revenge. And then there's that damn letter. I know you thought it was a hoax, but you're in real danger—"

Noah's gaze sharpened. "What letter?"

"Someone sent me a letter advising me not to hear the Dominguez case or I would regret it," she said reluctantly.

"And you still agreed to hear it?" he demanded incredulously. "Dammit, woman, are you out of your mind?"

"No, I'm a judge," she retorted, stung. "And a damn good one, which is why Dominguez didn't want to come into my courtroom. *He's* afraid of me, afraid that I won't let him get away with murder, and he has every right to be. I'm hearing this case fair and square, but if the jury comes back with a guilty verdict, I'm locking the monster up for as long as I can legally do it."

"You're going to have to have police protection," Sam said flatly, "and not just for a day or two. After tonight, we're not taking any more chances. I'll call and make the arrangements. Are you staying here tonight or going home?"

"Home!"

"Here!"

When she and Noah glared at each other, a smile tugged at Sam's mouth. "Why don't I leave you two to work this out?" he suggested, already heading for the door. "I'll call the station from out in the hall."

He disappeared outside, leaving behind a silence that was thick and tense. Scowling down at her pale face, Noah said huskily, "You'll be safer here tonight."

"I want to go home."

"It's more public here. If anyone tries to get to you, someone's bound to notice."

"I want to go home."

"Dammit, Sadie, you're not being reasonable!"

"I don't care," she retorted. "I was the one in that damn alley. I was the one who was threatened and drugged and thrown to the ground. I want to go home. I want to sleep in my own bed, to pretend, at least for tonight, that none of this ever happened. And *I can't do that here!*"

There was a note of hysteria in her voice, a panic she couldn't quite get a handle on, and it cut through Noah like a knife. What the devil was he doing? She'd been through hell already once tonight, and here he was giving her a hard time about where she was going to sleep.

Cursing himself for a fool, he slipped his arms around her and gently folded her against his chest. "Shhh. It's okay, honey. If you want to go home, I'll take you home. Whatever you say. It doesn't matter, anyway. Because wherever you sleep tonight, that's where I'm going to be, too. Lie back down and close your eyes. I'll take care of everything."

Chapter 10

While Noah went about the business of getting her released, Sam got on the phone and set up twenty-four-hour protection. By the time Noah drove her home nearly an hour later, the Lone Star Social Club was as secure as a bank vault. With a uniformed officer stationed on the front porch and another one at the back, on the River Walk, to make sure unwanted visitors didn't slip through the rear gardens undetected, no one was getting inside without satisfying the two policemen that they belonged there. Sadie couldn't have felt safer if she'd been in the White House.

Noah, however, wasn't taking any chances. The second he carried her into her apartment, he locked and dead-bolted her front door, then deposited her on the couch. "Stay right there," he said. "I'm just going to shut the blinds."

But when he'd closed the blinds on every window in the entire apartment, he moved to the closet in her living room. Surprised, she said, "What are you doing?"

"Just checking to make sure there're no nasty little surprises in here," he explained, then proceeded to check not only the closets in the bathroom and her bedroom, but under her bed, too.

Amused in spite of the exhaustion that pulled at her, Sadie couldn't help but laugh. "And I thought I was going to be the one who was paranoid. In case you hadn't noticed, Counselor, there's nobody here but us chickens."

"And I plan to keep it that way," he said without apology. Striding back to her, he scooped her up in his arms again.

"Noah! I can walk!"

"So can I." Grinning, he headed for her bedroom. "Indulge me, Your Honorableness. I like the feel of you in my arms."

Her heart jumped at that, but then he was walking straight through her bedroom into the bathroom. Her arms looped around his neck, her face on a level with his, she arched a brow at him in surprise. ''What are you doing?''

''Running a bath for you,'' he said simply as he stooped to deposit her on the vanity stool next to the old-fashioned claw-foot tub. ''I know they cleaned you up at the hospital, but I figured you'd like to wash off the antiseptic and smell like your old self when you crawl into your bed. So, Your Judgeship, you're taking a bath—if that's what you want, of course. Tonight, you're calling all the shots.''

Touched, she didn't mean to cry—not again, not after all the tears she'd shed in his arms at the hospital—but he just seemed to know how to touch her heart. Her eyes flooded. ''Noah…''

She couldn't manage anything but his name, but apparently that was enough. Leaning over her, he brushed a soft kiss to her mouth. When he pulled back, the heat in his eyes set her heart thumping.

''Where's that scent of yours that drives me crazy? I'll put some in the bathwater.''

''In the crystal jar on the vanity,'' she murmured. ''It only takes a little.''

A teaspoon would have been more than enough—he used two tablespoons and flooded the small, old-fashioned bathroom with the spicy, sweet aroma of her favorite scent. She wanted to laugh, but then, once the tub was filled and moist, fragrant steam was curling toward the ceiling, he turned back to her and moved to help her out of her filthy clothes.

Her smile fled. She swore she didn't make a sound of protest, but she didn't have to. He reached for her clenched hands, unfolded her stiff fingers and pressed a kiss to her palm as his steady eyes trapped hers. "I'm not making love to you tonight, and it's not because I don't want you," he said softly, roughly. "You turn me inside out, sweetheart, but right now, you need the security of feeling safe and protected. So I'm going to bathe you, then dry you off and put you in your nightgown and hold you close the rest of the night. That's all. I promise. Okay?"

He was a man who didn't give promises lightly, and she only had to look in his eyes to know that he meant every word. Something shifted in the region of her heart, and the tears she thought she was going to be able to hold at bay spilled over her lashes. She nodded, her smile watery. "I'm sorry. It's just…"

"Hush," he murmured, gently wiping away the tears that slowly trailed down her cheeks.

"You don't have to explain. Just let me take care of you."

Melting from his tender ministrations, she couldn't resist. Sighing in surrender, she dropped her head forward against his chest and let him undress her. For what seemed like hours, her nerves had been strung too tight and were the only thing holding her together. But now, as he eased the last of her clothes from her and tenderly placed her in the tub, the warm, fragrant water closed around her shoulders and felt like heaven. Slowly, the tension drained out of her, leaving behind a weariness that weighed heavy on her very soul. Suddenly so tired she couldn't keep her eyes open, she leaned her head back against the rim of the tub and let him do with her as he would.

"That's it, sweetheart," he growled softly. "Just relax."

Murmuring to her soothingly, he lathered a washcloth with a bar of scented soap that matched the bath salts he'd poured in the tub, then proceeded to bathe her with a thoroughness that turned her positively boneless. With agonizing slowness, he dragged the washcloth over her breasts and belly, arms and legs. Aches she hadn't known she had dulled, her mind blurred and the ugliness of those horrible moments in the alley slipped away.

Half-asleep, she never noticed the passing of time or the cooling of the water. Then he was pulling the plug on the drain and urging her to her feet in spite of her murmured protests. ''You can't stay in there all night,'' he rasped as he grabbed a towel and dried her with the same care with which he'd washed her. ''It's getting late and you need to be in bed.''

He tossed the towel aside, then pulled her nightgown over her head and threaded her arms through the sleeves. Then he was lifting her in his arms again. Switching off the light in the bathroom, he carried her to bed.

She was two heartbeats away from slipping into total oblivion when he gently laid her on her bed and crawled in beside her. She felt his arm settle heavily around her waist as he pulled her back against him, the arousal he made no attempt to hide, and tried to struggle back to consciousness. But his hands soothed as he murmured in her ear like a dream lover.

''Go to sleep, baby. Everything's all right. You're safe.''

The exhaustion that had been creeping up on her all evening finally overtook her then, and she fell asleep with him wrapped around her, his soft words a reassuring litany in her ear. And during the night, when dark, haunting images tortured her sleep, he was there to soothe and stroke and hold. Turning into his arms was as natural as breathing. His name a sigh on her lips, she buried her face against his throat and slipped deeper into sleep.

She was alone when she awoke the next morning. Stirring, she frowned at the rumpled pillow next to hers and couldn't for the life of her remember the night before. Then she heard the shower running and everything came flooding back in a dizzy rush. The man in the alley, grabbing her, hurting her, his cold voice threatening her even as he jabbed a needle in her arm and drugged her.

''Oh, God!''

All too clearly, she could feel the blackness that crushed her as the drug raced through her system. She'd never felt so helpless, so vulnerable, so totally at the mercy of another human being who didn't know the meaning of the word. That, more than the nausea that had followed, had been the real terror of the night.

''Don't think about it. It's over.''

Jerked back from her thoughts, she glanced up to find Noah standing in the doorway to the bedroom. Her heart turned over at the sight of him. His hair still damp from the shower, he'd nicked his chin shaving with her razor and wore nothing but jeans. He was, she thought, the one part of the night she didn't ever want to forget. When he'd shown up at the hospital, all she'd wanted was for him to hold her, and somehow he'd known that. He hadn't let her go all night.

When she'd needed him most, he'd been the one steady rock in her upside-down world, and for a woman who was determined not to need a man, she should have been more than a little bit alarmed. The fact that she wasn't was something she was going to have to deal with, but not now. Not when the frightening memories of last night were so fresh and she was still feeling vulnerable.

"No, it's not," she said quietly. Sitting up against the headboard of her ornate iron bed, she hugged her pillow to her breast. "It won't be over as long as the trial lasts, and it just started yesterday."

"You could step down and let someone else hear the case. After what happened last night, no one would blame you."

"Is that what you would do if you were in my shoes?"

It wasn't, and they both knew it. He was the same man who had given a small fortune to an orphanage rather than accept his fee from a man he knew to be an amoral murderer. There was no way he would let a coward in an alley scare him into backing away from doing the right thing. And she couldn't, either. Not if she wanted to look herself in the face in the mirror every morning.

"Admit it," she said softly. "You'd show up in that courtroom just to prove that you could. Why should I be any different?"

"Because you're a woman, dammit," he snapped, sudden fury burning in his eyes as he scowled at her. "Because you could have been seriously hurt last night. Because you could have been killed!" A muscle jumped in his clenched jaw. "I don't know if it was Dominguez pulling the strings last night or one of his Mexican mafia buddies—but I do know that these are people who don't make idle threats. And I don't mind telling you that scares the hell out of me. I want you safe."

"The police—"

"The hell with the police! Do you think

they're going to be able to protect you if someone decides to take you out from a rooftop across the river? Dammit, woman, you're in some serious trouble here! You show up in your courtroom this morning, and you may as well spit in Dominguez's face. At least postpone things for a couple of days. It'll give you time to get back on your feet, and you can use the excuse that you're still sick from whatever junk that bastard shot you up with last night.''

Hugging her pillow, Sadie wondered if he had any idea how he tempted her. It wasn't as if she *wanted* to face down the drug lord. Personally, she'd give just about anything if she never had to lay eyes on the man again. But in this particular matter, her personal likes and dislikes were immaterial. She was a judge and if she allowed him to intimidate her into backing off the case, he would do the same thing to the next judge and the one after that, until he finally found one to his liking he could control.

''I can't,'' she said quietly. ''That would be a sign of weakness, and this jackass has to know that no matter what, I won't back down from him. His thugs can threaten me and drug me and try to scare the hell out of me, but I'm still going to work and I'm still going to preside over his trial. He's not going to beat me, damn him!''

Exasperated, Noah wanted to shake her…and snatch her into his arms. It was common knowledge that Hanging Judge Thompson was as tough as steel, but he'd never suspected just how deep her grit ran. God, she was something! When it came to a fight, a man couldn't lose with her in his corner. But this wasn't a fight with just anyone—it was with a ruthless drug lord with long arms who wouldn't hesitate to crush her if he got the chance. And there wasn't a damn thing he could do to protect her.

Frustrated, worried sick about her, he couldn't keep his distance a second longer. Crossing the room to her, he sat on the side of the bed and took her hand, needing to touch her. It didn't help. Her fingers were so small and delicate under his, all he could think of was how easily the bastard in the alley could have hurt her last night if he'd wanted to.

''I understand,'' he said huskily, surprising her. ''I'd do the same thing if I were you. But knowing you're right isn't doing a hell of a lot for my peace of mind right now. I've got a trial starting in Houston in the morning, which means I've got to leave this afternoon, and I'll probably be gone the rest of the week. How the hell am I supposed to leave you when you've got this hanging over your head?''

Her fingers linked with his. ''I'll be fine,'' she said softly. ''The police—''

''Will do everything they can,'' he finished for her. ''I know. But I still hate to leave you alone. Why don't you go stay with my mother while I'm gone?''

She was so startled her fingers jerked in his. ''Your mother? But—''

''She's got two rottweilers in the backyard and a loaded shotgun under the bed. If anyone tries to get to you, she'll be ready for them.''

''But I could never put your family in danger! This isn't their fight.''

''They'd take on the entire Mexican mafia in a heartbeat if they knew how worried I was about you,'' he retorted. ''Dammit, I want you safe!'' Giving in to the need to hold her, he pulled her into his arms and crushed her close, burying his face in the cloud of her hair. ''Promise me you won't take any chances.''

She didn't even hesitate. ''I promise. No more walking to work. I'll leave in the afternoons when everyone else does, and I'll stay away from the windows. I'll be fine.''

He wanted to believe her, but later, when they were both dressed for work and had left the relative security of her apartment, he readily admitted to himself that she could have been surrounded by the Fifth Army, and he still would have been a nervous wreck. There was a uniformed officer waiting to drive them to the courthouse when they stepped out of the social club, and a plainclothes one who tailed them all the way, but Noah couldn't stop looking at rooftops. He'd never felt so paranoid.

When they got to the courthouse, however, he had to admit that it would take nothing short of a Sherman tank to reach Sadie once she was in the building. As promised, Sam Kelly had beefed up security, and it was evident from the moment they arrived at the courthouse parking garage and found impatient drivers backed up down the street and around the corner. The lot was closed to the general public for the course of the trial, and everyone but courthouse employees with the proper identification were turned away.

Inside, things were even more chaotic. Overnight, more metal detectors had been brought in, and not even the pope himself could have gotten into the building without passing through one. Upstairs, near Sadie's courtroom, security was even tighter. All entrances to the second floor were closed except for the elevator and the main stairwell, where additional metal detectors had been set up. Police roamed the hallway and only potential jurors escorted there from the central jury room or people who had been subpoenaed to testify in the case were even allowed on the floor. And at the short corridor that led to the private entrance to Sadie's chambers, a bulldog of a policeman stood right in front of the door, just daring anyone to try to get past him.

Immeasurably relieved, Noah still didn't like the idea of leaving her alone. He followed her into her chambers, lowered all the blinds at her windows and checked to make sure her closets were empty of unwanted intruders.

When she caught him at it, he grinned sheepishly. "I'm a worrywart. So sue me. I'm just making sure there're no rats in here. They have a habit of sneaking in in the middle of the night, you know."

"I'm perfectly safe. Sam would have never let me anywhere near the building if he thought there was any danger."

He knew that—that was the only reason he

wasn't a complete wreck. If there was one man he trusted to watch over her and keep her safe, it was Kelly. Moving to her desk, he grabbed a notepad and scribbled down the name of his hotel in Houston. ''This is where I'll be when I'm not at the courthouse,'' he told her, tearing off the sheet and handing it to her. ''If you need to talk, if you're scared—hell, if you just can't sleep—I want you to call me.''

''When you're in the middle of the trial? I don't think so!''

''Then I'm calling you every night at ten,'' he warned. ''If you don't answer within five rings, I'm calling the police immediately.''

He sounded like a concerned, possessive husband. Staring up at him, Sadie reminded herself that they weren't lovers in the truest sense of the word, yet he was behaving as though one act of passion gave him rights to her—the right to protect her and see to her welfare, the right to take care of her. Just weeks ago, that would have sent her running for cover, but now, somehow, his concern warmed her all the way down to her toes. How had this happened? And when? When had he gotten past her guard?

''Sadie? Are you listening to me? Dammit, I'm serious! If you don't answer within—''

Dazed, she blinked up at him, then suddenly realized that he thought she was deliberately putting him off. Holding up a hand that wasn't quite as steady as she would have liked, she stopped him in midsentence. "If you'll calm down a minute, you'll realize I'm not giving you an argument on this. It's a good idea. Call me. I'll be waiting, and if I don't answer, you'll know I'm in trouble."

He should have been pleased. Instead, he looked at her like she'd just set a trap in front of him. "You're giving in just like that? Why? Are you feeling okay? You do look a little out of it. Are you sure that damn drug's out of your system? Maybe I should call the doctor...."

"Oh, no, you don't! We've already had this discussion, and I'm just fine, thank you very much. In fact," she said, glancing at the clock on the wall, "I've got about two minutes before I have to be in the courtroom, so you'd better get out of here. I've got work to do."

She gave him the perfect excuse to leave, but he just stood there, his blue eyes dark with something that set her pulse skipping crazily. He didn't so much as lift a finger to her, let alone kiss her, but suddenly she felt hot and breathless and achy, just as she had when she'd awakened to find him in her bed. "Noah?"

"I'm not going to kiss you," he told her in a voice as rough as an unpaved road, "because if I do, I just might not be able to let you go again. But when I get back from Houston..." He didn't complete the promise, but left it hanging in the air to be filled in with her imagination. "I'll call you," he said hoarsely. "Tonight at ten. Take care of yourself."

If he hadn't left then, *she* would have reached for him. Instead, she waited too long. She took a step toward him, but he'd already turned and walked out and the chance was gone. The door shut quietly behind him, and once again, she was alone. Solitude had never looked so miserable.

When she walked into her courtroom two minutes later, she was once again the venerable Hanging Judge Thompson. Dressed in her black robes, her reading glasses perched on her nose and every hair scraped back in place, she stood proud and tall and didn't show a trace of fear. If her stomach was knotted and her palms a little damp, no one could tell it to look at her.

"All rise!"

At the sharp command of her bailiff, they all

came to their feet, tension vibrating in the air in the packed courtroom. Seated at the defendant's table, his black eyes narrowed like a laser on her face, Dominic Dominguez stood, his gaze never leaving hers. He didn't say a word, but he didn't have to. There in his eyes was the knowledge of what had happened to her last night.

A coldness invaded her blood. Up until that moment, she hadn't let herself think about whether or not Dominguez was responsible for what happened to her in the alley. There was no direct evidence linking him to the incident in spite of the fact that her attacker had tried to scare her into reversing her rulings on the pretrial motions. Anyone with a link to Dominguez could have carried out the attack without his having any knowledge of it.

Or at least, that was what she'd told herself. But now it was obvious that the man knew every disgusting thing that had been done to her last night and relished the thought of her helplessness. God, he was something! Even now, when she was surrounded by police and there was no way he could hurt her, he thought he could terrify her, break her, scare her so badly that fear, rather than the quest for justice, would dictate every decision she made in the court-room.

It wasn't going to happen. Not in her court-room, she assured herself grimly. If Dominguez didn't know it yet, he soon would—she didn't back down from a fight or her responsibilities. It was her duty to see that he was brought to trial, and by God, that was what she was going to do. Dismissing him as if he was of no consequence, she stepped up to the bench and sank into her chair. All business, she took up where they had left off the day before—with the selection of the jury.

It was a long day. By taking a short lunch and hurrying things along, they had a jury in place by two-thirty. After a very brief recess, the prosecution called its first witness, a senior citizen who had known Henry Bingham, the San Antonio businessman Dominguez was accused of killing, since he was a boy. Every seat in the gallery was filled as the old man described how he had seen Dominguez and Bingham having a heated argument just hours before the man was gunned down in cold blood.

It was riveting testimony—and damaging. Kingston, the defense attorney, tried his best to rattle the man and make him look like a senile old fool who couldn't remember his own name, but he made a serious mistake when he pressed too hard. He ended up turning the jury against him and his client by badgering the old man. Realizing he'd gone too far, he quickly back-pedaled, but the damage was done. By the time the witness was excused, the jury was regarding Dominguez and his attorney with decidedly hostile eyes.

From there, things only went downhill for the defense. Evidence was presented that placed the murder victim's blood in the defendant's car and Kingston could not only not discredit it, he couldn't offer a single logical explanation of how it had gotten there. He tried to imply that the police had planted it, but it was a half-hearted effort at best and you only had to look at the faces of the jurors to see that they weren't going to buy into the conspiracy theory. Unless Kingston was able to present a better case than that when he called his own witnesses, his client was in serious trouble.

Over the course of the afternoon, tempers shortened and expectancy gathered in the air like thunderheads before a storm. The D.A. and Kingston were constantly at each other's throats, trading sharp barbs, and Dominguez was in a rage. His hands clenched in fists and murder in his eyes, he looked like he was going to explode any second. And that appeared to be what the spectators in the gallery were waiting for. All eyes were on him as whispered murmurs made their way around the courtroom.

Afraid violence was going to break out any moment, Sadie called a halt to the proceedings at five-thirty, remanded the defendant into custody and cautioned the jury not to watch television or discuss the case with their friends and family. They were then dismissed to the central jury room, Dominguez was led away by a sheriff's deputy to the county jail and the circus was over, at least for that day.

That didn't mean, however, that she could relax her guard. A sheriff's deputy accompanied her to her chambers, where she lingered only long enough to remove her judicial robes, then escorted her down to a waiting patrol car stationed outside the east entrance to the courthouse. She'd hardly settled into the back seat before she was whisked away to the Lone Star Social Club, where another officer saw her safely inside the building, then took up a position on the front porch.

As she stepped into the entrance hall of the

social club, the peace and quiet of the old Victorian house surrounded her. With a tired sigh, she leaned back against the closed stained-glass front door and felt safe, really safe, for the first time in hours. She'd made it back home without mishap and could spend the rest of the evening relaxing. Besides the officer stationed at the house, a patrol car drove down the street every hour on the hour. Nothing and no one could harm her here.

Relieved, she deliberately pushed Dominguez and everything else connected with the trial from her mind and headed for her apartment at the rear of the house. Her key in her hand, she started to push her key into the dead bolt, only to have the doorknob turn easily in her hand before she ever unlocked it. Surprised, she froze, desperately trying to remember if she'd locked the door that morning when she'd left for work. God, she must have! She always had before. It wasn't like her to just walk out without making sure everything was locked up tight. Of course, she had been distracted by the thought of Noah leaving. And some of the drug her attacker had drugged her with could have still been in her body....

Images from last night that she had repressed

all day stirred to life, and all too easily she could picture the man in the alley coming back for her, this time surprising her in her own home. Even now, he could be waiting for her behind the door, ready to seize her the second she walked inside. Alarmed, her heart suddenly slamming against her ribs, she started to turn. She had to run, get help—

But before she could take a single step, the door swung open. Sick with fear, she opened her mouth to scream, only to gasp at the sight of her landlady standing before her with a mischievous smile on her face. Wilting, she impulsively hugged her. "Alice! Thank God! You scared me to death. What are you doing here? I thought you were one of Dominguez's thugs and was just going to scream the house down!"

"Oh, my!" The older lady laughed in chagrin. "I'm sorry, dear. When Noah and I set this up, we never meant to scare you."

"Set this up?" Sadie repeated, surprised. "Set what up? Alice, what's going on? Noah's not even here. He went to Houston."

"I know, dear. But before he left, he stopped by my apartment and we had a long talk. He was worried about you being by yourself tonight after everything that happened yesterday.''

''I told him I was fine—''

''I know, but you know how men are,'' Alice retorted with a grin. ''They like to think we can't get along without them, and we humor them. And he was really worried, dear. So I hope you don't mind, but I volunteered to spend the evening with you so you wouldn't have to be alone.''

Touched, Sadie hugged her again. ''Of course I don't mind, but you really don't have to if you have something else you need to do. I wasn't going to do anything but have an early supper and watch television.''

''Do you watch 'N.Y.P.D. Blue'?'' At Sadie's nod, she beamed happily. ''Wonderful! So do I. It was so hot today I thought chicken salad would be nice for supper, and it's already in your fridge. We can eat, then talk, while we're waiting for the show to come on. If that's all right with you, of course.''

''Are you kidding? I'd love the company.'' Slipping out of the jacket to her suit, she said, ''Give me a few minutes to change into something more comfortable, and I'll be right with you.''

After donning shorts and a T-shirt and letting her hair down, Sadie would have sworn that her nerves were still strung too tight for her to have much of an appetite, but she hadn't counted on Alice distracting her from the stress of the day. The old lady had Sadie laughing five minutes after they sat down. By the time they finished the meal, she'd not only eaten a healthy serving of the chicken salad, but she'd put away a more-than-respectable piece of the lemon meringue pie Alice had made for dessert.

"Oh, God, that was good!" she groaned, savoring the last bite. "Tell me you're going to give me the recipe, Alice. That was the best thing I've ever tasted!"

Pleased, Alice grinned. "Of course. Then you can make it for Noah. Not that you need to entice him with food to get his attention. He seems to be quite taken with you, dear. He asked me to remind you that he's going to call you tonight at ten."

Sadie blushed; she couldn't help it. "He's concerned about my safety."

"Oh, I think it's much more than that," Alice teased, her blue eyes twinkling. "I've never seen him quite so...restless. But there, I've said enough. I'm really not an interfering busybody, despite rumors to the contrary.''

Sadie started to laugh, only to frown in sudden confusion. Lifting her nose to the air, she sniffed delicately. ''Do you smell that? It smells like gardenias.''

''Oh, my, it is!'' Delighted, she laughed gaily. ''Oh, this is wonderful! Do you know what this means?''

Her lips twitching, Sadie could only shake her head. ''Only that the garden's in bloom.''

''But there're no gardenia bushes in the garden. And even if there were, your windows are closed because of the air-conditioning.'' Closing her eyes, she sniffed again and smiled. ''Smell. It's getting stronger.''

The scent *was* getting stronger. In fact, it was permeating her entire apartment, and Sadie couldn't for the life of her explain how. The windows *were* closed, and from what she could remember, the only flowers in bloom in the garden were roses. Frowning suspiciously at her companion, she said, ''Okay, Alice, what's going on? You obviously know and you're thrilled. Are you going to explain or do I have to guess?''

Happy to share the story, Alice settled back

for a long chat. "I don't know if you know it or not, but the living room and kitchen of your apartment were originally part of what was called the garden parlor back when the house was still a social club. It was a wonderful room, especially in the spring and summer when the flowers were in bloom, and a lot of weddings were held here."

Sadie blinked. "I knew there were a lot of dances up in the ballroom in the attic, but I didn't realize people actually got married here."

"Oh, yes. The lady who ran the place loved nothing more than putting on a wildly romantic wedding for couples she had helped bring together. But the first wedding, the very first one, was for her daughter." She smiled, picturing another slower, more romantic time. "According to the stories that have been handed down through the years, it was one of those perfect matches, the kind made in heaven that only comes around once in a lifetime. The bride carried a bouquet of gardenias and was said to look just like an angel. Ever since then, whenever you smell the scent of gardenias in the mansion, it has always been a sign that two soul mates have found each other."

Sadie was so entranced by the story that it was several heartbeats before she caught Alice's pointed look. Startled, she drew back. ''You think that Noah and I...that we—''

Her heart knocking crazily against her ribs, she couldn't even verbalize the thought, but Alice had no such trouble. Her blue eyes dancing, she nodded. ''You're the only single people in the house right now and you just happen to be seeing each other. I don't know how your arithmetic is, dear, but I've always found that one plus one adds up to two.''

''But we're just friends!''

''Of course you are,'' Alice said easily, patting Sadie's hand. ''And you should be. If a man and woman are going to spend the rest of their lives together, they don't have a chance if they don't like each other a great deal.''

If she'd been able to find her tongue, Sadie would have pointed out that no one had said anything about her and Noah spending the rest of their lives together. Just the thought of it was enough to start her fantasizing, and that scared the living daylights out of her. ''Alice, I think you misunderstood—''

She laughed, not the least troubled. ''That's what all my boarders say when they get touched by the magic of the social club. You can fight it, but it won't do any good. Not when it comes to love and this house. I warned you it works out every time, dear. Don't you remember?''

Oh, she remembered, all right, Sadie thought, trying to hide her growing panic. She just hadn't believed her. Now what was she going to do?

Chapter 11

Was she falling in love with Noah?

Long after Alice left, the thought pulled at Sadie, worrying her, destroying any peace she'd found in the evening. Restless, she told herself the very idea was ridiculous. Of course Alice would think that—she was a romantic and she loved that old legend about the house bringing true loves together. But that's all it was, just a legend, just wishful thinking on an old lady's part. She knew for a fact that fairy tales didn't come true in the real world—David had once been her knight in shining armor. She wasn't looking for another one.

If she found herself thinking about Noah at every turn, dreaming of him every night, she couldn't let herself fall into the trap of thinking it was because she was in love with him. It was just that he was the first man who ever...who made her...

Shying away from the images that sprang to mind, she told herself firmly it was just sex. She responded to him in a way she'd never responded to a man in her life, and only a naive, innocent girl made the mistake of thinking that was love. It was just a physical response that released a flood of emotions she hadn't been prepared to deal with. She was still heart-whole and intended to stay that way.

Yet, in spite of that, she couldn't stop anticipation from curling warmly into her stomach when he called sharply at ten, as promised. In the tub up to her neck in bubbles, she reached for the portable phone she'd laid on the stool next to the old-fashioned claw-foot tub. "'Lo?"

"Sadie? Is that you?"

At the sound of his sexy voice in her ear, she could no more hold back a smile than she could have stopped the moon from rising in the summer sky. "The one and only, Counselor," she said, chuckling, "all safe and sound. Just for the record, you can relax. There's not a bad guy in sight."

"I'm glad to hear it. How'd everything go in court today?"

She shrugged one bare shoulder lazily, disturbing the bubbles that swelled around her breasts. "That depends if you're putting your money on the prosecution or the defense. The jury was picked and the prosecution called its first witness. Kingston and his client took quite a few hits."

"Which means you're in more danger than ever," he said grimly. "The more hits the defense takes on the stand, the more desperate Dominguez is going to be. And a desperate man is just like a wounded animal—you never know what either is going to do. So watch yourself, okay?"

"Every time I so much as twitched an eyelash today, a constable or policeman was there to hover over me," she replied as she dipped her washcloth into the soapy water, then lifted a leg to sluice bubbles over it. "Sam had a patrol car waiting to drive me home after court adjourned. And I wish you could see the two giants who pulled guard duty over me tonight— they're both as big as a barn. Anybody who would try to get to me with those guys around would have to be a moron."

She expected him to point out that the man who grabbed her in the alley hadn't exactly been an Einstein and he'd still gotten away with drugging her, but she could almost hear him shifting gears, then he asked abruptly, ''Where are you?''

Surprised, she laughed. ''Where do you think I am? You called me, remember? I'm at home.''

''No, I mean where are you in your apartment? In the kitchen? I thought I heard water.''

''No. I'm…'' Later, Sadie couldn't have said why she hesitated and suddenly blushed like a peach in the sun. He couldn't see her, and even if he could have, it wasn't as if he'd never seen her naked before. The man had made love to her, for heaven's sake! There was no reason to be shy.

She ordered herself to act casual, but she couldn't. In spite of her best intentions, her voice was soft and husky when she admitted she was in the bathroom. ''I'd just stepped into the tub when you called.''

''Oh, God,'' he groaned. ''You're naked!''

She laughed; she couldn't help it. ''Most people generally are when they take a bath. Though I wouldn't say I'm completely bare,'' she added, glancing down at herself. "At least not yet. Once the bubbles melt, though…"

"Bubbles? You're taking a bubble bath?"

He sounded like a man on the rack, a tortured soul, and suddenly the shyness that gripped her eased. Leaning her head back against the rim of the tub, she found herself grinning foolishly up at the ceiling. "Mmm-hmm. I figured I deserved a nice long soak after the day I've had. So what about you? How'd your trial go?"

"Well enough," he said dismissingly. "Let's get back to this bubble bath. How high are the bubbles?"

"Well…" Her lips twitching, she studied the white stuff that surrounded her like mounds of meringue. "I guess it depends if I'm sitting up or lying back. Of course, the tub's very deep, so either way I'm decently covered…for now."

For a long, pregnant moment, his only answer was silence. Then, just when she thought he might have lost interest in the little flirting game they were playing, he said thickly, "You're a little witch, Your Judgeship. Are you enjoying yourself?"

Her eyes dancing, she giggled. "Actually, I am. What about you?"

If she could have seen him, she wouldn't

have had to ask. Stretched out on the bed in his hotel room, the TV on mute, he was hard as a rock and unable to stop grinning. She'd giggled. He'd seen her laugh, heard her chuckle, but never thought to see the day when she would do something as girlish as giggle. And he liked it, dammit. He liked it a lot.

''Actually, Your Honor, now that you mention it, I'm enjoying myself, too,'' he replied gruffly. ''Of course, I'd be enjoying myself a hell of a lot more if I was there with you and all those bubbles. You do know that you're driving me crazy, don't you?''

''One can only try,'' she said demurely, then gave in to another giggle.

Grinning, he growled, ''Do you know what I'd do to you if I was there right now?''

''What?''

''I'd crawl into the tub with you and wash every sweet inch of you. I'd start with your toes and work my way up, all the way to…''

He murmured hot, sexy words to her, telling her how he would stroke and tease and seduce her until they were both out of their minds with need. And then, only when they wanted each other so badly that they ached, he'd pull the plug on the drain and slowly dry them both off.

By then, he promised her, he'd be so desperate for her that he'd never be able to make it to the bedroom. He'd lie her down right there on the floor and have his way with her.

The trial and Dominguez's threats forgotten, he got her all hot and bothered, and she loved it. He could hear the breathlessness in her voice as she shyly responded in kind, and it nearly drove him right over the edge. Torture. With a few soft, husky words whispered in his ear, she turned his own game on him and never knew just how she drove him wild.

Cursing the distance between them, he could have talked to her all night. But they both had to work the next morning, and if they kept teasing each other, it was going to be a long time before either one of them calmed down enough to fall asleep.

"You need to be in bed, sweetheart," he told her huskily. "It's getting late and tomorrow's going to be another long day. If you're going to keep Kingston and Dominguez in line, you're going to need your sleep."

"Yeah, right. Like I'm really going to sleep *now*."

"Just close your eyes and think of me," he replied, wishing like hell he was there with her to hold her when she finally did fall asleep. "I'll call you again tomorrow, same time, same station. Okay?"

"I might be here and I might not," she teased. "Why would I want to talk to a man who enjoys tormenting me?"

"Because you love it," he retorted, laughing. "Nighty-night."

"Stuff it, Counselor."

Chuckling, he was still grinning when he hung up.

When Sadie walked into her chambers the next morning, she couldn't seem to stop smiling. She'd have sworn she'd never be able to sleep after Noah wished her good-night and hung up, but the second her head hit the pillow, she'd been out like a light. All night long, he'd walked through her dreams, and when she awoke as her alarm went off, he was the one she reached for. She felt like a teenager, her head reeling, smitten with the opposite sex for the first time in her life. And all she could think of was that he was calling her again that night at ten. She couldn't wait.

Replaying their entire conversation over and over again in her head, her eyes dreamy, she didn't notice the bulky letter addressed to her in a rough scrawl until she sat down behind her desk and bent to put her purse in the bottom drawer. Surprised, she instinctively started to reach for the padded yellow envelope, only to frown and slowly draw her hand away from it.

Sitting back in her chair, she studied the package critically. It appeared to be just a harmless piece of mail, but so had the threatening letter she'd found on her desk weeks ago, warning her to refuse to hear the Dominguez trial. Was this another threat? And how had it gotten on her desk anyway? The day's mail hadn't been delivered yet and she always cleared off her desk before she left at the end of the day. If something had arrived for her by messenger, Betty would have told her the minute she walked into the outer office.

Reaching for the phone, she buzzed the other woman. ''Betty, do you know anything about this padded envelope on my desk?''

Surprised, she said, ''No. What envelope? Where did it come from?''

Already pushing back from her desk in alarm, Sadie felt cold all the way to the bone. ''I don't know. I think you'd better call security and Sam Kelly. Something's not right here.''

In the time it took to hang up the phone,

Betty appeared in the doorway that adjoined
Sadie's chambers to the outer office. She took
one look at the brown envelope sitting squarely
in the middle of Sadie's desk and blanched.
''Oh, God. Do you think it's a letter bomb?''

Sadie didn't intend to stick around to find
out. Urging her back into the outer office, she
said, ''We'll know that when the police get
here.''

Security arrived almost immediately, took
one look at the package and immediately called
the bomb squad. Just that quickly, all hell broke
loose. An alarm sounded over the public-
address system, then a disembodied voice informed the jurors, lawyers and others already
in the justice center that everyone was to evac-
uate the building immediately. Suddenly the
halls were jammed with people streaming toward the exits, jostling one another to get out
as the speaker on the public-address system
warned them that this was not a test, but an
actual emergency.

Her heart in her throat, Sadie only had time
to grab her purse before she found herself
caught in the rush of the crowd. Flanked by two
beefy sheriff's deputies, she and Betty were

hustled outside to the square across the street just as police cars converged on the justice center like an invading army. Startled, Sadie and the rest of the gathering crowd stood in hushed silence as all streets within a three-block area were quickly cordoned off by every type of emergency vehicle available.

It was there in the square, protected by the sheriff's deputies, that Sam Kelly found her fifteen minutes later. ''Sam! Thank God,'' she said as he dismissed the deputies and escorted her toward a patrol car parked at the curb. ''I don't know how that thing got on my desk. Have you seen it? Is it really a letter bomb?''

''If it's not, it's a damn clever imitation,'' he said grimly. ''The bomb squad is checking it out right now, and you might as well know that the FBI's been called in. There's no way in hell anyone's going to get back into the building until they go over it with a fine-tooth comb.''

Startled, she paled. ''Are you saying there could be more than one of these things lying around?''

''That's what we're trying to find out. In the meantime, you can't stay out here—it's not safe—so I'm going to have Officer Barker here take you down to the station to wait until we get the all clear. I'll be in touch as soon as I know something.''

She would have preferred to stay where she was, but he was right. She might have been surrounded by hundreds of people, but most of them were strangers, and for all she knew, one of them could have left the letter bomb on her desk just to flush her out into the open. With the police distracted by the bomb and only two deputies to watch over her, she was an easy target for anyone who wanted to take her out.

So without a word of complaint, she let Office Barker drive her to the police station, where she was out of harm's way. She knew it was for the best, but that didn't make waiting any easier. Alone, completely out of sight of the courthouse and with no television or radio to tell her what was going on, she couldn't stop her imagination from going wild as one hour slipped into another and there was still no word from Sam. How long did it take to sweep an entire building for bombs?

Her stomach muscles knotted with tension, she prowled around the small office where she'd been spirited away to wait, too restless to sit. Someone brought her a cup of coffee and a Danish, but she couldn't touch either. What was going on, dammit? Had the bomb exploded? Surely she would have heard something. She didn't know much about letter bombs, but the padded brown envelope that had been left on her desk had looked large enough to hold a fair amount of explosives. If she'd made the mistake of touching it, she didn't doubt for a minute that she'd be dead now.

Too close, she thought, shivering. Dominguez—or whoever was carrying out this vendetta for him—had come much too close for comfort this time. Only a fool would think they wouldn't try again.

That thought was still worrying her when Sam walked in twenty minutes later. "Thank God!" she breathed. "What's going on? Was it really a bomb?"

His lean face carved in stone, he nodded curtly. "It was set so sensitive that it went off the second the bomb squad touched it."

Pale, she gasped. "Oh, God! Was anyone hurt? I didn't even hear anything."

"No, thank God, but that wasn't the jerk's intent...*this time,*" he stressed. "This was a warning, pure and simple. And at this point, we have to assume it's directly related to Dominguez."

"How did it end up in my chambers?"

"A man in a messenger service uniform delivered it this morning when your clerk was called away from the office for a few minutes to deal with a sick woman in the hallway. He walked right in, put it on your desk, then walked out again without anyone being the wiser."

"Then the messenger service should have a record—"

"It would if the bomb had actually been delivered by one of their employees, but it wasn't. The whole thing was a setup," he said flatly. "The sick woman who got your clerk out of the office, the messenger, everything. World-Wide Messenger Service has no record of any deliveries to the courthouse for the last three days. They were burglarized last week, however, and several uniforms were taken. As for the woman, the security cameras caught her rushing out of the building, looking healthy as a horse, just minutes after your clerk helped her to the restroom.

"These people are clever, Sadie," he said grimly when the last of the color washed out of her cheeks. "They've proven that they can get to you just about any time they want, and I would be remiss in my duties if I didn't tell you that you need to think about letting another judge take over for you. It's not worth getting killed over.''

''It's not going to come to that.''

''How do you know?'' he countered. ''You're dealing with the Mexican mafia here, not some two-bit thief on the street who likes to show how tough he is by intimidating women. These people are cold and ruthless and play by their own rules. They don't compromise with people who get in their way—they eliminate them. And right now, you're in Dominguez's way. If you continue to stand strong, you could end up in a body bag.''

The cold finality of his words sent a shiver racing down Sadie's spine, but she'd be damned if she gave in to fear. ''So I'm supposed to quit, right? Turn tail and save my own neck and to hell with justice? Then what? Dominguez gets a new trial, a new judge, and the game starts all over again. So where does it end? *When* does it end? When there are no more judges willing to hear the case and he's finally able to walk? I don't think so. Someone's got to draw the line with the jerk, and it looks like it's me. I don't like bullies.''

That, at least, was something he could agree on. "Neither do I. Every bully I ever met was a coward, and Dominguez is no different—he's just got more power than most. And that makes him doubly dangerous. If you're going to stand your ground on this and force him to deal with you, then you need to know that with this latest stunt, all the rules change. When you're not in the courthouse, the FBI wants you in a safe house and protected by a female agent at all times.

"There's no negotiating on this," he warned when she started to object. "If you're going to try this case, then you have to give us the opportunity to keep you alive long enough to get a conviction, or we're all just spinning our wheels. And it's not like it's forever—just until the trial ends. It's going to be an inconvenience, but better that than dead."

He had a point, one she couldn't deny. "Fine," she replied. "Whatever it takes to get a verdict."

Once the courthouse was searched and declared bomb-free, the Dominguez trial reconvened, but not in Sadie's usual courtroom on the second floor. The bomb had damaged part of her chambers and a wall near the witness box, and it was decided that it would be better if the sequestered jury didn't see the damage and start asking questions that couldn't be answered without influencing the outcome of the trial. So the proceedings were moved to a smaller, unused courtroom on the third floor. There, the trial picked up where it had stopped the day before, without an explanation of the cause of the delay to the jury.

Sam had warned her that facing Dominguez again would be like waving a red flag in front of a bull, and he wasn't far wrong. When she stepped into the courtroom and took her seat on the bench, the defendant glared at her with eyes that were black with hatred. Still, she was determined to be unfailingly fair. She didn't intend to give Dominguez's lawyers any grounds for an appeal if he was convicted, so she bit her tongue and bent over backward to keep her prejudices to herself. And it cost her. By the time she adjourned for the day, she had a pounding headache and a stomach that was queasy from tension.

The stress of the day, however, only intensified when she left the courthouse with Julie Danson, one of the female FBI agents who had been assigned to protect her for the rest of the trial. A tall, thin woman with sharp green eyes that missed little, she made sudden turns without warning and constantly checked her rearview mirror to make sure they weren't being followed as she drove away from downtown and headed toward the northeast part of town. Despite her best intentions to remain calm, Sadie found herself looking over her own shoulder, waiting for someone to come out of nowhere to attack her.

But Julie knew what she was doing, and it never happened. They reached the safe house, a small, unassuming ranch-style house on a quiet street in a neighborhood north of the airport, and Sadie was quickly whisked inside without incident. ''Don't let the simplicity of the house fool you,'' the other woman told her as she locked and dead-bolted the front door. ''All the windows are bulletproof glass and the doors are reinforced steel. The front and back yards are monitored by security cameras, and the houses on either side of us are occupied by agents whose sole job is to make sure no one even looks at this place, let alone tries to approach it. You're safe, Your Honor. No one's going to get to you on our watch.''

All business, the agent showed her to her bedroom, a small, interior room with no windows that was simply furnished with a double bed and dresser, where Sadie found some of her things already waiting for her. Surprised, she said, "How did you—"

"We couldn't take the chance on letting you go home to pack a bag," she explained, "so we did it for you. Your landlady let us in— *after* she called downtown to make sure we were really who we said we were," she added with a rueful smile. "She wanted me to remind you that Noah Baxter is supposed to call you at ten tonight."

"Oh, my God!" Stunned, Sadie couldn't believe she hadn't given Noah a thought all day. But she'd hardly had time. From the moment she'd arrived at work to find that letter bomb on her desk, it seemed like she'd been managing one crisis after another. "I need to call him. That's okay, isn't it?"

"Just don't tell anyone where you are." Nodding to the phone on the bedside table, she smiled. "Talk as long as you like—the call's on Uncle Sam."

When Julie excused herself to see what was in the refrigerator for supper, Sadie searched through her purse for the slip of paper Noah had given her with the name and number of his hotel on it. Punching it in, she slipped out of her shoes and sank onto the side of the bed as she waited for the hotel operator to patch the call through to his room.

She half expected him to be gone to supper, but the phone had barely rung, when it was snatched up. "Sadie?"

Surprised, she blinked. "Yeah. How'd you know it was me?"

"Where the hell have you been?" he demanded furiously. "Dammit, woman, I've been worried sick about you! I heard about the bomb on the five o'clock news and have been trying to track you down ever since. Are you okay? The news reports said the trial had to be moved to another courtroom because yours was damaged when the bomb went off. Where was security, for God's sake? Did they just stand by with their hands in their pockets and let some joker walk into your chambers with a bomb or what? You could have been killed!"

Practically roaring, he threw the words at her like an accusation, as if *she* was the one to blame for the whole incident. If anyone else had implied such a thing, Sadie would have snapped right back, but she knew Noah's anger was directed at the circumstances rather than at her. If she'd have heard such a thing on TV when she was two hundred miles away, she would have been upset, too.

"I never even touched the letter," she said soothingly. "It was on my desk when I came in this morning, and the second I realized that it had no business being there, I called security. The police evacuated the building immediately. And by the time the bomb squad set the thing off, I was down the street at the police station. The FBI has been called in, and I'm going to be kept at different safe houses until the trial's over with. That's why I called. I didn't want you to worry when you phoned the apartment tonight and I wasn't there."

She was fine. And safe. The bomb hadn't touched her, and now that the FBI had been brought in, the chances that one of Dominguez's men would be able to get to her were slim to none. She was in good hands and he didn't have to worry about her anymore.

Reassured, Noah told himself he could relax now, but the fear that had held him by the throat ever since he'd heard the first news reports about the bomb refused to ease its hold.

He didn't care if she was surrounded by every law enforcement officer within a hundred-mile radius of San Antonio, he wanted, *needed*, to be there with her. To see for himself with his own two eyes that she really was unharmed. To touch her and hold her and feel the reassuring cadence of her heart beating in time with his. As long as he held her close, he would know for sure that she was safe.

Because he was falling in love with her and he didn't want to lose her.

The truth snuck up on him like a thief in the night and caught him completely off guard. Stunned, he heard her explain how her clerk was lured away from the office so that the bomb could be delivered by a man in a stolen messenger service uniform, but the words hardly registered. How the hell had this happened? How had he *let* it happen? From the very beginning, the physical attraction had knocked him for a loop—he'd had to fight just to keep his hands off her—but he'd never suspected that the lady would get past the guards he'd erected around his heart so easily. Not when he had commitments to his family, his sisters, that he couldn't ignore.

There was no room in his life for a woman,

he thought grimly. Not yet. There might not be for years. Alex was still in high school, for God's sake! She hadn't even decided yet what she wanted to study and could still have years of schooling left to complete. Add the cost of Nat's law school, Kelly's years in medical school and Rachel's bachelor degree to that, even with scholarships and grants, and he was still looking at a mountain of debt. Of course, the girls would pay once their careers were established, but in the meantime, he was the one who signed the checks.

Time. He needed time, dammit, and that could be the last thing in the world they had. He didn't care how many agents were protecting her or how many safe houses they took her to, danger was bearing down on her like an out-of-control freight train. Dominguez wasn't going to sit back and let his fate be decided by a court of law or a spunky judge who was a constant irritant in his side. He was a man of incredible power who crushed anyone who had the temerity to get in his way, and right now, Sadie was right in the middle of his path.

"I wish I was there," he said roughly, irritably. "You know that, don't you? I don't like being this far away from you when we don't know what kind of garbage Dominguez is going to pull next. The bastard could strike from anywhere.''

''Sam and the FBI have covered all the bases,'' she assured him. ''The trial's going to be moved to a different courtroom every day, and security is so thick around the justice center now that an ant couldn't get in without the proper credentials. Trust me, nothing's going to happen.''

For her peace of mind, he didn't argue with her, but he wasn't nearly as optimistic. Long after he hung up, he paced the confines of his hotel room, fighting the need to drop everything and rush back to San Antonio. And that need only got worse with the passage of time. Over the course of the next few days, his gut told him the danger around her was intensifying like a fire that was quickly reaching flash point. Out of the loop and too far away to be of any help, he could do nothing but wait for her to call every night from the different safe houses she was transported to each evening after work.

From the nightly reports she gave him, it was obvious the trial was proceeding much more rapidly than expected. The prosecution was expected to rest its case on Thursday; and on Friday, the defense, fighting an uphill battle all the way, would begin calling its first witnesses. If everything went according to plan, the case would go to the jury on Tuesday or Wednesday of the following week. If Dominguez was going to do something to cause a mistrial, he was going to have to do it damn fast.

Worried sick and cursing the distance between them, Noah got a break in his own case when his client, who had been adamantly opposed to settling with a former business partner he had accused of embezzling funds, decided Thursday morning to cave in and work out an equitable agreement that both parties could live with. He had the deal worked out and accepted by lunchtime and was on the road to San Antonio by one.

He'd told Sadie he would be in late on Friday, but it was actually a little after four on Thursday when he passed through the tight security outside the door of the fourth-floor courtroom where the trial had been temporarily moved to for the day. He'd hoped to slip inside unnoticed and take a seat in the back, then surprise her later when court adjourned for the day. But at the sound of the door quietly swishing open, she dragged her attention from the witness, who was being questioned by the D.A., and quickly glanced toward the entrance to the courtroom.

Blue eyes met brown, and time just seemed to grind to a halt. It couldn't have lasted more than a few heartbeats, and to the casual observer, Sadie didn't appear to react one way or the other, but Noah knew better. Even from a distance, he saw the slight, revealing color that flared in her cheeks and the pleasure that abruptly warmed her eyes behind the lenses of her reading glasses. If they'd been anywhere else but where they were, he would have gone right up to her and pulled her into his arms. God, he needed to touch her! Instead, all he could do was take a seat in the last row and wait for the moment when she adjourned for the day and he could be alone with her.

In the time it took for him to stretch out his legs, he, like everyone else, was caught up in the drama of the trial as the prosecution called its last witness. A forty-year-old Hispanic woman who nervously twisted her hands together, Gloria Valdez was obviously scared to death as she stepped into the witness box and shot Dominguez anxious looks as she swore to tell the truth. She was a maid in his household, and when the D.A. asked her about her boss's temper, she admitted that it was volatile and unpredictable. Shaking with fear, she told of other employees who had displeased him who'd disappeared overnight and were never seen or heard from again.

"Objection!" With a roar of outrage, Kingston jumped to his feet as all hell broke loose in the courtroom. "Move to strike, Your Honor! The witness is drawing a conclusion based on speculation."

"To the contrary, Your Honor, she is only reporting what she has seen with her own two eyes," Michael Dunn, the assistant D.A., argued. "Employees at Dominguez's compound have been known not to show up for work the next morning. That's not idle speculation."

"Objection overruled," Sadie stated with a bang of her gavel. "You'll get your chance to cross-examine the witness, Mr. Kingston. Continue, Mr. Dunn."

Pleased with the ruling, the D.A. told the maid reassuringly, "Just a few more questions, Ms. Valdez. First, how many people do you personally know of who walked away from their jobs and families at the Dominguez mansion with absolutely no warning?"

"Three."

"And as far as you know, did their families ever hear from them again?"

With a scared look at Dominguez that said more clearly than words just how much she feared him, she shook her head. "No."

Satisfied, Michael Dunn smiled. "No further questions, Your Honor."

Ethan Kingston was on his feet in a shot. "Ms. Valdez, you said these three employees disappeared overnight. Weren't all three residents of Mexico?"

"Yes."

"And they had only worked for Mr. Dominguez a matter of weeks. Isn't that correct?"

Confused, she nodded. "Yes."

"Then isn't it a possibility that they might have just decided that they were homesick for Mexico and just walked out?"

"Well, yes, I suppose so, but—"

"Have other employees quit without notice?"

"Of course, but—"

"In the years that you worked for Mr. Dominguez, did you ever personally see him hurt or harm anyone?"

"Not personally, no, but—"

''Just answer the question, Ms. Valdez. Did you actually see Mr. Dominguez hurt any of the three employees who walked away from his employment?''

Clutching her hands in her lap, the poor woman could do nothing but shake her head and look miserable. ''No.''

As pleased as a snake that had just swallowed a rat, Kingston returned to the defendant's table. With a few quick questions, he had defused whatever damage the witness had done. ''No further questions, Your Honor.''

It was fifteen minutes until five o'clock, and the defense would begin presenting its case next. Not surprisingly, Sadie excused the witness and called it quits for the day. With a bang of her gavel, she announced, ''We will reconvene at nine o'clock in the morning, when Mr. Kingston will call his first witness. Members of the jury, you are reminded not to discuss the case among yourselves or watch or read any media coverage. Court is adjourned.''

Her heart thumping, Sadie saw Noah immediately start toward her, only to be stopped by Julie Danson, who, along with a handful of deputies and other agents, moved to surround her as the courtroom began to empty. She wanted to call out to the two of them, to tell Julie it was all right to let him pass, but she never got the opportunity. Taking no chances with her, her bodyguards quickly hustled her out the back way before she could do anything but sputter a protest. Her last view of Noah was of him being turned away by Julie and slipping out the front entrance of the courtroom.

"This way, Your Honor," one of the agents told her as he urged her into a service elevator that had already been secured for her use. "We weren't expecting you to adjourn quite so early today, so it'll be a few minutes before we can get a car downstairs and make sure the area is secure. In the meantime, you can wait in your chambers. That'll give you time to get some work together to take with you, if you like."

She didn't want to think about work, not when Noah was right there in the building and could, even now, be leaving because no one would let him get close to her. He should have told her he was coming back early, she thought in frustration as the elevator doors rumbled open and she was rushed down the hall to the short corridor that led to the private entrance to her chambers. She would have made arrangements for him to bypass all the added security.

As it was, she didn't even know where he was. Once she was whisked off to the safe house, she wouldn't have a chance to see him until tomorrow.

Her heart twisted at the thought, and suddenly she knew she couldn't wait that long. "Where's Julie?" she asked, balking at the entrance to her chambers. "I need to talk to her. There's someone I need for her to find for me."

Lifting his radio to his mouth, the agent spoke into it, listened to the response and grinned. "She's on her way. Go on inside and she'll be right with you. I'll be out here if you need anything."

Relieved, Sadie quickly unlocked the door to her office and stepped inside. Almost immediately, two strong arms closed around her and pulled her back against a hard male body. "Finally!" a familiar rough voice groaned in her ear when she gasped. "You're a hard lady to get ahold of, Your Judgeship. C'mere."

"Noah!"

That was all she had time to say, just his name, then he was turning her in his arms and kissing her like he was never going to let her go. And she loved it. She'd missed him, missed the feel of his arms around her, the sparkle in his eyes when he teased her, the fire he lit in her blood with just a whisper of a touch. When she'd seen him slip into the courtroom earlier, the rest of the world had ceased to exist.

When, she wondered, had he come to mean so much to her? She'd been so sure that after David's betrayal, she would never let anyone get close enough to her to hurt her again, but she hadn't counted on meeting someone like Noah. He was a man who cared about family and doing the right thing and everything she believed in, and even though she knew she was leaving herself wide open to heartache, she couldn't summon any defenses against him anymore. She just couldn't.

Shaken, she pulled back to look up at him searchingly. "What are you doing here? I thought you were going to be tied up in Houston until tomorrow."

"So did I, but we settled." He reached for her reading glasses, pulled them off and sat them on her desk, then cupped her face in his hands and kissed her again. "Your watchdog, Julie, let me in here and said you'd be leaving for the safe house once she gets the call from downstairs that it's all clear. I want to go with you."

His husky words stroked her, setting her heart hammering against her ribs, then she realized that he probably meant he was still worried about her safety. Every night when she'd called him in Houston, he'd asked her about the security at the different safe houses she'd been taken to and the number of agents guarding her. He'd made it clear he hadn't thought she was being protected as she should be.

"I don't need another bodyguard, if that's what you're concerned about," she said quietly, hurt. "I can't turn around now without running into one."

She tried to draw away, but he was having none of it. Linking his hands behind her waist, he held her in front of him. "I wouldn't care if you were surrounded by a hundred agents and cops, I would still be worried about a slime like Dominguez getting to you. But that's not why I want to be with you. I missed you," he said honestly. "I couldn't wait to get back here, and I promised myself that when I did, I wasn't letting you out of my sight for at least twenty-four hours, and maybe not even then. I want to be alone with you, to kiss you all over, to make love with you until we're both too weak to move. And I can't do that when you're God knows where and I'm all alone in my apartment. So since you can't go to my place, I'll go with you…if that's okay with you, of course.''

Heaven. He'd just described exactly what she needed, what she'd dreamed of and never told him. How had he known? Tears welling in her eyes and thickening in her throat, she nodded and buried her face against his chest. ''Okay.''

Chuckling, he crushed her close and kissed her hair. ''Now I've made you cry. Don't look now, Your Honorableness, but your mascara's running and the car's going to be downstairs any second.''

''Oh, God!'' Horrified, she pulled back just far enough to swipe under her eye, only to cringe at the black smear that smudged her finger. ''I can't go downstairs looking like this. If a reporter sees me, it'll be all over the morning paper that I'm crying my eyes out over this trial. Give me a second. I'll be right back.''

After standing on tiptoe to press a quick kiss to his mouth, she grabbed her purse, slipped out the door and hurried down the hall to the restroom. As expected, agents were at both ends of the hallway, watching everyone who stepped foot on the second floor and refusing to let anyone pass without proper identification. Smiling to them, she signaled that she was just going to the restroom and slipped inside.

Already digging for her mascara in her purse, she never saw the cleaning woman with her cart until she almost ran her down. "Oh, I'm sorry," she gasped, laughing slightly. "I wasn't watching where I was going. I just need to put on a little makeup, and then I'll get out of your way."

"There's no hurry," the woman said easily, and turned to face her. A split second later, Sadie found herself staring down the barrel of a gun.

Chapter 12

What the hell was taking her so long?

Pacing the hallway in front of the women's restroom, Noah shot the closed door a frown and glanced at his watch for the third time in as many minutes. How long did it take a woman to freshen up her makeup? A minute or two? Surely five at the most, and he'd given Sadie more than that while he'd waited for her in her chambers. Impatient to have her back in his arms, to kiss the stuffing out of her, he'd finally come out into the hall to wait. What the devil was she doing in there?

Half-tempted to press his ear to the door, he told himself he was being paranoid and turned away to pace again. At each end of the hallway, the two FBI agents guarding the elevator and stairs stood tense and straight with their eyes trained on the door to the women's restroom. They didn't seem any happier about the situation than Noah, and as he watched, one of them spoke into his radio. Was he calling to report that there might be a possible problem?

Maybe she was sick.

The thought stopped him in midstride before he remembered that she'd been perfectly fine when she'd left him in her chambers to freshen up. If she'd been sick, he'd seen no sign of it then or earlier when he'd watched her in the courtroom. No, she probably just needed some time to herself and would be out when she was ready.

He told himself he wouldn't rush her—he'd give her another five minutes before he knocked on the door to make sure there wasn't anything seriously wrong. But in the end, he could only give her two minutes. He needed to see her again, dammit, to assure himself that she was all right. If he had to chance making a fool of himself to do that, then so be it.

Throwing caution to the wind and not giving a damn what the agents down the hall thought, he approached the door and pushed it open without bothering to knock. If he embarrassed her, he'd apologize later. "Sadie? What's wrong? What's taking—"

That was as far as he got. A woman in a cleaning service uniform whirled to confront him, the small, but deadly .38 she held pointed right at his midsection. "What the hell!"

Sadie's heart stopped dead in her chest at the sight of him. *No!* she wanted to cry. *Get out of here before you get yourself shot!*

But he didn't move, didn't take his eyes off the gun, and Sadie could almost feel the cleaning woman's panic. She had to know she was trapped, that there was no way out. Noah hadn't exactly been quiet when he'd discovered the woman holding a gun on her, and she had to know that even now the agents out in the hall were closing in to investigate the ruckus in the restroom. The only exit was the door, and Noah was standing in the way.

She would kill him. Sadie had spent the last ten minutes pleading with the woman, trying to reason with her, to *reach* her, but nothing she'd said had registered. The woman kept saying she had to kill the judge—it was the only way. And she would have done it if Noah hadn't opened the door when he had. She was desperate, irrational, filled with rage and looking for a reason to pull the trigger. Cornering her was all it would take.

Her blood roaring in her ears, Sadie knew she had to do something. Now! While the woman was distracted. As she glanced wildly around, her eyes fell on the cleaning cart. Lightning quick, she snatched up a broom. Without a thought to the danger she was putting herself in, she brought it down with bruising force on the cleaning woman's right arm.

''No!'' she screamed.

The gun went flying, but instead of scrambling for it, the woman turned on Sadie with a cry of rage. Launching herself at her, she closed her hands around her throat and sent them both crashing to the floor. Gasping, Sadie clutched at her fingers, but the woman had the strength of a bear and outweighed her by a good forty pounds. Spitting curses at her, she literally tried to choke her to death.

Black spots swimming before her eyes, Sadie never heard Noah's bellow of rage. Then he was ripping the woman's hands from Sadie's throat and hauling the cursing woman to her feet. Out of control, she turned on him in a flash and would have gouged his eyes out, but the FBI agents exploded into the small restroom then and grabbed her. In ten seconds flat, they took control and subdued her.

As quickly as it had begun, it was over. One of the agents got on the radio and summoned backup, and within minutes, the place was surrounded by agents and cops. Julie, who had been downstairs arranging transportation, glared at the two agents whose responsibility it was to secure the second floor. "How the hell did she even get up here in the first place?" she demanded. "You know the cleaning crew isn't allowed on this floor until after seven."

"She had the right identification," the younger of the two men said grudgingly. "And her name was on the list of the cleaning crew. She said she'd been given permission to clean the second floor early because her mother was in the hospital and if she had to wait until after seven to do her work, she'd miss visiting hours."

It was a logical excuse, one Sadie might have fallen for herself, especially given the fact that the woman had all the right credentials. "Are you sure she's with the cleaning service?" Sadie asked with a frown as she studied the woman. "I work late fairly often and thought I knew most of the crew. I've never laid eyes on this woman in my life. What's her name?''

The older agent checked the list of people scheduled to work that evening. ''Maria Gonzalez.''

Stunned, Sadie gasped. ''No, it's not! I know Maria. She's small and petite, with red hair.'' Frowning at the woman who had tried to kill her, she said in bewilderment, ''Who *are* you? Why did you did this? What did you hope to accomplish?''

For a moment, Sadie didn't think she was going to answer. Handcuffed, her black hair hanging around her face, she glared defiantly back at Sadie, refusing to say so much as a word. Then, with no warning, she burst into tears. ''I'm sorry! I wasn't going to kill you— not really. I was just going to kidnap you to stop the trial. Dominic—''

Before she could go any further, Sadie quickly held up her hand. ''Stop right there. I can't hear the rest of this, not if it involves the defendant. Julie, is the car downstairs? I need to get out of here.''

The agent didn't have to be told twice. Motioning three agents to join them, she whisked Sadie and Noah downstairs and out a side entrance to where a blue van with dark windows was parked at the curb. Sadie and Noah took the middle seat, the agents took the front and back, and within moments, they'd left the courthouse far behind.

The safe house they were taken to was, in actuality, a working ranch that was located right outside the city limits on the northwest side of town. Surrounded by a thousand acres of grazing land, the adobe-style house was set back a half a mile from the road, and you could scream until the cows came home and the nearest neighbors still wouldn't hear a thing. The owners, who were spending the summer in Europe, were old friends with the national director of the bureau and had graciously offered the use of their home while they were gone in the event that it was needed. Quiet and secluded and just over the hill from a spectacular view of the city, it fairly oozed peace.

Her nerves still shot from what happened at the courthouse, Sadie took one look at the thick white walls, arched doorways and graceful, romantic lines of the place and felt the tension begin to ease out of her. This was what she needed, she realized. Total isolation from the real world...with Noah.

They hadn't said two words to each other over the course of the long drive from downtown, but they hadn't needed to. He'd held her hand the entire way. And for the first time since he'd left for Houston, she realized that she felt totally and completely safe. Because he was close.

She wanted to tell him, to show him how glad she was that he was back, but supper was waiting for them when they stepped through the front door and there was no time. The housekeeper, a gray-haired woman with an ageless face and kind eyes, showed them to the dining room, where candles had already been lit and wine poured.

''The guard at the gate buzzed me when you arrived,'' she said softly. ''Please...sit. I'll bring the food.''

She didn't have to say that twice. Sadie took the seat across from Noah as Julie and the rest of the agents found places at a table that could easily accommodate twenty. They'd all barely settled into their chairs when the housekeeper returned with platters of grilled steak and baked potatoes. Sadie felt her mouth water, and suddenly, it seemed like days since she'd eaten. Starving, she took a bite and looked up to find Noah watching her with a grin. Under the table, he nudged her foot with his, just as he had at the charity dance for the Safe Haven Children's Ranch. And just that easily, despite everything, she was happy.

She wanted to be alone with him. Her heart was in her eyes and she knew he saw it. His smile faded, his eyes darkened with emotion, and under the table, where no one could see, he slipped off a shoe to press his foot warmly over hers. Conversation flowed over and around them, but they never noticed. *Later,* he promised her without saying a word. Later, it would be just the two of them.

But later never seemed to come. Once the meal was completed, security for the night was discussed. The ranch hands would keep an eye on the perimeter of the ranch and make sure there were no unexpected visitors while the agents stayed closer to the house. The odds on anyone actually reaching the house and harming Sadie were slim to none, but no one was taking anything for granted. Hourly patrols were arranged and the drive into work the following morning talked over. It was agreed that they would leave forty-five minutes early in the morning to allow for the extra distance they had to travel and the traffic they would run into on the way downtown.

That meant a five-thirty wake-up call.

Everyone groaned at the thought and the topic of conversation immediately switched to bedroom assignments. Unlike the other safe houses, which had an interior bedroom where Sadie could stay without worrying about someone coming through a window, all six bedrooms of the Spanish-style house had exterior windows. There was, however, a maid's room off the kitchen that was currently in disuse and had apparently once been used for storage. Small and narrow, it had only one window, and that was a single pane high on the wall. The only source of natural light in the dark room, it didn't even open.

Julie took one look at it and nodded. "Perfect. I'll take the room next door, and there'll be someone outside the back door at all times. Tom, where're the judge's things?"

Sadie's overnight bag was produced, and within minutes, she found herself alone in the small room. It wasn't quite the way she'd expected the evening to end, not after she'd spent most of dinner playing footsie with Noah under the table and reading promises in his eyes. When she'd stepped into her room, she'd truly thought that he would be right behind her, but he'd disappeared into the room two doors down the hall instead.

Staring forlornly at the bed, she tried to tell herself that it was probably for the best that she didn't jump right back into bed with him the first night he was back in town. She'd missed him too much, thought of that one time they'd had together so often that she could replay every touch, every kiss, in her head. If they made love tonight, she knew her heart would never be hers alone again.

That didn't, however, make crawling into her lonely bed any easier. She changed into her nightgown, then turned out the light, but instead of sliding between the sheets, she couldn't stop her eyes from drifting to the closed bedroom door. As the house grew quiet and everyone settled down for the night, all she could think of was that Noah was just two doors down the hall. If she was careful, she could let herself out of her room and slip into his, and no one would be any the wiser.

Tempted more than she'd ever been in her

life to actually chase after a man without any shame, she'd actually taken a step toward the door when it suddenly began to slowly open. Freezing, she told herself there was no way Dominguez could know where she was or get to her. There was no reason to be alarmed. It was probably just Julie checking on her.

But even as she tried to convince herself she was perfectly fine, her heart was doing a slow roll in her chest. She couldn't move, couldn't do anything but stand there in the dark and hold her breath as the door was pushed open wider and wider.

Unconsciously, she braced herself, ready to scream if anyone but Julie was standing there. But when the door was finally pushed open far enough to reveal the person on the other side, the only sound she made was a faint gasp as the light streaming in through the room's single high window etched Noah's rugged features in silhouette.

He quickly shut the door, and was beside her in a heartbeat. "Shhh," he whispered in her ear, pressing his fingers to her mouth. "I want you all to myself, and if we make too much noise, that bodyguard of yours is going to come running and get an eyeful."

In the darkness, her luminous eyes met his. ''I didn't think you were coming.''

''Nothing short of an act of God could have kept me away,'' he murmured huskily. ''Not tonight.''

Turning into his arms, she lifted her mouth to his and silently reminded herself that they had to be quiet. She'd just die if somebody heard them and came to investigate. But then his fingers tangled in her hair, his mouth lowered to hers, and all she could think of was how miserable she'd been while he was gone. She'd never been so lonely in her life, and it was all his fault. He'd made her want him, need him, and only now was she realizing how much. Even her heart ached.

To her horror, she felt tears welling in her eyes. God, she couldn't cry! Not now. But she was. The tears spilled over her lashes to trail slowly down her cheeks, and with a broken sob, she tore her mouth from his and buried her face against his throat.

Holding her cradled against him, he went perfectly still. ''Sadie? Honey? What's wrong?''

Her throat tight, she crowded closer and felt his arms tighten with satisfying fierceness around her. ''I just…missed you,'' she said softly. ''Love me, Noah. I need you to love me.''

The admission reached right into his chest and squeezed his heart. He did love her. The strength of it took his breath away and almost drove him to his knees, and even though he knew she wasn't ready to hear the words yet, he had to show her. Scooping her up, he carried her to bed.

Slow. He had to go slow. Somewhere in the back of his brain, a voice kept telling him that he still had to take care with her and not rush her, but then her arms were around his neck, her mouth soft and welcoming under his, and she was pulling him down to her, on her. Every sane thought he had flew right out of his head. Groaning, not giving a damn who heard them, he kissed her hotly, hungrily, like a man who hadn't had a decent meal in days and he could eat her right up.

If she'd shown the least sign of hesitation, he would have found a way to slow things down. But her mouth was as frantic as his in the dark, and when he reached for the hem of her night-gown, her fingers were already there, pulling it up and over her head. Then his hands were on her, molding themselves to the soft, enticing fullness of her breasts, and he felt like he'd died and gone to heaven. Soft. Good God, she was soft! How could he have forgotten the sweet, tempting texture of her skin in just a week? It was enough to drive a man mad.

Needing to feel every sweet inch of her against him, he tore at his own clothes, swearing when his fingers fumbled with buttons and the zipper of his jeans stubbornly refused to work properly. Then he was naked and they were between the sheets and skin to skin. She reached for him, her hands skimming over him, lighting little fires under his skin, and he knew he was never going to be able to give her anything close to the patient loving he had the first time.

Groaning, he trapped her fingers under his. ''Sweetheart, I love it when you touch me, but if you keep doing that, I'm going to lose it.''

Gazing up at him trustingly in the darkness, she said quietly, ''You don't have to treat me like I'm made of glass, Noah. I won't break.''

''I would never do to you what Lincoln did,'' he said tightly. ''I'd rather cut off my right hand.''

He'd meant to reassure her, but it wasn't relief that flashed in her eyes. It was anger, hot and quick, and directed solely at him. ''Do you think I don't know that? That I would be here with you now, like this, if I thought you were anything like him? I trust you,'' she said with soft fierceness. ''Do you need me to prove it?''

''No, of course not—''

He might as well have saved his breath. Pushing him to his back, she moved over him like a temptress out of his dreams, kissing and stroking and caressing her way down his body and back up again with a hunger that left him reeling. She stole the air from his lungs and the thoughts from his head, then used lips and tongue and teeth in a kiss that drove him mad. He was still gasping when she took his hand and placed his fingers on her breast, then guided his touch to show him just where she wanted to be touched and how. Far more intimate than a mere caress, it quite simply destroyed him.

There was never any question of control after that. He just wasn't capable of it. Not when her eyes were dark and slumberous and her hand guided his down every sweet curve and valley of her body. By the time she brought his fingers to the hot, wet heart of her desire, he knew the struggle was lost.

He never meant to say the words—it was too soon and she wasn't ready to hear them—but he could no more hold them back than he could hold back the hands of time. "Sadie, I love you," he groaned, kissing her fiercely.

It was a mistake—he knew it the second he saw the flash of something that looked like fear in her eyes—but before she could say anything more than his name, he stopped her. "No," he said in a hoarse whisper that wouldn't carry beyond the four walls of the bedroom. "You don't have to say anything. Not now, not ever if you don't feel like it. Just let me love you."

Not giving her a chance to say anything else, he covered her mouth with his and settled between her thighs, and the time for talking was past. Heart to heart, he eased into the hot, wet warmth of her and began to move. Her arms surrounded him, her body welcomed him, embraced him. And he knew that if he lived to be a hundred, his world could be falling down around his ears and he wouldn't give a damn if he had her in his arms to love. Because she made him complete in a way that no woman ever had before, and somehow, once the trial was over and life returned to normal, he had to find a way to convince her that she was, and always would be, his.

He loved her.

Staring at herself in the mirror the next morning as she dressed for work, Sadie told herself she must have dreamed the night before, or at least parts of it, anyway. There was no question in her mind that, just as he'd promised, he'd made love to her until they were both too weak to move, and it was wonderful. But he couldn't possibly have told her that he loved her. That wasn't a word he would use lightly, and right from the beginning, he'd made it clear that he wasn't looking for love any more than she was. She must have just misunderstood.

But later, when they all gathered in the dining room for the homemade sweet rolls and coffee the cook had set out for a quick breakfast, Noah was waiting for her. She only had to take one look at him to know that nothing about the previous night had been a dream. He met her gaze unflinchingly, his blue eyes direct and unblinkingly honest, and told her without saying a word that he loved her.

And deep inside, her heart whispered the words in return.

Panic hit her then, the kind that was soul deep and frightening. She wanted to throw herself into his arms...and run for the hills. How had she let this happen? When? Their arrangement was never supposed to come to this! Just sex. That was all it was ever going to be, all it could be. How could she have forgotten so quickly?

Shaken, she needed some time to think, to figure out how her life had become so complicated when she'd been so sure she was in control of it, but there was no time. The trial had to be her number-one priority right now—everything else had to wait. But God, it was hard. As soon as everyone was finished eating, they were hustled out to the van. She'd barely claimed a seat in the back when Noah slid in beside her and settled next to her, his thigh provocatively rubbing hers. Between one heartbeat and the next, her heart was doing double time.

He had to know something was wrong— she'd hardly said two words to him during breakfast and didn't speak all the way into town—but he didn't push the issue. Not until they reached the courthouse and passed through security at the personnel entrance.

Uncaring that they were surrounded by agents, he took her arm and pulled her into a small alcove that led to another judge's offices. "Excuse us, guys," he told the startled agents as he blocked their entrance into the alcove. "Her Judgeship and I need to talk."

"Noah! What—"

"I'm not going upstairs with you, so I'll say goodbye here," he said quietly as he turned his back on her entourage to face her. "But first I want you to know that I don't want you to worry about what I said last night. I didn't tell you I love you to pressure you, so put it out of your mind. Okay? You've got enough to deal with today without worrying about my feelings."

She wanted to tell him it wasn't that easy— how was a woman supposed to forget the first time a man told her he loved her?—but he didn't give her the chance. Drawing her into his arms, he gave her a tender, too-short kiss; then, before she was ready to let him go, he was gone.

If she'd been anywhere else but where she was, she probably would have cried, which was, in itself, surprising. She didn't consider herself one of those emotional females who got all weepy at the drop of a hat. But there was something about Noah and the way he touched her heart that just got to her.

There was, however, no time for tears today. Not when she had six agents watching her as if they half expected her to fall apart any second. And not when she still had a trial to oversee. Stiffening her spine, she dragged on a cool smile. ''Let's get upstairs. I'm sure the defense is ready to get started.''

The defense was, in fact, chomping at the bit, but the prosecution had other ideas. The second Sadie called court into session, Michael Dunn was on his feet to announce that the prosecution had one more witness to call before turning things over to the defense.

Outraged, Kingston wasted no time in objecting. ''This is outrageous, Your Honor! Mr. Dunn rested yesterday. He can't drag in a secret witness at the last minute without giving the defense a chance to know anything about this person.''

''We only became aware of this person's existence late yesterday, Your Honor,'' Michael replied quietly when Sadie called both attorneys to the bench to discuss the matter out of the hearing of the jurors. "I would have liked more time myself to question the woman, but life isn't always accommodating. If she isn't allowed to testify, there'll be a grave miscarriage of justice."

"This is nothing but histrionics, Your Honor," Kingston hissed. "If you go along with it, you'll be doing nothing but aiding and abetting in the lynching of an innocent man."

Sadie sincerely doubted that Dominguez had been innocent fifteen seconds after he'd been born, but that was hardly something she could say to his attorney. Giving Kingston a stern look, she said, "No one is lynched in my courtroom, Counselor. If, after the prosecution questions the witness, you need time to investigate the witness and prepare a defense, I'll grant you the rest of the day and the weekend. But I won't disallow a witness with information pertinent to the case just because they didn't come forward in a timely manner."

Instructing both men to step back, she said, "Objection overruled. Mr. Dunn, call your next witness."

"The prosecution calls Felicia Cantu."

The main doors to the courtroom opened, and

the bailiff escorted a short, stocky woman in a somber black dress to the witness box. Her hair was pulled back and neatly secured in a ponytail, her eyes lowered timidly, and at first, Sadie didn't recognize her. Then she lifted her head and looked straight ahead as the bailiff swore her in, and Sadie quickly swallowed a gasp. Felicia Cantu was the same woman who'd pulled a gun on her in the restroom.

Seated at the defendant's table, Dominguez swore and would have jumped to his feet if Kingston hadn't grabbed him by the arm and hauled him back down into his chair. A heated, whispered debate ensued, with neither man happy about the results. However, there was nothing they could do but sit there, grim-faced, as Michael Dunn began to question the woman about her relationship, if any, with the defendant.

''I'm his fiancée,'' she said quietly.

If the lady wanted to drop a bomb, she couldn't have found a better way. A sudden, horrified gasp drew all eyes to the first row of the gallery behind the defendant's table, where Dominic Dominguez's wife had dutifully sat from day one of the trial. Like a sudden tidal wave, whispers rippled out from her across the gallery.

"Shut up, Felicia!"

Shooting Dominguez a warning glare, Sadie told his attorney, "You will silence your client, Mr. Kingston, or he's going to find himself in contempt of court."

"Your Honor, I must object—"

"Objection overruled," she said flatly, and nodded to the prosecutor to continue.

Barely able to contain his satisfaction, Michael Dunn never took his gaze from the witness. "So you're Mr. Dominguez's fiancée. How long have you been involved with him?"

"Six years."

"That's a long time. Do you see him on a regular basis?"

"Every day. He bought me a house and does a great deal of his business there. In fact, he has his office calls referred there during the day."

His face mottled with fury, Dominguez growled low in his throat, but he stayed in his chair and kept his mouth shut. His eyes, though, were as cold as death as he listened to his mistress describe the business meetings he frequently had at the house they shared when he wasn't with his wife. Business meetings that, she admitted when questioned, were frequently with Henry Bingham, the man Dominguez was accused of killing.

"Were you present at a meeting on February 3, 1998, when the defendant and Mr. Bingham had a falling-out that led to a fight between the two men?" the D.A. asked. When she reluctantly nodded, he said, "Tell us what happened."

Pale, her hands twisting in her lap, she looked anywhere but at her lover. "Dominic accused Henry of going behind his back to buy a piece of property that the city was considering for a new sports arena. When Henry denied it, Dominic hit him and told him no one cheated him and lived to talk about it. If he wanted to save his family some grief, he'd start picking out his casket. The next morning, Henry was dead."

"You bitch!" Exploding out of his chair, Dominguez launched himself toward the witness box, spewing rage even as an FBI agent and two undercover cops threw themselves at him and tackled him before he could reach the cowering woman. "You sold me out! You stupid fool, did you think just because I told you

I'd marry you that I'd let you get away with something I wouldn't let Henry get away with? Weren't you paying attention at all? Nobody stabs me in the back. *Nobody!*''

Furious that a defendant would dare make a threat in her courtroom, Sadie slammed down her gavel. ''You're in contempt, Mr. Dominguez. Bailiff, handcuff him and get him out of here.'' Turning her attention to the gallery, where spectators were whispering excitedly, she banged her gavel again. ''Order! I will have order in this courtroom or I'll clear it in a heartbeat—the choice is yours.''

She didn't make idle threats, and those causing all the whispering in the gallery knew it. Silence fell like a stone. Satisfied, Sadie turned to the prosecutor. ''Do you have any more questions for this witness, Mr. Dunn?''

He did indeed have a lot more questions for Felicia Cantu about the business Dominic Dominguez conducted in front of her for the six years they were involved. She answered every question and, with every response, nailed another nail into her lover's coffin. She knew dates, names, hidden accounts, bodies and crimes that Dominguez had thought were long buried. She painted a picture of a violent, arrogant man who was so confident he was above the law that he didn't even bother to hide his illegal activities from a mistress he'd mistreated and strung along for years. She admitted on the stand that she would have, at one time, done anything short of murder for him. But she wouldn't go to jail for him. Not when she knew in her heart that no matter what he said, he was never going to leave his wife for her.

After such damning testimony, there was no question that Kingston needed more time to prepare his cross-examination. Sadie was willing to give him until Monday, but he only wanted until noon to confer with his client. When the trial reconvened after lunch, he tried his damnedest to shake Felicia Cantu's testimony, but she refused to budge so much as an inch.

Haggard, Kingston was no idiot and obviously knew he was fighting a losing battle, but he stubbornly called three different witnesses for the defense. Then he surprised everyone by announcing that the defense rested. By three-thirty, both sides were presenting closing arguments. By five-thirty, the jury came back with a verdict. Guilty. Dominguez was sentenced to life in prison, then immediately charged with the attempted murder of a judge. That conviction, which was all but guaranteed with Felicia Cantu's testimony, along with the first, would keep him in jail for the rest of his life.

Noah was at home when he got word that the trial was finally over. Stunned, he'd spent the day planning a celebration, but he hadn't expected to put it together so soon. Sadie could go home now, he thought, relieved. Convicted and sentenced, Dominguez would gain nothing but more jail time if he persisted in seeking revenge, and he wasn't that stupid. Quickly calling Sadie's office, he left a message for her to meet him at his place, then rushed around like a madman to get everything ready before she got there.

Then he got out the ring that his father had given his mother the day he'd asked her to marry him. It had become his the day he turned twenty-one to give to his future bride. Tonight it would become Sadie's...he hoped.

He was rushing her. And after he'd assured her he wasn't putting any pressure on her. He'd planned to give her time, as much as she needed, but after thinking of nothing but her since he'd left her that morning, he'd realized that he couldn't let the day pass without letting her know what his intentions were. He loved her, dammit. He wanted her in his bed at night when he went to sleep and in his arms when he woke up every morning for the rest of his life. Starting tonight. She might bolt when he told her, but he couldn't put it off any longer. She had to know.

So he set the scene for a proposal, then paced his living room like a nervous teenager and watched the clock. He expected her there by six-thirty, but it was actually after seven before she knocked softly on the door. "I'm sorry I'm late," she said breathlessly as she stepped inside. "It's been crazy—"

That was as far as she got. Looking past him to the dining alcove, she stopped short at the sight of the flowers he'd snatched from the garden to decorate the table with. A slow smile of delight stretched across her face. "You did this for me? To celebrate the end of the trial?"

"And your return to the social club," he said huskily.

It seemed like ages since he'd had her there to himself, where they could be totally and completely alone and didn't have to worry about anyone walking in on them. Suddenly, he knew he was never going to be able to wait until later, as he'd planned, to propose. Not after he'd waited a lifetime for her already. He wanted his ring on her finger and her in his arms. Now!

Not wasting another second, he took a step toward her, eliminating the space between them, and tenderly captured her face in his hands. When her eyes widened in surprise, he smiled crookedly. "This isn't the way I'd planned this," he told her huskily. "I was going to light candles and put a Nat King Cole CD on the stereo, and dance with you after we ate. You deserve the romance, and I swear I'll give it to you…later. But right now, I have to tell you how I feel. I love you."

Tears welled in her eyes. "Oh, Noah, you don't have to bare your soul to me."

"Yes, I do," he said, dropping a quick kiss to her mouth. "I need you to know this. I thought I had my life all planned out—I wouldn't look at any woman seriously until my sisters were all grown and out of school and on their own. Then you walked in and knocked me out of my shoes. You scared the hell out of me."

"I did?"

"You're damn straight. I'd never dealt with anyone like you before. You were so prim and proper, and you put me in my place the way no woman ever has before or since. You didn't let me get away with anything, and I thought you didn't like me at all. Then when I kissed you the first time, I felt like I'd just got run over by a freight train. And you did, too."

She didn't deny it—she couldn't when her cheeks were warm with color and the memory of that kiss was warming her eyes to a beautiful sable brown. Giving in to temptation, he leaned down and kissed her again.

"I know that jackass of a husband of yours hurt you," he murmured, gathering her close against him, "and that you're afraid of putting your heart on the line again. But you don't need to be—not with me. I love you, and I'll never hurt you. Ever. I want to spend the rest of my life with you. No," he corrected himself quickly before she could say anything, "I didn't phrase that quite right. I don't want to just spend the rest of my life with you. I want to go through forever with you by my side and in my arms."

He pulled a ring box from his pocket and

flipped it open to reveal an antique, square-cut diamond ring that was as old and uniquely beautiful as the Lone Star Social Club itself. ''I'm asking you to marry me, Sadie Thompson,'' he said quietly. ''To love me, to have my babies, to let me spend the rest of my life showing you how much I love you. Say yes and you'll make me the happiest man on earth.''

Sadie stared helplessly at the ring. It was the most beautiful thing she had ever seen in her life and couldn't have been more perfect if it had been designed especially for her. She hadn't even touched it and already she could feel it on her finger, the old-fashioned rose gold smooth against her skin, linking her to Noah…the man she loved.

Dear God, why had it taken her so long to see what was right in front of her nose? she wondered, stunned. When she was so sure she wouldn't let another man near her, she'd let him into her life, her heart. Because he wasn't like David, wasn't like the men her mother had warned her about. He was a man of principle and integrity and she could, she knew, trust him with her life.

Blinking back tears, she looked up at him with her heart in her eyes. ''I never expected someone like you to walk into my life,'' she said huskily. ''You made me feel things I'd never felt before. You made me love you even when I didn't want to. I just couldn't help myself.''

A slow grin spread across his face as his arms tightened around her possessively. ''So you'll marry me? When? Give me a date. If you want a big, fancy wedding, I guess I can suffer through it, but don't make me wait too long for you—''

''I can't marry you, Noah. Not now.''

She hadn't meant to be so blunt and saw in an instant she had hurt him. Tears clogged her throat. More than anything, she wanted to accept his proposal, his ring, but she couldn't. Not yet. She wasn't like the other women he'd dated—she wasn't beautiful or sophisticated or experienced in the ways of men. Or confident of her own sexuality. If they were going to ever have a future together, she had to be sure of not only him, but of herself.

''I'm not turning you down flat. I just need some time,'' she assured him quietly. ''To figure some things out. To make sure this is right for both of us.'' Taking the ring box, she shut it and closed his fingers around it. ''Will you keep this for me? Just for a while until I'm ready for it? I wouldn't trust it with anyone else.''

For a moment, she thought he was going to refuse. Beneath her hand, she could feel the tension in him as he gripped the ring box as if he wanted to throw it across the room, feel the disappointment he couldn't hide. His eyes searching hers, he obviously saw something there that reassured him, because he suddenly sighed, a small, rueful smile propping up one side of his mouth.

''I don't know why I ever thought this would be easy. Take your time, sweetheart. Whenever you're ready, just say the word and I'll have the ring ready.''

If she hadn't loved him before, she would have fallen head over heels right there and then.

She didn't tell him how much time she needed and he didn't ask. He would have waited a lifetime if that was what she thought she wanted and somehow found a way not to go quietly out of his mind, but he still carried the ring with him everywhere he went...just in case. Days passed, then a week. The subject of marriage never came up again, and he readily admitted to himself that he was getting more than a little antsy. They saw each other just about every evening, but Sadie seemed distracted and, at times, downright secretive. He couldn't figure out what was going on in her head, and she wouldn't talk about it.

By the following Friday, he was convinced that she had decided to turn him down. When he called her right before court started and asked her about going out to dinner that evening, she put him off with the excuse that she had made other plans. He'd never considered himself a jealous man, but suddenly, he felt like a Neanderthal on the verge of losing his woman to another caveman. He wanted to charge over to her chambers and demand some answers, to claim her as his once and for all.

But she had court, and even if he managed to get in to see her, there was no time for the type of conversation he really wanted. He would, he decided, try to catch her at her apartment after work. If things went the way he hoped they would, she'd cancel her plans and they'd spend the evening planning the rest of their life.

He should have been home by five-thirty, but he witnessed a hit-and-run accident on the way and had to stop and give the police a report. By the time he walked through the front door of the Lone Star Social Club, it was going on seven, and Sadie was nowhere to be found.

Swearing, wondering where she was and when she'd be back, he went upstairs to his own apartment, only to stop short at the sight of the note taped to his front door: *Noah, come upstairs to the attic.* Lifting a brow in surprise, he started to grin. There was no signature, but he didn't need one. What, he wondered in amusement, was the woman up to now? And in the attic, of all places?

Curious, he unlocked his front door, tossed his briefcase inside, then took the stairs to the attic. He'd never been up there, but Alice had told him all about the dances held in the huge ballroom at the top of the house when the place was still a social club. He thought it had been converted into storage space years ago.

When he reached the top of the stairs, he couldn't really see if that was the case or not. Heavy drapes had been drawn across the room's four gabled windows, filling the entire attic with thick, murky, all-concealing shadows. He thought he saw something move across the room in the darkness and started to fumble for a light switch, but before he could find it, Sadie appeared out of the shadows right in front of him.

''There you are,'' he began, grinning. ''What—''

''Shh,'' she said quietly, pressing her fingers to his mouth. ''You'll understand everything in just a second. First I have to tell you something. I love you, and I do want to marry you. But I can't accept your proposal until you know what you would be giving up by marrying me.''

''Giving up?'' he repeated in puzzled amusement. ''Honey, what are you talking about?''

For an answer, she hit the light switch and flooded the ballroom with light. And there before him was just about every woman he'd dated in the last five years.

Stunned, he just stood there, unable to believe his eyes. There was Mary Jo Pazuki and Susan Larson and Dani Gorham and a dozen other beautiful, successful women he'd wined and dined and remained friends with long after he had, for whatever reason, stopped dating them. And they were grinning like Cheshire cats, delighted that they'd actually surprised him.

Not sure if he wanted to laugh or groan, he

turned to Sadie with a grin. "What'd you do? Run an ad in the paper? *Wanted—old girl-friends of Noah Baxter*?"

"Not quite," she said, laughing. "I had a little help from your mother and sisters. It seems they've been keeping pretty good track of what you've been doing over the last few years. Do you mind?"

"Are you kidding? Sweetheart, I'm thrilled! You wouldn't have gone to all this trouble if you really didn't love me." Not the least bit concerned that every female eye in the room was on them, he pulled her into his arms. Lord, he was crazy about her. No one knew more than he did how difficult it must have been for her to gather women she considered so much sexier than she was, then stand next to them so that he could compare her with them. Humbled, he said in a voice that was loud enough to carry to the farthest corner of the attic, "I appreciate the gesture, but if you'd have asked me, I would have told you it wasn't necessary. I gave up every other woman on this planet the day I met you. I love you."

To the cheers and applause of his old girl-friends, he kissed her then because he couldn't help himself, because the love shining in her eyes made it impossible for him to do anything else. When he finally let her up for air, he would have liked nothing more than to carry her down to his apartment and show her just how much she meant to him, but they had one more order of business to clear up.

He set her gently from him, then reached into the inside pocket of his suit coat and drew out the document he'd drawn up right before he'd left his office. Handing it to her, he said, ''Before I pull out the ring, I want you to have this. I know I can't make up to you for what Lincoln did to you, but I can assure you that it won't ever happen again with me. Read it.''

Surprised, Sadie took it and opened it, only to glance back up at him when she realized what she held. ''This is a prenuptial agreement.''

He nodded. ''If you want to have your attorney look it over or make any changes, just say the word. I'll do whatever will make you comfortable.''

Stunned, Sadie glanced back down at the document and read the words he had written promising he would never make any claims on anything that was hers except her heart. This was not, she knew, just a gesture on his part.

He wasn't interested in what she owned or her bank statement—he never had been. He'd never been anything but good and loving and protective of her, and if she needed proof, she had it right there in her hands. He loved her.

A load she hadn't even known was there lifted off her shoulders, and without a word, she ripped the prenuptial agreement in two and launched herself into his arms. "I don't need it," she said, laughing tearfully. "I trust you. I didn't realize how much until just now. You were never the one who hurt me, and you never will. I love you. And just for the record, Counselor, the only thing I want to sign when we get married is our marriage license. How soon do you think you could arrange that?"

Grinning, he crushed her close. "I'll see what I can do, Your Judgeship. I'll see what I can do."

Epilogue

Wrapped close in her husband's arms, Sadie sighed in contentment as the night breeze whispered through the open window, bringing with it the soft, distant sounds of music from the River Walk. Down in the entrance hall, the grandfather clock struck midnight, signaling that they had been husband and wife for all of five hours. Smiling, she still couldn't believe that they were even married. It was just two weeks ago that she'd surprised Noah in the attic with all his old girlfriends.

Just thinking about it made her giggle, and his arms immediately tightened around her.

''What's so funny, Mrs. Baxter?'' he growled, nipping at her ear.

''Your face when your old girlfriends confronted you in the ballroom,'' she said, chuckling. ''I should have had a camera.''

''I should have paddled your backside for ever thinking that I would regret giving up any of them when I could have you,'' he retorted. ''You had me from the first time you knocked on my door and chewed me out.''

Surprised, she lifted her head from his chest. ''Are you kidding? That long ago?''

Grinning, he nodded. ''I was toast, honey. Couldn't you tell? Why else do you think I agreed to that crazy proposal of yours? I was afraid you'd go to somebody else if I turned you down, and I wanted you any way I could get you.''

''All this time...'' Overwhelmed at the thought, she could do nothing to stop the tears that spilled over her lashes to trail down her cheeks. ''We've wasted so much time.''

''Hush,'' he said softly, drawing her back down to him for a tender, lingering kiss. ''What matters is that we found each other. We could have spent years passing each other in the hallway in the courthouse and never known what we were missing.''

He had a point, one she readily agreed with, but just then, the curtains at the window stirred and another breeze caressed them, bringing with it the strong, sweet scent of gardenias. In the darkness, his eyes met hers and they both grinned. "It looks like we have somebody's approval from higher up," he said. "We never stood a chance, did we?"

"Not in this lifetime," she said, laughing. Sending up a silent prayer, she thanked God for whatever spirit watched over the inhabitants of the house and played matchmaker so well. Without that romantic soul, she might not have ever met the man of her dreams.

*   *   *   *   *

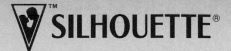

LARGE PRINT TITLES FOR
JULY – DECEMBER 2000

SPECIAL EDITION

July:	FORGOTTEN FIANCÉE	Lucy Gordon
August:	THE NINE-MONTH MARRIAGE	Christine Rimmer
September:	WANTED: HUSBAND, WILL TRAIN	Marie Ferrarella
October:	WHITE WOLF	Lindsay McKenna
November:	WITH THIS WEDDING RING	Trisha Alexander
December:	THE LITTLEST ANGEL	Sherryl Woods

July:	THE YOU-CAN'T-MAKE-ME BRIDE	Leanne Banks
August:	THE PATIENT NURSE	Diana Palmer
September:	BABES IN ARMS	Sara Orwig
October:	LOOK WHAT THE STORK BROUGHT	Dixie Browning
November:	NOBODY'S CHILD	Ann Major
December:	THE PRINCESS BRIDE	Diana Palmer

Sensation

July:	FRISCO'S KID	Suzanne Brockmann
August:	THE AMNESIAC BRIDE	Marie Ferrarella
September:	A MARRIAGE-MINDED MAN	Linda Turner
October:	THE OVERNIGHT ALIBI	Marilyn Pappano
November:	DEFENDING HIS OWN	Beverly Barton
December:	THE PROPOSAL	Linda Turner